FIGHTIN' WORDS

"I'm arresting you, Bo Altero," the ranger said in an official-sounding voice, "for the murder of Sheriff Mack Dolan."

"You've got to be joking," said Altero, offering a weak smile that looked hard for him to support. A twitch ran the length of his jawline.

"Murder's no joking matter," said the ranger, his hand hanging comfortably beside his big Colt, not poised, but appearing relaxed and ready. He drooped a bit, putting the gun butt at palm level.

"If it's a straight-up gunfight you want, Ranger, I always knew it would come down to you and me."

"That's up to you," said the ranger calmly. "I've made plans for it going a couple of different ways."

Altero's expression changed. "You've underestimated me, Ranger," he said. "I'm not some fool you can lead away to jail and off to a gallows. If I'm going down I'm taking you with me. . . ."

SHOWDOWN AT RIO SAGRADO

Ralph Cotton

Ralph Cotton

A SIGNET BOOK

SIGNET
Published by New American Library, a division of
Penguin Group (USA) Inc., 375 Hudson Street,
New York, New York 10014, U.S.A.
Penguin Books Ltd, 80 Strand,
London WC2R 0RL, England
Penguin Books Australia Ltd, 250 Camberwell Road,
Camberwell, Victoria 3124, Australia
Penguin Books Canada Ltd, 10 Alcorn Avenue,
Toronto, Ontario, Canada M4V 3B2
Penguin Books (N.Z.) Ltd, Cnr Rosedale and Airborne Roads,
Albany, Auckland 1310, New Zealand

Penguin Books Ltd, Registered Offices:
80 Strand, London WC2R 0RL, England

First published by Signet, an imprint of New American Library,
a division of Penguin Group (USA) Inc.

First Printing, July 2004
10 9 8 7 6 5 4 3 2 1

 REGISTERED TRADEMARK—MARCA REGISTRADA

Printed in the United States of America

For Mary Lynn . . . of course.

PART 1

Chapter 1

Ranger Sam Burrack rode into Redemption in the noonday heat when most travelers across the desert floor would have taken shelter in whatever sparse shade they could find. Most travelers would have been well advised to wait out the scalding sun, let it burn out its rage of the stark empty land as it had for millions of years past. Ordinarily the ranger would have done the same, but at first light he'd spotted five men headed in the direction of Redemption. He'd recognized one of the five riders to be Giles Capp, youngest of the infamous Capp brothers; and his interest in Giles Capp had caused him to push on in the scorching heat.

"Let's go, Black Pot," he'd said, nudging the big Appaloosa stallion forward. It only stood to reason that the four men riding single file close behind Giles Capp would be part of the Rio Sagrado Gang, venturing back across the border into the territory.

Sam knew that the real leader of the gang was Axel Capp. But with a murder charge hanging over his head, Axel Capp must've decided to stay on the far side of the border. Sam knew of no charges against Giles Capp. But with men like the Capp brothers and the rest of the Rio Sagrado Gang, Sam knew that could change at any turn in the trail. Trouble had summoned the ranger to Redemption. Now that he'd seen Giles Capp, he had a growing notion that Capp and his Rio Sagrado boys played a hand in things.

The town's sheriff had been killed, and Captain Dawes of the badlands outpost had sent Sam to take charge of the town until Redemption appointed itself a new lawman. This was Sam's first time taking charge of a town, most of his experience having been in tracking down hard cases, thieves and murderers on the run. But he felt up to the task, and the fact was, Captain Dawes had no one else to spare. He'd looked Sam up and down skeptically when he told him about the assignment. "There'll only be you, Ranger Burrack," he'd said, "you against that whole bad element. Can you make do?"

"I'll make do," Sam had told him flatly; and that had been the end of the discussion. What Sam didn't know about taking charge of a town he'd have to learn as he went along. That suited him. A lawman was dead, he reminded himself gravely, riding the big Appaloosa at an easy gait. It was his job to catch the killers.

From what the ranger knew about Giles Capp, the man relied heavily on his brother Axel's reputation. With the right amount of pressure, the ranger wondered if he might be able to use Giles to roust Axel out of hiding, see what role these two might have played in the death of Sheriff Mack Dolan. It would be worth a try, he told himself, reining the stallion down to a walk along the dirt street.

There were only a few people on the boardwalks of Redemption, but the hitch rail out front of Swain's Even Odds Saloon held eleven dusty horses. The rattle of piano music spilled freely from the saloon's bat-wing doors as the ranger reined his big Appaloosa over to an empty hitch rail out front of the sheriff's office. On a post above the sheriff's office a large wooden star hung low and lopsided by one chain, the other chain hung loose and broken, swaying slightly on a hot breeze. Someone had pulled the wooden star to the side out of the way and hooked it to a window frame.

Stepping down from his saddle, Sam led the Appaloosa to a water trough and let it drink as he looked along the street toward the far end of town, seeing three black men standing out front of a ragged tent. They stared toward the sheriff's office from seventy yards away.

When Black Pot finished drinking, Sam led the big stallion back to the hitch rail and wrapped his reins. He then took a closer look at the large wooden star, noting over a half-dozen bullet holes in it. Well, that was the *first* thing that had to be done here, he told himself. No self-respecting town could allow such blatant contempt for the law.

Before stepping onto the boardwalk and into the sheriff's office Sam gave another look back and forth along the street, taking in the same five horses he'd seen earlier as he'd watched Giles Capp and the other riders cross the desert floor. The horses stood across the street at the hitch rail out front of a small restaurant three doors down from the saloon. On the boardwalk out front of the saloon, two of the men he'd seen stood holding frothing beer mugs and smoking thin black cigars. One wore a broad dusty black sombrero. That was the *next* thing he'd have to do here after fixing the big wooden star. He'd get rid of loafers out front of the saloon. It made a town look bad, he thought. Drinking on the boardwalk showed disregard for the law.

"So, there is what they sent to settle the trouble here," said the drinker in the black sombrero. The two watched the ranger step onto the boardwalk and reach for the doorknob. "He ain't looking all that tough to me, Danny Boy."

"Well, Snake," Danny Boy Wright said, "I reckon looking tough to you wasn't what he had in mind when he woke up this morning." The two stared hard until the ranger stepped inside the office and shut the door behind himself. "He's the one who brought down Junior Lake and that bunch after they killed old Outrider Sazes." He nodded toward the ranger's Appaloosa stallion. "Right there is Sazes' Bear-claw Appaloosa stud to prove it. Folks up around the badlands say it was plumb spooky how that stud took up with this man after Sazes went down. Most everybody figured if anything ever happened to Sazes, that stud would have to be destroyed. But no-sir. The stallion slid up under this man's rump like Sazes called down to him and told him to."

"I've heard that same story from men who tell it a hell of a lot better than you do," said Snake Bentell, sounding unimpressed. He spit as if in contempt. "I didn't believe it then . . . and I especially don't believe it now . . . not after seeing this ranger in person."

"What's *wrong* with how I told it?" Danny Boy Wright eyed him closely.

"Nothing," Snake said flatly, not wanting to turn it into a fight. "I reckon my problem was I never counted Sazes as highly as some folks did. I never thought Junior Lake and his boys was that much either. So it just stands to reason this ranger ain't causing me any nervous jitters."

"I never said anything about having nervous jitters,

Snake," said Danny Boy, not liking the implication. "I just told you what the story is on him. Damned if you ain't getting harder to talk to every day."

"Yeah?" Snake grinned. "That's good to hear, Danny Boy. It lets me know I'm keeping my life on course."

"Come on," said Danny, turning toward the batwing saloon doors, "let's let Capp know there's a ranger in town."

The two walked inside the Even Odds Saloon, where Giles Capp stood at the bar flanked by Charlie Floose and Bo Altero. Across the bar, the owner, Andrew Swain, poured their drinks while the bartender took care of the rest of the drinkers. "Bad news, Capp," said Danny Wright, stepping up close to Giles Capp and leaning in between him and Charlie Floose to keep his words private among his companions. "A ranger just rode in off the flats."

His words had an affect on Giles Capp, who had raised his drink, but stopped and lowered it, his expression going sour. "Damn it." He looked back and forth at his men and Andrew Swain, then said, "That settles it. We can't make a move on the bank here till he leaves."

Charlie Floose winced a bit and said, "One ranger ain't worth changing our plans. I've got all stoked up and ready for that bank. I hate standing down for anybody."

"Don't forget I'm supposed to be getting this town set up so my brother can come here without the law being all over him," said Giles Capp. "Robbing the bank is just something extra. We're *standing down,* for now," Capp said firmly, looking Floose up and down, "unless you figure you've got enough bark on to rob it by yourself."

"All right." Charlie Floose nodded slightly. "You're the boss, Giles."

"Keep that in mind from now on, Floose," said Capp. He tossed his drink back and set the shot glass down solidly. "What about you, Swain? You're the one who set this up for us. Have you got any objections to us waiting for this lawman to leave?"

Swain tweaked the end of his thin waxed mustache as if considering it. "Well, I've been holding back depositing any of my money in it." He grinned slyly. "I hate stealing money from myself. It could look suspicious afterward, though, if I quit making my daily deposits just about the time the bank gets robbed." He shrugged. "At the same time, I hate keeping too much cash in this place." Again he grinned. "Never know when some desperados might ride through and take advantage of an honest merchant."·

"I see what you mean," said Capp, not sharing his humor. "How much are you talking about depositing every day?"

Thinking about it, Swain scratched the front of his bald head. "On a good day, I'll take in seven, maybe eight hundred dollars, counting the gaming tables." He gestured a hand toward the half of the Even Odds Saloon that had been sectioned off for gambling. A group of miners stood bunched together with their heads bowed over a roulette wheel as if in prayer. "Some weekends when everybody comes to town, I'll take in over a thousand a day . . . sometimes close to two thousand!"

"To hell with the bank," Charlie Floose kidded to the others. "Let's rob Swain!"

Giles Capp only stared at Floose for a second, his expression showing that he was in no mood for joking around. When Floose's smile faded, Capp said to

Swain, "Hold your money back for now. But if this ranger stays in town very long, start making your deposits again. We'll give your money back to you when we split everything up."

"I don't know," said Swain. "I'd rather not have my own money involved. It makes things easier all the way around."

"Don't you trust us?" Giles Capp asked flatly.

"Of course I trust you," said Swain.

"Then show me any deposits you put in right before we make our move; I'll see to it you get your money back . . . end of talk." He slid his glass forward for Swain to fill and asked, "You *do* keep all your deposit receipts?"

"Of course I do," said Swain. "I have every receipt for every dollar I've ever put in that bank. Trusting banks is one fault I've never had."

"Then we've got no problem," said Capp. He raised a finger for emphasis. "But don't ask for nothing unless you've got the receipts to back it up, agreed?"

"Certainly," said Swain. He poured drinks for the rest of the men.

Danny Boy Wright cleared his throat and said to Capp, "This ranger looks like the one who killed Junior Lake and his bunch."

Giles Capp turned facing him. "The one who rides Sazes' big Appaloosa?"

"Yep, that's the one," said Danny.

"I've heard of him," said Capp. "They say he's a crack shot with a big .45 Colt."

"A real fast draw?" Swain asked.

Giles Capp considered it for a second, then said, "No, come to think of it, I never heard anything about him being *fast* . . . only that he's a crack shot."

Snake Bentell cut in. "Being a crack shot doesn't

buy a man much where I come from. You can shoot straighter than a tight string, but it won't keep a bullet out of your belly, 'less you're fast enough to clear leather before the man facing you."

"I couldn't give a damn less how fast he is," said Giles Capp, sounding tired of the conversation. "I came here to build a safe place for my brother Axel to come to, not see who's the best shot *or* the fastest."

"I understand that, Capp," said Snake Bentell, not dropping the subject. "To you it might mean nothing. But take somebody like myself or Bo there"—he nodded at Bo Altero—"who prides themselves as a gunman, it means a lot."

Bo Altero leaned slightly forward and said to him along the bar, "Leave my name out of anything you've got to say about gunfighting, or anything else, Snake. I can speak for myself any time I feel the urge."

"Alls I'm saying, Bo," said Snake, "is that men like you and me have to keep an eye on whoever starts gaining a reputation with a gun."

"There you go putting my name in your mouth again, me just telling you not to," said Bo Altero, setting his full shot glass down without drinking from it. "What do I have to do to get you to keep your mouth shut?" His hand fell loosely poised beside his holstered Colt.

"Do what makes you feel best," Snake Bentell said, not backing down from such a blatant threat. His hand fell poised near his holster as well.

"All right, shut up, *both* of you!" said Giles Capp, cutting Bo Altero off before he could respond. He looked at Snake and said, "Why don't you and Danny Boy fill your mugs and get back out front. Let me know when that ranger leaves the sheriff's office. I want to get a good look at him. He just got here;

already he's messing things up for us." He grinned cruelly. "I was looking forward to seeing Swain and his townsmen hang that black rabbit they've got in the jail." He tossed a look at Swain. "Don't tell me you hung him while we weren't here?"

"You mean Henry Dove?" Swain asked absently.

"Yes, Henry Dove," said Giles Capp, giving Swain a bemused look. "How many other Negroes have you got waiting to hang?"

"None," said Swain. "We haven't hung him yet." He shrugged. "Now that I see he's kept his mouth shut, I'm not as concerned about hanging him as I was before."

"Neither am I," said Giles Capp, "but you have to admit it would be some good entertainment."

Swain gave a smug grin. "Far as I'm concerned, I'd like to see the man set free. It's easy to put a bullet in a target that big. Now that there's no fingers pointing at us, I'm at peace with the world," said Swain. "Delbert Watts will soon be acting sheriff. We'll let things settle down, then go on about our business . . . let things keep going our way."

"Suit yourself, then, Swain," said Giles Capp, raising a shot glass in salute. "Here's to things *going our way.*"

Inside the sheriff's office, the ranger stopped and looked at the young woman seated behind the battered oak desk. "Ma'am," he said, removing his tall pearl-gray sombrero, "I'm Sam Burrack. You sent for a ranger?"

She stared blankly for a moment, taken by surprise. He could see that she had been crying. She touched a handkerchief to her eye and sniffed and said, "Oh, of course, Ranger Burrack. I sent for you." She stood up as she spoke and wadded the handkerchief and shoved it into the pocket of her doeskin riding skirt. "I'm Julie Ann Dolan . . . Sheriff Mack Dolan's daughter."

"Yes, ma'am," said the ranger. "I never met your father, but I'm sorry to hear about his death."

"You didn't know my father, Ranger Burrack?" she asked, finding that fact difficult to accept, given Mack Dolan's reputation as a lawman.

"No, ma'am," said Sam, "but again, I'm awfully sorry about him getting killed. I plan on bringing his killers to justice . . . although I realize that's little consolation to you right now."

She'd looked him up and down as he talked to her. He appeared to be in his early twenties with a clean-cut look to him in spite of his brush-scarred trail clothes and his sweat-stained sombrero. He stood no taller than average, yet there was a quiet presence of strength to him. "How old are you, Ranger Burrack?" she asked bluntly. Then before he could attempt to answer her, she asked, "How long have you been a ranger?"

The quick velocity of her questions gave Sam pause for a moment. "Ma'am, I realize these are hard times for you. But I'm here to help. I haven't been a ranger as long as your pa was a sheriff." He waited for a second, then said, "My age shouldn't matter. I work hard at my job and I get it done." He took a step forward and stopped close to her desk. She noted that the big tied-down Colt on his hip seemed to cause his right shoulder to droop just a bit. "I wish I could tell you that if you aren't satisfied with me, the captain will send you somebody else. But that's not the case. Truth is, we're short of help in the badlands outpost. I'm all you get."

"I see," she said. Easing her tone and attitude. "I apologize, Ranger Burrack. I'm more distraught than I realized. My telegraph from your captain said he would send me the man who brought down the Junior Lake Gang, not to mention a few other unsavory types."

"Yes, ma'am," Sam said modestly, giving a slight bow of his head, "that's me."

"You?" She seemed even more surprised.

"Yes, ma'am," said Sam. He stood silent, leaving the next words up to her.

She stammered, "I—I feel so foolish, Ranger Burrack. Of course you're the one he told me about." Recognition came to her face. He told me your name, Ranger Sam Burrack! It must've slipped my mind. Please forgive me . . . it's just that you look so young."

"I *am* young, ma'am," he said, allowing himself a trace of a smile, "but the longer I stand here, the older I'm getting." He'd grown used to this sort of thing over the past year and a half. "Think we ought to talk about the situation here in Redemption?" Before she could answer, he continued, "I take it that's the prisoner your wire talked about?" He nodded at a sweaty black face staring at him between the bars of one of the jail cells along the back wall.

"Yes," Julie Ann said, "that's Mr. Dove, the man I'm concerned about. Please, sit down, Ranger Burrack," she said. "I'll draw us some fresh water while you rest for a moment, then we'll have you talk to Mr. Dove. I know that he had nothing to do with killing my father."

"I see," said Sam, not wanting to ask her why just then. "Water sounds good." But instead of sitting down, he gestured with his hat toward the jail cells.

"I might as well go ahead and talk to the prisoner while you do that."

"Oh, well, let me introduce you, then," said Julie Ann.

"That won't be necessary, ma'am," said Sam. "Henry Dove and I are already acquainted.

"Indeed . . . ?" Julie Ann looked more than a little surprised that the two should know one another. "Well, then . . . I'll only be a moment." She left the front office and walked back along a narrow hall past the three iron-barred jail cells and out the back door, picking up a small oaken bucket on her way. The ranger walked along slower in the same direction. As he walked along, he slowly lifted his big Colt from his holster, reached around behind his back and shoved it down in his belt. He stopped in front of the cell where two large black hands gripped the bars. "Howdy, Henry."

"Howdy, Ranger," said Henry Dove. He nodded at the ranger's empty holster and said, "You didn't need to tuck that gun on my account. I ain't grabbing it."

"I know, Henry," said the ranger. "Call it force of habit." Sam placed his sombrero back atop his head. "What have you done now?"

The big man said in a deep gruff voice, "I told you before, Ranger, I don't have to do nothing to get in jail . . . a man my color gets in jail if he ain't gone straight from one place to the next. Long as a man my color keeps moving, he's all right. But if he ever stops, shame on him. White man can't stand to see a black man standing still. A black man got to keep moving . . . you know that."

"Then why'd you stop, Henry?" the ranger asked.

"I just got tired, Ranger." Henry Dove shook his big head wearily. "Sometimes a man just gets tired . . . you know that. "

The ranger nodded. "Yep, I know that. How'd you get tangled up in all this, Henry?"

"I just told you," Henry Dove shrugged. "I *stopped* . . . it made everybody nervous."

"Come on, Henry," said the ranger.

"All right," said the big man. "I came to town, drank me some whiskey, went to sleep in the alley alongside the saloon, next thing I know I woke up hearing gunshots. I got to the street, found the sheriff dead. Lamps started lighting up, here they come! Everybody yelling, carrying on. I started to run! Bunch of them overpowered me. Here I am . . . they saying I killed the sheriff." He stopped for a moment. "Everybody except his daughter, Miss Julie. She say she knows I didn't kill her father. But she's the only one."

"Did you have a gun on you?" the ranger asked.

"I don't never carry a gun, Ranger," said Henry Dove. "I ain't carried no gun since I rode with the cavalry. I don't know if I could even hit what I shoot at anymore."

"So, no gun was found?" Sam asked.

"No, there weren't no gun found." Henry Dove shook his head. "But you know how it is . . . the saloon owner started hollering, getting everybody all riled up. They kind of settled down now. But for a while there I thought they'd come through the door any minute, snatch me up and drop a loop around my neck."

"What brought you to Redemption to begin with?" Sam asked.

"I came here to buy some mules for some folks from Kansas," said Henry Dove.

"Would that be the three men I saw up the street out front of a big tent?" Sam asked.

"If their face was the same color as mine it would be," said Henry. "I met them on the trail. They come through here with their families, headed back to Nicodemus, Kansas. They lost two mules crossing the desert." He stopped there as Julie Ann Dolan came back in carrying the water bucket.

"And you rode in here to purchase fresh mules for them?" the ranger asked, finishing his words for him. "Did you know these people before?"

"No." Henry Dove shrugged his broad shoulders. "But they asked me to do that for them, on account of them being strangers around here."

"I see," said the ranger. "How much money did they give you to buy the mules for them?"

"Sixty dollars," said Henry.

"Where is that money now?" Sam asked.

"Fellow by the name of Delbert Watts took it," said Henry. "But he denies it."

"Who is Delbert Watts?" the ranger asked, looking at Julie Ann as she appeared with two tin cups full of water. Sam took them from her and handed one to Henry through the bars.

"Delbert Watts is the town's new and struggling blacksmith," Julie Ann said, cutting into the conversation. "His business hasn't been going well. He began looking after things here after my father's death. Now he has been appointed temporary sheriff."

"And he says Henry here didn't have any money on him when he was arrested?" Sam asked.

"That is correct," said Julie Ann. "I'm sure Mr. Dove has told you how the townsmen were up in arms at first, talking about lynching him. Thank God that has settled down some."

"Yes," said the ranger, "thank God for that." He appeared to be thinking things over for a moment. Then he said to Henry Dove, "when you woke up, you didn't see anybody on the streets . . . maybe somebody running away?"

"I never saw nobody nowhere, Ranger," said Henry. "I just had woke up like I told you . . . and I was still drunk."

"Now the folks from Kansas can't go on home because they can't get any mules," the ranger said.

"That's the whole of it," said Henry Dove. "I feel awful bad about it. But that's how it is, Ranger. Even if the judge lets me out of here . . . I still have lost their money." He shook his head. "Umm, umm, the trouble a man gets into when he *stops*. I ever start back up, I'll never *stop* again. I strike me an oath to that!" He gave the ranger a tired sad smile.

"This man didn't kill my father, Ranger," Julie Ann said quietly between Sam and herself. "I'll tell you why when we speak privately." She gestured for Sam to follow her away from the cells and back to the battered desk.

"Yes, ma'am," said the ranger, "I already knew that."

She gave him a curious look over her shoulder but said no more as they walked away from Henry Dove, who stood sipping his tin cup of cool water. "I'm glad you're here, Ranger Sam," Henry Dove called out in his gravely deep voice. "I know you won't forget about me."

"No chance of it, Henry," Sam called back to him. He raised his Colt from behind his back and slipped it into his holster.

Chapter 2

Sam looked around the sheriff's office as he pulled out the chair for Julie Ann, and she sat back down behind the desk. On the desktop he saw a framed picture of a young man wearing a dark suit, holding a battered Stetson on one knee and supporting a little girl on his other. He wore a sheriff's badge on his chest. The ranger concluded that this had to be Sheriff Mack Dolan when he was a younger man and his daughter Julie Ann Dolan as a child. The position of the picture atop the desk told him that Julie Ann must have been sitting here staring at it when he'd arrived. As he assisted her with the chair, he noticed a weathered gun belt hanging on the chair back. The worn walnut grips of a big Starr Arms .44 caliber pistol stuck up from an equally worn Mexican-style single-loop holster.

Noting the wear along the Starr's trigger guard, the ranger said, "Ma'am, would you like for me to put this gun belt away for you? It's not a good idea leaving it out like this."

"Yes, thank you, Ranger Burrack," she said. "I would like that very much. I hung it there, but oddly enough I have had difficulty wanting to put it away."

"I understand, ma'am," Sam said.

"It has been difficult for me to come here and go through my father's belongings. Being a lawman's daughter, I suppose I should have been better prepared to hear that something tragic had happened to him, but I wasn't."

"Some things we can't get prepared for," said the ranger. He gestured a hand toward her chair. "Why don't we sit down and you tell me what you know about who killed your father. In your telegraph you told the captain that the saloon owner here killed him?"

"Yes, that's what I said," Julie Ann replied, her eyes taking on a sharpness fueled by both hurt and anger. "Andrew Swain is a low-down murdering coward."

"That may be, ma'am," Sam said, "but what makes you think he had anything to do with your father's death?"

"Because Andrew Swain has taken over Redemption, Ranger Burrack," she replied a bit defensively. "My father wrote me only a month ago, right before his death. He said Andrew Swain had bribed his way into owning the town council. He told me that he alone stood between Swain and his criminal friends running this town. He said that Swain had offered him a handsome sum to step down from office . . . but of course my father refused the offer."

"How long until the next sheriff election?" Sam asked, trying to connect her story into something that might offer any foundation for her belief.

"Not for another year and a half," Julie Ann replied. "Too long for a man like Andrew Swain to want to wait." She searched the ranger's face, wanting to see a sign of his agreeing with her.

Sam saw what she was looking for, but he shook his head slowly, not wanting to confirm for her something that might not be true. "Ma'am, I agree that it looks suspicious, your father being killed shortly after confiding in you that Swain wanted him out of the way. But the fact is, I need more than that before I can go arresting Swain for murder."

"I—I realize that you can't arrest him right off, Ranger," said Julie Ann, sounding a bit in despair. "But if you will at least question him, I'm hoping that he might reveal something of himself to you . . . give you something more to go on."

Sam weighed his words then said them quietly. "Ma'am, I want to be honest with you. Men who murder other men don't make it a practice of revealing anything about themselves. I don't want you getting any false hope about us finding your father's killers. If I thought that talking to this Swain fellow would be worth—"

Before Sam could finish his words, the office door swung open and two men in business suits stepped curtly inside without closing the door behind themselves. "There you are, little lady!" said the first one in. He wore a neatly brushed bowler hat cocked a bit far to one side of his head. A well-attended black mustache mantled his lip. A matching goatee came down to a sharp point beneath his chin. Without acknowledging the ranger, he sternly cocked a hand on his hip and said to Julie Ann Dolan, "I'll take the key to this office now, and on behalf of Redemption bid *you* farewell! You have had plenty of time to gather your father's belongings!"

The other man rushed forward nervously and said, "Miss Julie Ann, what Councilman Avondale means is, you need to go ahead and gather your father's personal belongings and make arrangements for your trip back to Ohio." He passed an overly sympathetic glance to Sam, adding, "This poor young woman has been through so much, we hate to see her prolong her grief."

"Pipe down, Meaker!" said Councilman Willis Avondale. "I made it clear exactly what I mean! I'm tired of pussyfooting around here. Grief or no *grief*, we need this office cleared out so our newly appointed sheriff can step in and get to work here! We still have a town we're responsible for!"

Julie Ann Dolan stood up shaking. Tears welled in her eyes. Seeing how pale her face had suddenly become, Sam stepped around the desk and steadied her with his hand on her arm. "Take it easy, ma'am," he said quietly to her. Then he turned facing the two men.

"And who might you be?" asked Councilman Avondale. But before Sam could speak, the councilman's eyes glanced at the badge on Sam's chest. "Oh, a ranger, I see," he said impatiently. "Well, I suppose we all know who sent for you!" He gave Julie Ann a look of disgust.

"He is Ranger Sam Burrack," said Julie Ann, her voice shaky but determined and defiant. "And, yes, I did send for him! I saw that no one in Redemption was going to arrest my father's killers!"

Sam stood in silence, watching and listening closely, recalling everything Julie Ann Dolan had told him about what was going on in Redemption and deciding for himself if there might be some merit in what she'd said.

"Arrest your father's killers?" said Avondale. "Miss Julie, no one here knows who killed your father, or why! It could have been any number of men your father became involved with over the years. I daresay there are some who wonder just which side of the law your father was on most of his life."

"How dare you!" Julie Ann shouted. Sam had to grab her firmly to keep her from going around the desk after Avondale. "You wouldn't say that to my father's face if he were alive!"

The ranger gave both of the councilmen a firm stare. "I think you better leave."

"Oh, do you?" said Avondale, looking down his nose. "Well, this may come as a surprise to you, Ranger . . . but we don't want you here in Redemption. Your services aren't needed, and your presence isn't welcome!"

Instead of responding to Avondale, the ranger asked Meaker in a quiet tone, "Do you know where to take him?"

"Take him?" said Meaker, bewildered, beads of nervous perspiration forming on his brow.

"Yes," Sam said, calmly drawing his big revolver slowly as he stepped around the desk toward them. "He's going to need your help getting around for the next twenty minutes or so."

Avondale backed up a step, seeing that the ranger held the pistol without his finger on the trigger, ready to swing the barrel like a billy bat. "No, hold on, Ranger!" said Avondale, back stepping. "You can't come into Redemption bullying the town leaders!"

"I'm here to investigate the murder of Sheriff Mack Dolan," Sam said. "If I have to crack your head with this gun barrel to get you out of here so I can get started, I'll just call that part of us getting acquainted."

"You haven't seen the last of me, Ranger!" Avondale threatened as he backed away, Meaker pulling him by his arm.

"I hope I haven't," said Sam, stalking forward with the pistol barrel poised for a sudden swipe at any second.

When the two were out and off of the boardwalk, the ranger closed the office door quietly and turned to face Julie Ann Dolan.

"Then you will be questioning Andrew Swain?" she asked hesitantly.

Sam offered a slight smile. "I never said I wasn't going to, ma'am."

"But you sounded like you were about to say it would be pointless to talk to Andrew Swain," said Julie Ann.

"It might be pointless talking to Swain about your father's murder," said Sam. "But I wonder what Swain's going to think when he hears I'm talking to everybody else in town about it."

"Oh . . ." Julie Ann Dolan cocked her head, seeming a bit impressed at what he'd just said. "How long did you say you've been a ranger?" she asked, managing a slight smile herself.

Sam holstered the big Colt and said, "Long enough to know that we can't leave that star hanging out front with its chain broken." He nodded toward the front of the building. "With it pulled over to the side, we can't even see out the window."

Julie Ann said, "I suppose I've been so consumed by bigger problems, I've let something like a broken sign go unattended. It seemed like such a minor detail with everything else that's going on."

"I understand," said the ranger, looking toward the blocked window. "But I've found that the more I attend to the *minor details* on this job, the easier it is for me to attend to the *big problems.*"

Julie Ann considered the ranger's words for a moment, hearing something familiar in them. "Much obliged, Ranger," she said at length, her eyes once again welling with tears, only this time tears of a different nature. "Come with me, I'll help you get some tools."

"Are you sure that's the same ranger who killed Junior Lake and his bunch?" Snake Bentell asked Danny Boy Wright. The two still stood on the boardwalk out front of the Even Odds Saloon drinking from frothing mugs of beer. They watched Sam Burrack and Julie Ann Dolan repair the chain and raise the big wooden badge back into its proper position. Moments earlier Bo Altero had stood with them, but he'd walked back inside the saloon when the two councilmen left the sheriff's office in a huff.

"I told you I recognize that big Appaloosa more than I recognize the man," Danny Boy said to Snake. "But I'm damn sure that's him. The story is he learned to shoot from none other than Lawrence Shaw himself."

Snake Bentell's eyes snapped around at Danny Boy almost in disbelief. "Fast Larry Shaw taught *this man* to handle a gun? You mean *the* Fast Larry? From down in Somos Santos, Texas?"

"None other," said Danny Boy with a proud grin for having known such a choice piece of information.

Catching himself, Snake Bentell shrugged it off and tried to look bored with the whole subject. "Well, I never got the chance to see Lawrence Shaw in action, so I can't say how fast he is."

Still watching the ranger and Julie Ann work on straightening the sign, Danny Boy said, "Lawrence Shaw is known as the fastest gun alive, if that gives you any idea how *fast* he is."

"So much for Shaw, then," said Snake Bentell, also watching the work going on out front of the sheriff's office. "That doesn't mean this ranger is anything spe-

cial. Shaw might've taught him to shoot, but that
doesn't mean he learned, now, does it?"

"I guess if you put it that way, no," said Danny
Boy, shaking his head, "it doesn't make him nothing
at all."

"Oh, Lord, look at this!" said Snake, his eyes rivet-
ing more intently on Julie Ann. The ranger stood atop
a ladder he'd carried from around the side of the sheriff's office and leaned against the front of the building.
Sam reached down as Julie Ann stretched upward,
handing him a hammer. "I would've helped that sweet
woman thing hang that big ole sign. She didn't need
to get no *ranger* to do it."

Also watching Julie Ann more intently, Danny Boy
grinned. "Do you reckon he'll be warming his belly
against her back?"

"If he doesn't, he's a damned fool," said Snake.
Watching the ranger and the woman, the two raised
their beer mugs to their lips and drank.

Inside the Even Odds Saloon, Bo Altero had
walked to the table where Andrew Swain and Giles
Capp sat playing cards and pouring shots from a bottle
of bourbon Swain had shipped to him all the way from
Kentucky. "Thought you'd want to know, Giles," said
Bo, leaning down on his palms atop the table, "our
pal Willis Avondale just left the sheriff's office, had
that other mousy-looking councilman with him. They
didn't look real happy."

"Oh?" Giles Capp cocked his head slightly to the
side. "How come *you're* the one telling me? I told
Snake and Danny Boy to keep an eye on things for
me."

"They're both busy watching the ranger and the
Dolan girl straighten up the star we all shot up the
last time we was here," Bo Altero said in a critical

tone. "That is when they're not discussing the fastest gun, the biggest horse and all that other important stuff."

"Those two sonsabitches!" Giles Capp slapped his cards onto the tabletop and started to get up from his chair.

"Hold on, Giles," said Swain, stopping him. He looked up at Bo Altero and nodded him toward an empty chair. "Now that we've got this ranger to deal with, maybe this is a good time to cull out any dead-weight we've got hanging around."

"You mean sic Snake and Danny Boy on the ranger?" said Giles Capp, reseating himself, liking the idea.

"Sure, something like that," Swain smiled, motioning for his bartender to bring Bo Altero a shot glass. The bartender came hastily with the clean glass, sat it down and disappeared. As Swain filled the shot glass from his bottle of prize bourbon, Bo Altero gave Giles Capp a look, both of them realizing that Bo's standing in the Rio Sagrado Gang had just risen greatly. Swain continued, saying, "Tell those two to goad the ranger into a gunfight." Swain shrugged. "If they kill the ranger, good enough. If he kills them, we'll get Councilman Avondale to raise the old *blood in the streets* issue, get the townsfolk in an uproar."

Giles Capp grinned. "Yeah, I like that. Either way it comes out, we get rid of the ranger."

"Precisely," said Swain, rolling a cigar back and forth between his lips. He tossed the subject aside and said to Bo Altero, who had just taken a sip of the bourbon, "What do you think of that stuff, Altero? I have it sent here from a little town halfway between Louisville and Nashville."

Bo Altero smiled tightly with pride, held up his shot

glass and said, "I could stand to drink like this from now on."

"Then you stick with us, Bo," said Swain. "You'll see how well us Rio Sagrado boys take care of our own, eh?"

Us . . . Giles Capp smiled to himself, noting the way Andrew Swain had just included himself in the Rio Sagrado Gang.

Bo Altero nodded and smiled. But even as he went along with Swain, he realized that he had just heard these two plan a scheme that could get two of the Rio Sagrado boys killed, for all they cared. "I'll stick with you," he said. "Just so long as you stick with me."

Swain and Giles Capp gave one another a look, then brushed it aside and raised their shot glasses as if in a toast before drinking. "Don't worry about us, Bo," said Swain, setting his glass down. He nodded toward the front of the saloon where Danny Boy and Snake Bentell stood on the boardwalk. "Those two have grown lax on their job. They would rather stand around and talk about what they want instead of going out and taking it." As he spoke, he grasped some imaginary object from the air with his fist and held it firmly. "Us Rio Sagrado boys take what we want with no apology. We've got a system worked out between us, me setting things up in a town like Redemption, then Giles here and his brother Axel bringing in the rest of the gang and cleaning the place out anytime we're good and ready."

"Sounds like a pretty sweet way to do business to me," said Bo Altero. "I'm glad to be a part of it."

Giles Capp cut in, saying, "I like the idea of owning the local politicians the way we do here."

"Is it just Avondale you own?" Bo asked, watching Swain reach over and refill his glass for him.

Before Giles Capp could reply, Swain answered for him. "Right now it's just Avondale, but it looks like it won't be long until he'll bring Meaker in with us. I own Willis Avondale, lock, stock, and barrel," Swain grinned slyly. In a lowered voice he said, "Nobody knows it around here, but Avondale is a back-stabbing sporting man from Tupelo, Mississippi. His real name was Willis Flick—most sporting folks called him 'Flick the Blade,' owing to his use of a long Arkansas toothpick knife on more than one or two occasions. Avondale is a name he picked up somewhere . . . probably from some poor sumbitch he robbed in his sleep."

"Flick the Blade! I read about him in a periodical a couple years back, how he disappeared in New Orleans." Bo Altero looked amazed and shook his head. "How the hell did you ever find out something like that about this *Councilman* Avondale?"

Swain chuckled and replied as he rolled the cigar back and forth in his mouth, "I make it a point to keep myself on the good side of a lawman or two anywhere I go. You never know how much good a *bad* lawman can do for you."

"What lawman told you something like that?" Altero asked.

"Anyway," said Giles Capp, cutting in, avoiding Altero's question, "we've got Avondale dancing to whatever tune we play. Now he's gotten Meaker to take some money we shoved his way. We told him it was to help get an ordinance passed to keep folks from throwing litter on the streets." Giles Capp grinned. "All it takes is something small like that to buy a politician. They figure what the hell, that won't hurt nothing, it's a good ordinance anyway. But once they start taking our money, we never let them off the ook. So we'll soon have sweaty little Horace Meaker oing our bidding for us too."

"Not bad," said Bo Altero with admiration in his yes. "I've always wanted this kind of setup. I knew ere was more to life than shooting some stagecoach river and taking off with the money. I just wished e pa could have lived to see me here, sipping fine ourbon . . . smoking cigars." His voice turned a little ght in his chest.

Rising from his chair, Andrew Swain patted the oung outlaw's gloved hand lying on the tabletop. You've proved you're one of us now, Bo. Just don't t us down." He turned and walked away to the rear oor of the saloon, the door leading to the privies ut back.

Feeling a little embarrassed by Swain's hand-patting esture, Altero raised his shot glass and drained it. urning to Giles Capp, Bo Altero saw the flat expres- on on Giles' face as he stared him in the eyes. "Are ou all through?" Giles Capp asked flatly.

"Through?" Bo looked bewildered.

"Yeah, through." Giles nodded at the shot glass in ont of Altero.

"Sure," said Altero, pushing the empty shot glass way from him. "What do you want me to do?"

"First of all," said Giles Capp, raising a finger for mphasis, "I want you to clear your mind of all the orse shit Swain just shoveled into your face. He's not part of the Rio Sagrado Gang. Me and my brother in this gang. We say who is and ain't a member of . So don't go letting this four-flushing saloon keeper t you to thinking otherwise, understand?"

"I understand," said Bo Altero, getting more seri- us, sitting straighter.

"And keep this between us," said Giles Capp in a lowered tone. "I'm watching this sumbitch. If he's got the guts to do this business, we'll go from here to another town and do it all over again. But if he looks like he can't hold his water when the going gets tough, he's going to be feeding buzzards out on the badlands. So, don't go making *good friends* with him."

"Good friends? What are you getting at?" Bo Altero looked puzzled at the way Giles Capp had said the word.

"Nothing," said Giles, "forget it. I want you to go tell Danny Boy and Snake that I told you—"

"Hold on," said Bo Altero, cutting him off. "I don't know what you meant by that 'good friends' remark."

Giles Capp stared at Bo Altero for a second, as if deciding whether or not to go any further on the subject. Finally he said, "I told you to forget it. Now, are you going to do like I tell you or not?"

Chapter 3

When Bo Altero stepped through the bat-wing doors of the Even Odds Saloon onto the boardwalk, he found that Danny Boy Wright and Snake Bentell had seated themselves in two wooden chairs and leaned back against the front of the building. They sat staring at Julie Ann Dolan as if dumbfounded by her. Their beer mugs were nearly empty, with no more foam left in them. Looking down at Bentell's mug, Bo Altero saw a fly walking along the glass rim. Unaware that Altero had joined them, Danny Boy whispered side-long to Bentell without taking his eyes off of Julie Ann. "I'll be honest, I've never been in bed naked with a woman that pretty in my whole miserable damn life. Have you, Snake?"

Bentell tried to act like it was no big deal to him, yet his eyes were fixed wide and unblinking on the woman. "Oh, yeah, many times," he said. "Although I have to admit that it's been a while."

Behind them Bo Altero cut in saying, "Yeah, a really *looong* while, I bet."

The two turned in surprise and saw Altero standing near them. The suddenness of his voice had startled them a bit. Their hands had instinctively gone to their holstered pistols. "Damn it, Altero!" said Snake, "that's a good way to get yourself shot!" But realizing who he was speaking to, he added quickly, "By accident is what I mean."

"Yeah, that better be what you mean, Snake," said Altero. His hand also lay on his gun butt. He stared at Snake until Snake averted his eyes and nodded at Julie Ann out in front of the sheriff's office.

"If that wasn't what I meant," said Snake Bentell, not backing down, "you'd already know it."

"We're just admiring the scenery here," Danny Boy cut in, hoping to detract any trouble between the two. "Get yourself a beer and join us."

"Not me," said Altero, "I'm busy taking care of business. If you two are smart, you'll do the same."

"What business are you talking about, Bo?" said Danny Boy, standing, stretching, giving one more look toward Julie Ann Dolan.

"Giles wants you two to push on that ranger a little, see what he's made of," said Altero with authority.

Snake also stood up. "Since when has Giles started sending you to give his orders for him. Are you the *segundo* now?"

"No," said Altero, "I'm not the second in charge. But he told me to tell you both, and I did. If you don't like it, go tell him so. I did my part." He started to turn and walk back inside.

"Wait a minute," said Bentell. "What about you?"

"What *about* me?" said Altero.

"Ain't you going with us?" asked Danny Boy.

Looking back and forth between the two, Altero said with a smug grin, "What do you need me for, two big gunslingers like you?"

"What Danny Boy meant is that we usually all work

together on stuff like this," said Snake Bentell. "You ain't been with us long . . . maybe you don't know how things work yet."

"I know how it *works*," said Altero. "Giles said for me to tell you two to do it. He didn't mention me going along with you. Do you figure you two together can't handle one ranger?" His voice took a sarcastic tone.

Bentell's face reddened in anger. "You're damn right we can handle him, Altero! In fact, I can handle him by myself. So you can go on back inside; Giles might need you to shine his boots."

"Save your bark for the ranger," said Altero. He walked back inside the saloon and left the two standing alone on the boardwalk.

"Well, hell . . ." said Danny Boy. He reached up under his hat brim and scratched his head. "I expect we best go do what Giles told us to."

"I never heard Giles say a gawdamned word!" said Snake, still smoldering with anger at Altero. "For two cents I'd go in there and ask Giles myself!"

"Yeah, you do that, Snake," said Danny Boy. "Then you'll have Giles and Axel Capp both down your shirt from now till judgment day."

Snake grumbled but settled down. "I feel like doing it, though," he said, glaring at the doors to the saloon.

"Feel like it all you want to," said Danny Boy, "just don't go *doing* it." He looked along the street at the ranger and Julie Ann still working on the sign. "Come on, let's go poke some sticks at this ranger, see if we can make him hiss."

"I told you I can handle this ranger by myself," said Bentell, "and I meant it. All I want you to do is be my backup."

"Are you sure about this, Snake?" Danny Boy asked. "Giles wants us both to do it; maybe we best stick to what he said."

"Stay back and let me handle him, Danny Boy," Snake insisted. He looked all around, then added, "Just let me get a good swallow of rye whiskey first. Whiskey always helps me get my bark on."

Glancing at the bat-wing saloon doors, Danny Boy said, "We can't go back in there right now, Snake."

"I know we can't," Snake replied, nodding down at their horses standing at the hitch rail. "But I've got a swig or two left in a bottle I keep hidden in my saddlebags."

Danny Boy followed him down off the boardwalk and between the two horses. Bentell gave a glace back over his shoulder at Julie Ann Dolan as he flipped up his saddlebag flap and pulled up a bottle of red rye whiskey. He looked at the contents of the bottle as he pulled the cork.

"Hell, Snake, that bottle's over half full!" said Danny Boy.

"I didn't realize it," said Bentell, lifting a long swig of warm whiskey from the bottle, then passing it to Danny Boy as he let out a hot gasp of a breath. "Lord, that gets my bells ringing."

"I'm better with a gun half drunk any day than I am stone sober. What about you?" He lifted a long drink and passed the bottle back to Snake.

"I'm good either way," said Snake, "so I never thought much about it." He took another deep swig and wiped his hand across his lips. He stuck the cork back into the bottle, tapped it tight with his palm and dropped the bottle back down into his saddlebags. "Come on, Danny Boy, watch me put this ranger in his place."

*   *   *

In front of the sheriff's office, the ranger and Julie Ann Dolan had just finished rehanging the big wooden badge on a new length of chain. "So you do agree with me that Mr. Dove is innocent?" she asked, having spent most of their time together talking about her father's death and why she was convinced it was Swain and his men who had killed him.

Sam spoke as he reached down and helped Julie Ann gather the hand tools from the boardwalk. "Yes, I'm convinced Henry Dove is innocent, ma'am," Sam said. "But I'm also convinced he's lying through his teeth about not seeing anybody that night. I think he saw who killed your father but is afraid of telling me."

"Mr. Dove doesn't appear to me to be the sort of person who would fear man or beast," said Julie Ann.

"Oh, he's not afraid for his own safety, ma'am," the ranger said. "He's probably afraid of what the killers might do to you, or any other innocent person who might try to stand up to them."

"Doesn't he believe the law would protect me?" Julie Ann asked.

"Henry Dove grew up a slave, ma'am. It hasn't been so long ago that he was not a free man under the white man's law. I reckon he has reason to distrust the law. He's never seen the law as something that protected folks in his world."

"He seems to trust you, Sam," Julie said. Then catching herself, she said, "I mean, *Ranger* Burrack."

The ranger felt himself blush. "Ma'am, feel free to call me Sam. It looks like you and I are going to be seeing a lot of one another over the next few days." He offered a shy smile. "Who knows, we might become friends in all this."

"I need a friend right now, Ranger—I mean, Sam,"

she said, catching herself again. "Feel free to call me Julie." She said it quickly, then said, "If you think he is lying about seeing someone, why do you believe him when he says he didn't kill my father?"

The ranger rolled his shirtsleeves down and buttoned them as he spoke. "Because last year when I met Henry, he told me that when he left the cavalry and the Indian war, he struck an oath against the side of an oak tree that he would never shed the blood of another human being."

"He did what?" Julie Ann asked.

"He struck an oath," said Sam. "It has something to do with his religion I expect."

"And you believed him?" asked Julie Ann, trying to understand.

"Under the circumstances, yes, I believed him," said the ranger. "You see, Henry had been stabbed by a buffalo skinner over near Apache Wells. And he wouldn't lift a hand to defend himself. After the man had stabbed him three times, Henry just sank to his knees and bowed his head. He accepted his death so to speak. But luckily there were some people there who stopped the skinner from killing him. Still, poor Henry almost bled to death. I arrived the following day, heard what had happened and went and arrested the skinner. Henry Dove wouldn't bring charges against him. He said it would be an act that would cause more violence to follow. That's when he explained about striking an oath. Can you see why I believed him?"

Julie Ann stared for a moment, speechless. Finally she said, "Is Henry all right? I mean, you know . . ." She tapped the side of her head.

"He's as sane as any man I've ever met," Sam shrugged, "unless we think his being nonviolent makes him crazy. I know how strange that sounds, especially for somebody his size . . . but that's Henry Dove. He struck an oath against the side of an oak tree." He shook his head slowly. "I hate to think what he must've seen in the Indian war to make him turn that way."

"He was a buffalo soldier, then?" said Julie Ann.

"That's what some called the colored troops," said the ranger, "but I never heard them call themselves that." As Sam spoke he looked past her and saw the two men walking along the boardwalk toward them. Something in their swagger told him they were trouble. He said calmly to Julie Ann, "Anyway, that's who Henry rode with, the 10th Cavalry, part of the United States Colored Troops." As he finished buttoning his shirtsleeve, he said, "Why don't you step inside out of the evening heat. I'll put the tools away."

"No, indeed," said Julie, "I'll help you." She stooped down and picked up a hammer and a leftover length of chain lying at their feet.

"Please, Julie Ann," said Sam, raising her to her feet, taking the hammer from her hand. "I'd like for you to go inside."

"But I—" Julie Ann started to speak, but Sam's sudden movement cut her off. Seeing he wouldn't have time to explain to her what was about to happen, he sidestepped around her and stood in front of Snake Bentell as Bentell came to a halt with his hand poised near his pistol. Danny Boy stopped a bit to the side behind Snake Bentell.

"Well, well," said the gunman, pushing up his black sombrero, "if it ain't the ranger we've all heard so much about . . . the one who—"

Snake's words stopped short as the first sudden blow of the hammer handle cracked him across the jaw. Behind Snake, Danny Boy stood stunned, seeing the ranger quickly swing the handle back, the second blow batting Snake's head in the opposite direction. Snake spilled backward into Danny Boy's arms. Danny Boy caught his downed partner instinctively. Then realizing he'd made a mistake, he dropped Snake to the boardwalk and made a grab for his gun. But his move came too late. Standing crouched, his hand on his empty holster, Danny Boy stared down the barrel of his own pistol pointed at him. "Aw, Jesus!" he murmured. The ranger had him cold.

Sam shoved the tip of the barrel in close to Danny Boy's forehead. Behind Sam, Julie Ann, who had also been stunned by the ranger's suddenness, managed to say in a shaky voice, "Oh, God!"

Her words unnerved Danny Boy Wright. "Please, Ranger, don't shoot me! We didn't come looking for trouble! We just wanted to talk!"

The ranger gave him a dubious look and cocked the hammer on Danny Boy's pistol.

Danny Boy flinched. "No! Wait! Please! I mean, all right! We did come looking for a little trouble, but not like this! He just wanted to goad you some! That's all! Just in fun!"

"One," said the ranger with calm resolve.

"Huh?" Danny Boy looked confused, unsure what to do.

"Two," the ranger said in the same calm flat tone. His hand tightened on the pistol butt.

"Wait!" A sharp light of realization came on in Danny Boy's wide frightened eyes. He backed away a few quick steps, then turned and raced along the boardwalk toward the Even Odds Saloon, leaving his pistol and his pal behind.

Sam uncocked Danny Boy's Colt and shoved it

down behind his belt. He stooped down and lifted Snake Bentell's pistol and did the same thing with it. He poked his boot toe into Snake's ribs. The gunman only groaned and stared up at him through drifting unfocused eyes. Both of his jaws were already swollen and turning red-purple. A trickle of blood ran down from his nose.

"You—You weren't really going to shoot him, were you, Sam?" Julie Ann Dolan asked in a trembling voice.

Sam didn't answer. Instead he looked along the boardwalk in time to see Danny Boy Wright disappear through the bat-wing doors of the Even Odds Saloon.

Seeing that she wasn't going to get an answer to her last question, Julie Ann tried another. "How did you know they were coming to start trouble?"

"The way they walked," the ranger said flatly. He stooped down, got his hands beneath Snake Bentell's shoulders and dragged him over to a wooden chair that sat against the front of the sheriff's office.

"The way *they walked?*" Julie asked, still sounding a bit stunned. "What if you had been wrong?"

Sam lifted Snake Bentell enough to place his limp body in the chair. He pulled the chair forward enough to tilt it back against the wall, the angle being sufficient to keep the knocked out gunman from sliding back down onto the boardwalk. "But I wasn't wrong," Sam replied. "You heard what he said." He gave a jerk of his head in the direction of the saloon.

"Yes, I heard him admit they were coming to goad you, to start trouble," Julie Ann said, not seeming to be able to let it go. "But what if they weren't out for trouble? What if you had been *wrong*?"

"I wasn't wrong," Sam insisted with a trace of a smile. "That's as much as I can say about it."

Julie Ann shook her head as if she were put out with him. Yet she returned the ranger's smile, saying, "I can't tell you how much that sounds like something my father might have said."

Sam gave a glance back toward the Even Odds Saloon. "Let's go inside, in case any of his pals wants to come and get him."

Julie Ann looked at the dazed gunman as Sam reached down, scooped up Snake Bentell's battered sombrero, shook it out and stuffed it down on Snake's head. Snake lay sprawled limply in the tilted chair, his hands dangling down over the chair arms almost to the boardwalk. His head rocked back and forth, then settled as he mumbled something under his breath. "He's one of Swain's men," she said. "I've heard his name is Bentell."

"You mean Buel Bentell?" Sam asked, "Better known as Snake?"

"Yes, I believe Snake is what they call him," said Julie. "You've heard of him?"

"Yes, I've heard of him," said the ranger. Sam didn't mention that he'd seen this man riding toward Redemption with Giles Capp and the others. Instead he opened the door to the sheriff's office for her and looked up at the newly hung wooden badge for a moment and said, "Now, that's better. I couldn't stand seeing that badge hanging crooked. It gives the wrong image."

"I know," Julie Ann said. "It happened after my father's death. He would never have allowed such a thing to go unattended."

"I'm sure he wouldn't have, Julie Ann," Sam said as they stepped inside. Sam closed the door behind them and walked over and looked out the window down at Snake Bentell. From this angle all he saw of the knocked-out gunman were his legs from the knees down and his dusty boots lying motionless on the boardwalk. Sam gave a sidelong glance in the direction of the saloon and said, "Now we'll see who comes to get Buel Bentell. That'll tell us who's really in charge of things here."

Sam searched the opposite side of the street along the row of storefronts until his eyes found one that reflected the street like a dark mirror. He smiled to himself, watching the reflection of a freight wagon roll slowly down the rutted street. He looked at the ghost-like image of the Even Odds Saloon, seeing two men in business suits step out through the doors and walk away along the boardwalk. Stepping back from the window yet still keeping an eye on the reflection of the Even Odds Saloon in the storefront, Sam said, "I bet your pa spent a lot of time gazing out this window before that wooden star blocked the view."

"Yes, it seems he did," Julie Ann said, giving Sam a curious look. She stepped forward and looked back and forth along the street, not noticing the reflection in the storefront. "What makes you say that?" she asked.

Not wanting to tell her just yet, Sam nodded down at coffee cup rings on the window ledge and said, "I can see where he sat his coffee."

"Oh . . ." Julie studied the rings for a moment, then said, "That's very attentive of you."

Sam only watched her as she once again looked back and forth along the street. Before stepping away from the window, she started to close the curtain, but Sam stopped her, saying, "Leave it open for a while. Let's keep an eye on the comings and goings along the street. You never know what we might see out there." He walked over to the oak desk, took out the big Starr pistol and checked it. Then he handed it to her, saying, "I'm getting ready to leave here for a few minutes. I want you to leave the door locked and don't unlock it for any reason. No matter what anybody says out there, don't answer them."

Julie gave him a curious look. "But if the door is locked from the inside, they'll know somebody is in here."

"That's what I want them to know. But don't say a word. If anything serious happens, you fire a shot and I'll come running . . . but I don't think there's anything to worry about." He gave a stern look and said, "It's important that you do just like I ask, all right?"

"All right," she said, "but where are you going?"

"I'm going to see Andrew Swain and let him know how innocent I think he is," said the ranger.

Chapter 4

Inside the doors of the Even Odds Saloon, Danny Boy
Wright had skidded to a halt and tried to look as if
nothing had happened. But his red sweaty face and his
panting breath told on him, as did his empty holster.
Conversation stopped; all the faces along the bar
turned toward him. The piano player stopped abruptly
in mid song. At the table in the far corner Giles Capp,
Bo Altero, Charlie Floose and Andrew Swain stood
up slowly, staring hard in his direction. Danny Boy
looked away from the faces along the bar and hurried
across the floor to Giles Capp. Passing the piano he
shouted at the old piano player, "What the hell are
you waiting for? *Play!*" He whirled toward the bar
and shouted at the staring faces. "What the hell are
you fools gawking at?" The drinkers turned away, but
watched him in the mirror as he hurried on to
Swain's table.

Staring at Danny Boy Wright, Giles Capp said
sternly, "Where is your pistol, Danny Boy?"

"He took it, Giles!" Danny Boy replied, scared, em-
barrassed, not knowing what to expect from Capp.
Before Capp could respond, Danny Boy said, "I swear
I never seen nothing like it! He beat Snake senseless,

left him laying on the boardwalk . . . he could be dead for all I know!"

"Oh, yeah?" said Capp. "In other words you threw in your gun and hightailed it so fast you don't even know if one of our *own* is dead or alive?"

"That ain't how it happened, Giles! I'm telling you, this ranger moved so fast I never had time to get my gun before he got ahold of it somehow and cocked it right in my face!" Danny Boy shook his head vigorously. "He's faster than anything I've ever seen! And he's as cold-blooded as anything walking this earth!"

Giles Capp gave him a disgusted look. "Take it easy, Danny Boy, or you might never be able to father children." He kicked a chair out with his boot. "Sit down so people will quit staring at you . . . you're shaming every one of us."

Danny Boy reached with a shaky hand toward the bottle of bourbon sitting on the table. But Giles Capp pushed the bottle away from his hand. "Huh-uh! This is for us workingmen." He looked at Charlie Floose and said, "Charlie, go get this man a beer. His hands are shaking so bad he couldn't take a piss without abusing himself."

Bo Altero chuckled under his breath. Swain stared at Danny Boy Wright with a look of concern on his brow. Charlie Floose grumbled to himself but walked over to the bar and ordered Danny Boy a tall mug of beer. Danny Boy gave Bo Altero a cold stare, saying, "You wouldn't think it was so damn funny if it happened to you!"

"It wouldn't *happen* to me, Danny Boy," said Bo Altero. "My hand never shakes that bad." He grinned, making a loose fist and shaking it back and forth in Danny Boy's face.

"You son of a bit—!" Danny Boy blew up, but

Giles Capp shoved him back down in his chair, cutting him off.

Looking at Bo Altero, Giles Capp said, "Everybody settle down, damn it!" He looked at Swain. "Is there still a sawed-off behind that bar?"

"Well, yes, of course there is," said Swain, looking curious as to what Giles Capp had in mind. "What are you thinking about doing?"

"I'm thinking about splattering that ranger all over the front of the sheriff's office, is what I'm thinking about doing!" said Capp.

Charlie Floose returned to the table with a frothing mug of beer and set it down in front of Danny Boy. "Obliged, Charlie," Danny Boy said in a lowered voice. He lifted the mug with both hands and took a long swig. When he set the mug down and wiped his hand across his mouth, he saw all four men staring at him in tense anticipation.

"So? What went wrong, Danny Boy?" Giles Capp asked impatiently. "And keep your voice down so the whole damn saloon don't hear about it."

"We didn't do anything wrong," said Danny Boy, lowering his voice a bit. "We walked down to the sheriff's office to feel the ranger out just like you told us to. Snake started to say something to him, but he never even got his words out of his mouth! The ranger flew into him with a hammer! Beat him cock-eyed right down to the boardwalk!"

"My God, a hammer?" said Swain, giving a slight wince of pain at the image inside his head.

"He hit him with the handle," Danny Boy said. "But he must've hit him a half-dozen times!"

"And all this time you couldn't do nothing to help Snake?" said Capp.

"Maybe it wasn't a half-dozen times," Danny Boy

said, changing his story. "But he hit him so quick I couldn't count . . . and I couldn't make a move to stop him. Then, when I did go for my gun, it was gone!"

Bo Altero and Charlie Floose gave one another a disbelieving smirk. Danny Boy saw their reaction but was powerless to do anything about it at the moment. Giles Capp leaned down close to Danny Boy's face and said, "You expect me to believe that the ranger did all that so fast that all you could do was turn and run? Where is Snake now?"

"Still laying there is what I'm thinking," said Danny Boy, "unless the ranger hauled him in and put him in jail."

"In jail for what, you damned idiot," Giles Capp growled, "for bleeding on a public walkway?"

Bo Altero and Charlie Floose stifled a laugh. Swain saw no humor in any of it. He cut in saying to Danny Boy, "The ranger didn't mention me, did he? I mean he didn't ask any questions about me, or the saloon?"

All four eyes turned to Swain. "No," said Danny Boy, "the ranger never said a word about you or the saloon or anything else. He just commenced beating the hell out of Snake."

"I never heard of a ranger doing something like that." Giles Capp shook his head as if to clear it and get a better picture of what had happened. "Let me get this straight," he said to Danny Boy. "The two of you walked up, never said a word, never did anything? The ranger just started beating Snake with a hammer?"

Danny Boy shrugged in his bewilderment. "Yes, that's the size of it. Snake might have said something like, 'Well, well . . . you're the ranger we heard of.' But I swear that was all he got out of his mouth! Next thing I knew, Snake was falling all over me, the ranger had my gun . . . and I was staring death in the eyes! He would have killed me too. But luckily I got out of there before he said *three*."

"Before he said what?" asked Capp. All four men listened intently.

"When he cocked my gun in my face," said Danny Boy, "he started counting. He counted real slow and cold-blooded like. He counted to two and I saw he was about to pull the trigger. So, I lit out . . . figuring it was best I hurry back here and let you know what happened. We can't leave Snake laying knocked out on the boardwalk!"

Giles Capp just stared at him for a moment. "No, we can't," Capp finally said, without taking his eyes off of Danny Boy Wright. "Charlie, go get that sawed-off from behind the bar," he said to Charlie Floose.

Charlie Floose gave Bo Altero a look of exasperation, but then he hurried away to the bar and walked behind it. Bending down, he picked up the shotgun.

Danny Boy looked scared. "Giles, you ain't going to shoot me are you?" he said in a broken voice.

"No, but I'm damn close to it," Giles Capp said. "We're all going to go get Snake and bring him back here. If that hammer-swinging ranger pokes his nose in, I'll blow it off myself! Seems doing everything myself is the only way to get anything done *right* around here."

"Going there now is a bad idea," said Andrew Swain, speaking with the authority he thought he held among Giles Capp and the Rio Sagrado Gang. He rose halfway up from his chair. "We're going to wait and see what this ranger does next."

"Sit down and shut up!" Giles Capp hissed, keeping his voice down, but not keeping his hand from almost snatching his pistol from its holster. "You're not calling any shots! You're here because we saw a way for both of us to make some money. Don't think that gives you any rights!"

Andrew Swain wasn't going to be put off that easily. "Your brother and I made an agreement. This is as much my show as yours!" said Swain, standing his ground.

"Oh, that's right, I almost forgot," said Giles Capp, appearing to settle down a bit. But then he suddenly snatched the sawed-off shotgun from Charlie Floose's hands as Charlie returned with it from the bar. Giles threw the gun across the table into Andrew Swain's hands, Swain catching it in reflex action.

"What the hell is this for?" Swain asked, looking at the shotgun as if it had just dropped from the sky.

"You're going to lead us down the boardwalk to get Snake," said Giles Capp.

Swain's face took on a sickly expression. The shotgun fell to the tabletop as if it were red-hot. "I'm no gunman, Giles!" he said, coming unnerved at the thought of such a thing.

"You are now," said Capp. "And if you think we won't put you in front and make you go faceup with that ranger, then you've seriously misjudged us. Right, boys?"

None of the men replied, but Swain saw each of them take a short step forward, closing in tighter around him. He held his hands chest-high. "All right, Giles. I admit I spoke hastily. You know this side of the business better than I do. Like I said, I'm no gunman."

"Then sit your ass down and stay out of a *gunman's* way," said Capp.

Swain dropped back into his chair without hesitation.

Giles Capp picked up the shotgun, then reached down and pulled Danny Boy Wright to his feet. "Come on, Danny Boy."

"Me?" Danny Boy said in surprise, still shaken from his encounter with the ranger.

"Yeah, you, Danny Boy," said Giles Capp. "I know you're wanting to go get your gun back."

"It's an old gun . . ." Danny Boy said weakly, not wanting to face the ranger again. But seeing the sharp expressions on the faces of the rest of the men as they turned their eyes to him, he quickly said, "But you're damn right I want it back. He might have caught me and Snake off guard once, but he'll never do it again."

The ranger stepped away from the window when he looked out and saw the reflection of the men come out of the Even Odds Saloon and stand looking toward the sheriff's office. He noted the sawed-off shotgun in Giles Capp's hand. "All right, Julie, it's time for me to go," Sam said, closing the curtain quickly and turning to her. "Remember what I told you. I'll be right back."

"Be careful, Sam," Julie Ann said, holding the big Starr pistol against her chest with both hands.

"Yes, ma'am, I will be," he replied. "Now, come back here and lock this door behind me."

"What have you got up your sleeve, Ranger Sam?" Henry Dove asked, staring out between the bars of his cell as Sam rushed past him on the way to the rear door.

"Nothing for you to concern yourself with, Henry," the ranger said in passing.

He hurried out the back door and only hesitated long enough to hear Julie slip the big cross bolt in

place. Then he ran along the alley to the rear of the
Even Odds Saloon and walked in through the back
door, slowing down to an easy walk as he spotted
Andrew Swain based on a description Julie Ann had
given him of the man. Richly dressed in a boiled white
shirt and a flashy brocade vest, the bald man with the
thinly trimmed mustache sat alone at a table with a
bottle of bourbon in front of him. Sam walked unnoticed to the table, not having to pass the drinkers at
the bar on the way to the table.

"Andrew Swain," Sam said quietly, catching Swain's
attention as the saloon owner wiped a red gentleman's
handkerchief across his sweaty forehead.

"Ye—Yes," Swain stammered, seeing above all else
the ranger badge on Sam's chest, then the way Sam
came toward him with his hand poised near the big
Colt on his hip.

Swain started to rise from his chair, but the ranger
motioned him back down with his free hand.

"Keep your seat, Mr. Swain," said Sam. "I'm here
to talk to you about the death of Sheriff Mack Dolan."

"Sheriff Mack Dolan?" Andrew Swain gave a nervous glance toward the bat-wing doors, hoping that
Giles Capp and the others hadn't already gone to the
sheriff's office. But he realized it was too late. He'd
seen them pass the large windows only seconds ago.

"That's right, Swain," said the ranger, keeping a
low-level tone of voice. "You haven't forgotten Sheriff
Dolan have you? He died right out there in the
street."

"Of course I haven't forgotten him," Swain said.
"But surely you don't think I had anything to do with
that! My goodness, Ranger!"

"Hold it, Swain," said the ranger, holding up a

hand, stopping him. "Did I say that you had anything to do with it?"

"Well, I assumed that was what you were implying," said Swain, sweating heavier than before.

"Oh?" Sam's tone of voice softened a bit. "Then I beg your pardon, Mr. Swain. I know you didn't have anything to do with his death."

"Really?" Swain looked surprised. He seemed to relax a little. "His daughter has accused me of killing him. I must've thought that perhaps she'd convinced you. Women can be so convincing as we both know." Swain raised a hand for the bartender to bring over a fresh glass. "Care for a drink, Ranger?" he asked.

"Obliged, but no thanks," Sam said. He looked over at the bartender and motioned for him to stay put behind the bar. "I never drink when I'm working. I'm after the sheriff's killer. I've got an idea you know who it is."

Swain's expression turned worried again. "Me? Of course I have no idea who killed the sheriff," he said. "If I did I would have already told someone . . . either the new acting sheriff, the territorial judge or someone like yourself."

The ranger just stared at him for a moment, then said, "I believe you know who did it and you're afraid to say anything about it. You're afraid they'll kill you next."

"*They?*" said Swain, starting to feel better again. He cocked his head slightly and gave Sam a questioning gaze. "Ranger, who do you mean by *they*?"

"We both know who I mean, Swain," said Sam. "I'm talking about the Rio Sagrado Gang. I'm talking about Axel and Giles Capp and their band of murderers and thugs. Somehow they have taken you into their midst . . . and I imagine that about now you're looking for a way out before they turn on you, the way they always do sooner or later."

Swain fidgeted in his chair. "The way they always do, you say? What do you mean by that, Ranger . . . not that I *am* involved with them in any way."

Sam nodded slowly. "I understand, Mr. Swain," he said sympathetically. "If I were in your boots, I would be awfully careful who I confided in and what I admitted to. After all, you don't know me. But if you've been consorting with the Capps and their pals, you know by now what they're capable of doing. There'll come a time when these men will turn on you like wild dogs."

Swain tried to form a nervous smile. "Ranger, you're misinformed about me. I run this saloon, I do some gambling, that's it for me. I have nothing to worry about from the Capps, because I have nothing to do with them. We certainly have no alliance or partnership of any sort."

"If that's true, then I suppose you have nothing to worry about. You're the only who knows if it's true or not." Sam raised a finger for emphasis. "I'm going after whoever killed Sheriff Dolan. When they begin to realize there's a noose with their name on it, you better hope they don't push you up onto that gallows ahead of them."

"For God sakes, Ranger," said Swain, trying to chuckle a little to show how unconcerned he was by all this, "you make these men sound like something straight up from hell."

Sam held up his hand. "Enough said, Mr. Swain. But just remember, my job is to protect innocent people like you from getting tangled up with the likes of the Rio Sagrado Gang. Don't wait until it's too late for me to help you. Do you understand?"

"Sure." Swain shrugged, trying to appear uninterested.

Sam backed away, then turned and left quietly through the back door. As soon as the door closed behind the ranger, Andrew Swain stood up on shaky legs, picked up his black linen suit coat draped over the chair next to him and put it on quickly. He headed for the bat-wing doors; but before he'd gone three steps, he stopped and considered everything the ranger had said. Rubbing his chin, he walked back to the table and plopped down into his chair. Not so fast, he told himself. This ranger thought he was innocent. *Good enough* . . . Maybe he better take a few breaths, clear his mind and think this over before mentioning it to Giles Capp.

Chapter 5

On the boardwalk in front of the sheriff's office, ten feet from where Snake Bentell lay sprawled in the chair tilted back against the building, Giles Capp stood with the shotgun poised and said to Charlie Floose, "I've got you covered, Charlie, go get him."

Floose looked doubtful. He glanced at the window above Snake's head. "What if this is a trick? It looks like it could be a trick to me."

"He said he's got you covered, Floose!" said Bo Altero, giving Floose a hard shove forward. With daggers in his eyes, Floose looked back at Altero; but he rushed the rest of the way to Snake Bentell in a crouch.

"Where we going?" Snake asked in a groggy voice, his jaws swollen twice their size.

"Keep quiet, Snake," Floose whispered. He turned the tilted wooden chair around and dragged it back to where the other three gunmen stood waiting. Snake's head lolled back and forth like a drunkard's.

When they had arrived moments earlier, Giles Capp had called out three times for the ranger, but he'd gotten no answer. Now that Snake was back in their fold, Giles Capp called out loudly again. This time when he got no response, he said to the others, "I'm going to check that door, cover me." He walked down off of the boardwalk and circled halfway across the street, keeping an eye on the window until he stepped back onto the boardwalk and stayed close to the building as he sidestepped over to the door and tried turning the handle. Grinning at the others, he said in a raised whisper, "It's locked. Looks like our ranger is a little shy when company comes calling."

The other gunmen relaxed a bit. "I'll be damn," said Bo Altero. "I've never seen a ranger lock himself indoors and hide!"

Floose and Danny Boy both chuckled. "Guess he's not so tough when he doesn't get the drop on somebody," said Danny Boy. He raised his voice to the window, saying, "I'm getting my gun back, Ranger. Hear me? First time I see you out on the street, I'm taking my gun back!"

"Think he hears you, Danny Boy?" Floose asked.

"He hears me all right," Danny Boy called out, "don't you, Ranger."

In the alley behind the sheriff's office, Sam hurried to the back door and rapped softly, until Julie Ann asked in a hushed tone, "Who is it?"

"It's me, Sam, let me in," the ranger said.

Julie unlatched the door and Sam came in quickly, latched it and hurried to the front window. Pulling the curtain open enough to look across the street, he saw the gunmen's reflection in the store window. They walked back toward the saloon, two of them dragging Snake Bentell along by his chair back. Sam smiled slightly, went to the front door, unlocked it and stepped out onto the boardwalk with his thumbs hooked in his belt. He stood in full view, making sure the men dragging Snake's chair got a good look at him.

"Giles! There he is!" said Danny Boy, turning loose of Snake's chair, leaving all the weight on Floose.

"Jesus!" said Floose, letting the chair go. Snake crashed to the boardwalk and let out a groan.

Bo Altero's Colt came up from his holster as he turned. Giles Capp crouched with the shotgun ready, his thumb over the hammers. But upon seeing the ranger staring at them from a hundred feet away, his thumbs hooked in his belt, both men eased up and lowered their guns. "Get him up from there," said Capp, giving a nod down at Snake Bentell. This ranger ain't interested in tangling with us."

"Are you damn sure this is the same ranger who done so much damage to Junior Lake and his bunch?" Bo Altero asked Danny Boy, putting a sarcastic snap to his tone of voice.

But Danny Boy didn't answer as he and Floose righted Snake's chair and dragged their knocked-out comrade into the Even Odds Saloon. Giles Capp and Bo Altero stood for a moment longer, staring back at the ranger until they saw him turn and go back inside the sheriff's office. "What do you make of this?" Altero asked, lowering his Colt back into his holster.

"I think he's scared, is what I think," said Capp. "He's heard who we are by now. That sheriff's daughter has told him enough that by now he knows he's fooling with the Rio Sagrado Gang." He grinned. "It ain't the first time I've seen men turn yellow at the mention of our name."

"If you're right," said Altero, "we'll soon have him out of our hair." Turning, the two pushed open the bat-wing doors and entered the Even Odds Saloon.

Capp and Altero swaggered a bit as they walked over to Swain's table, where the saloon owner had stood up when Floose and Danny Boy came dragging

Snake's chair across the floor toward him. "What—What happened?" Swain asked Floose, stepping around his table and looking down at Snake's battered face. "Is he . . . ?" His words trailed.

"Naw, he's alive," said Floose. He shook Snake by his shoulder until Snake groaned and held his head upright for a moment. "See, he's all right . . . or he will be, once these jaws heal."

Swain turned his attention away from Snake and toward Giles Capp as he and Altero came closer and stopped beside the table. He'd decided not to mention that the ranger had left there only moments ago. He would wait and see what they had to say first. "Well?" Swain asked, looking them up and down.

"Well, what?" Capp replied. He reached out, picked up the bottle of bourbon, bypassed a glass and raised the bottle to his lips. He swallowed freely, Swain watching his expensive bourbon disappear without being savored.

"Well . . . what happened?" said Swain, taking the bottle as soon as Capp lowered it.

"I don't think we'll have any more trouble out of that ranger," said Capp.

"Oh?" Swain didn't want to say too much; he wanted to listen. As he stood staring at Capp, Altero snatched the bottle from his hand and threw back a long drink before Swain could grab the bottle back. This time he clasped it to his chest.

"He wouldn't even step out and face me when I called him out," said Capp.

"Maybe he wasn't there," said Swain, feeling his way along in the conversation.

"Oh, he was there all right," Altero cut in, wiping a hand across his mouth. Swain watched his prized bourbon run down Altero's beard-stubbled chin. "We looked back and saw him standing on the boardwalk after we'd already got back here."

Swain looked puzzled by Altero's words. "You saw him? On the boardwalk?"

"Yep," said Capp. He started to reach for the bourbon, but Swain backed away a step and motioned for the bartender to bring a bottle of cheap rye. "He was too scared to show his face while we were there."

"But you did *see him*?" Swain asked, wondering for a second if there could possibly be more than one ranger in town.

"Why the hell do you keep asking me that?" said Capp, giving the saloon owner a curious look.

"Nothing, never mind," said Swain, shaking his head as if to clear it.

The bartender hurried up to Swain with a fresh bottle of red rye. "Here you are, sir," he said to Swain.

"Thank you, Dick," said Swain, taking the bottle of rye and handing the bartender the bottle of bourbon. "Put this away for me. I'll save it for a special occasion."

"Don't tell me never mind!" said Giles Capp. "Twice you asked me if we saw the ranger . . . twice I told you *yes*. Why does that strike you as strange?" He narrowed a gaze at Swain.

The bartender, hearing Capp say they had just seen the ranger, gave Swain a bemused look. Capp saw the look and said, "Whoa, what was that?"

"What was what?" said Swain.

The bartender ducked his head and turned to leave, but Capp caught him by his arm and stopped him abruptly. "I got enough sense to know when somebody is passing looks back and forth! Now, spit it out, one of you!"

"Let him go, I'll tell you," said Swain. He swallowed

a knot in his throat as Capp turned the bartender loose. Then he said as the bartender hurried away, "He gave me that look because the ranger was just here."

Capp and the others looked confused. "He couldn't have been," said Altero. "We just saw him standing out on the boardwalk!"

"How long ago was he here?" Capp asked.

"It hasn't been but a few minutes," said Swain. "I stood right here talking to him."

"Oh, yeah? Talking to him about what?" asked Capp.

"He asked me about Sheriff Dolan's death. I never told him a thing, that's the truth so help me God!" said Swain, his words spilling out nervously.

"Hey, slow down, take it easy," said Capp, giving Swain a questioning stare. "Why didn't you tell me about it as soon as I walked through the door?"

"Why?" Swain stalled for a second, then said, "Well, I wanted to hear what you had to say first, that's all."

Capp looked the saloon owner up and down, then chuckled and said, "Somebody get Swain here a rag, or a mop, or something, before he drowns in his own sweat." To Swain he said, "What the hell is wrong with you anyway?"

"Nothing, it's just that the ranger coming here caught me by surprise. He's like some strange stalking cat. All the time he was here, I kept feeling like any minute he was going to pounce!"

Capp looked at the back door of the saloon. He looked down at Snake Bentell's battered face, then at Danny Boy's empty holster. "Looks like *surprise* is that ranger's strong suit. He might appear like a stalking cat to you," Capp said to Swain, "but if he keeps

this up, he better hope he's got nine lives to spare."
Turning to Charlie Floose, Capp said, "Floose, get
yourself a beer and a cigar and get on the boardwalk.
Keep an eye on the sheriff's office. If he sticks his
neck out that door and looks this way, I want to know
about it. He can't see us unless he comes out and
shows himself. So, there goes his element of surprise
from now on."

"He ain't . . . human," said Snake's strained rasping voice.

All eyes went down to Snake, who had come
around and sat touching a hand to his battered jaw.

"Don't you ever let me hear you say something like
that again, Snake," Capp warned him. "He's no different than we are! He just made a fast move and
spooked a couple of yas. But that's all in the past now.
Don't make him bigger than what he is . . . just one
more lawdog with his tail in the air."

"Sorry, Giles," Snake murmured.

"Snake, you all right now?" Danny Boy asked,
stooping down beside his partner.

"Do I look all right . . . to you?" Snake groaned.

In the sheriff's office, the ranger looked out through
the window and saw Charlie Floose walk out onto the
boardwalk and look in his direction. Sam smiled to
himself and stepped back. "Did you talk to Swain?"
Julie asked as he turned facing her.

"Yes, I spoke to him," said Sam, "just enough to
introduce myself and let him know that I can come
walking up to him at any time, in spite of all his gunmen friends."

"Did he say anything that might help you charge
him with my father's death?" she asked.

"No," Sam replied. "But I wasn't expecting him to.

gave him some things to think about. If he and the
io Sagrado Gang are involved in your father's death,
e'll soon hear something from him. I told him I think
e's innocent, but that I know Giles Capp and his
ang are guilty. Once Swain realizes that the law is
oing to make somebody answer for your dad's death,
e's going to think things over and start looking for
omebody to ally himself with on this side of the law."

"He'll blame my father's death on the others and
ope to go free himself?" Julie Ann asked.

"That's what I'm hoping for," said Sam. As he
oke he looked back toward the cell where Henry
ove stood looking at them between his bars. He
new that he and Julie Ann had not been talking loud
nough for Dove to hear them. He raised his voice
nd said, "Henry, I'm going to bring Sheriff Dolan's
illers to justice. Until I do, if you saw anything that
ight, your life is in danger walking the streets of
edemption."

"I didn't see anything, Ranger Sam," said Henry
ove. "I told you I was asleep . . . asleep on whiskey.
nderstand?" he said firmly.

Sam walked closer to the cell and said, "Yes, I un-
erstand. But do the killers understand? Maybe you
idn't see anything that night. But what if they *think*
ou saw something? These men hold life pretty cheap,
lenry. If they have the slightest doubt, they'll kill just
 cover their tracks. So, I'm not the one you have to
orry about believing what you say . . . they are."

"I know all that, Ranger Sam. I've had plenty of
me to think about it from every which angle ever
nce I got put here. I never saw anything that hap-
ened that night, and there ain't nothing more for me
 say about it."

"These men don't think anything about you taking

the blame for Sheriff Dolan's murder, Henry," Sam
said in a quiet tone just between the two of them.
"Nothing would suit them better than to watch you
hang for a crime they committed."

"I know that too," said Dove, the ranger's words
not budging him. "I've seen many of these kind of
men, Ranger Sam. Trouble is, I've seen as many of
them on the *right* side of the law as I have seen against
it. I trust only the Lord, Ranger Sam. And I don't
even tell him *everything* I see."

The ranger started to say something more, but before he could speak, the front door opened and Councilmen Avondale and Meaker walked in, this time
accompanied by a tall, broad-chested man carrying a
Remington rifle at port arms. "Ranger Burrack," said
Avondale, without so much as a tip of his hat to Julie
Ann, "this is our acting sheriff, Delbert Watts."

Watts gave Sam a sheepish look as he stepped forward and said, "Ranger, I'm here to fulfill the duties
of sheriff until a permanent sheriff is elected."

"Glad to make your acquaintance, Sheriff Watts,"
said Sam. "Is this your first experience upholding
the law?"

Watts looked surprised at the ranger's welcoming
attitude. But he also looked a bit embarrassed at his
lack of experience as he said, "Yes, this is my first
time wearing a badge." His hand went to the new tin
badge on his chest for a moment, then dropped to his
side. "I've been the blacksmith here ever since I arrived two years ago."

"Well, I wouldn't worry about it if I were you,"
said the ranger. "I'll be here to help you any way
I can."

"You won't be needed here, Ranger," Councilman
Avondale cut in.

Ignoring Avondale as if he weren't there, Sam said to Watts, "It's a ranger's duty to assist local law authority. I'll stay here as long as it takes, to see to it that you uphold the law properly."

Watts looked puzzled. He turned a gaze to Avondale and Meaker. "I just told you, Ranger," said Avondale, "you are free to leave Redemption now that we have ourselves an appointed sheriff."

"I heard you, Avondale," said Sam. "But I'm still investigating a robbery here in Redemption, and until I'm finished, I'll expect full cooperation from your new sheriff."

"A *robbery?* What robbery?" Avondale fumed.

Sam gestured a hand toward Henry Dove standing with his hands clasped around the bars, staring out at them. "This man was robbed of sixty dollars in his sleep the night Sheriff Dolan was killed. I intend to find the person who stole it before I leave town." As he spoke, Sam's eyes locked onto Delbert Watts' for a moment, just long enough to force Watts to look away. Then Sam turned to Avondale, seeing he was about to say something. "Before you say anything, Councilman," Sam said calmly, "let me caution you that I won't tolerate any interference while I'm solving this case."

"That does it," Avondale said, his voice controlled but trembling with anger. "I'm contacting your captain! We'll see how long you stay here after I tell him you're not welcome."

"You do that," said Sam. "I'll be contacting him myself afterward just to make sure you didn't skip any details. I might even want him to see if he can round up a couple of more rangers and have them stop by here. Even though we're short of men, I think he'll want to see to it I get some help solving the robbery."

Avondale's face reddened. Councilman Meaker

tugged his coat sleeve, nudging him toward the door. "Come along, Willis, let's let Sheriff Watts deal with the ranger. It's his job now."

"I told you before, Ranger," said Avondale, shaking his finger toward Sam, "you haven't seen the last of me!"

"I told you before, Councilman," said the ranger, "I hope not."

Once again, Avondale and Meaker found themselves stomping out of the sheriff's office in a huff. As soon as they were gone, Julie Ann closed the door behind them and turned alongside the ranger, facing Delbert Watts.

"Well, now, Sheriff Watts," said Sam. "I guess I'll start my robbery investigation by talking to you."

"To me?" Watts' eyes looked worried. "Why with me?"

"According to Henry, you were the person who brought him to the jail the night Sheriff Dolan got shot. Did you see anybody who might stoop so low as to rob a man in his sleep?" Contempt showed in Sam's voice. "Somebody who might use the death of a good man like Sheriff Mack Dolan as an opportunity to hide their crime. Pretty cowardly, wouldn't you say?"

Watts couldn't look the ranger in the eyes. "I have no idea who would do something like that, Ranger Burrack," he said. "But where did a man like Henry Dove get sixty dollars? And if he had it, who can say he didn't steal it himself?"

Sam looked confused by Watts' words for a moment. But then, as if it became clear to him what Watts meant, he said, "Oh, I see what you're doing. You're giving me the answers some low despicable sneak-thief might use to justify such an act." Sam smiled, looked at Julie Ann, then back to Watts.

'That's good thinking on your part. Knowing how a poltroon like that thinks might help us find him."

"Us?" said Watts.

"Yep," said the ranger. "I want you by my side all the while I search for this thief. When we find him, we'll expose what he did to the whole town. How would that make him feel?" His eyes burrowed deep into Watts'. "Then we'll see to it he goes to prison over in Yuma for a year or two. Would that be justice enough for you, Mr. Dove?" he asked, turning to face the dark face staring at Watts through the bars.

"Yes, Ranger Sam," said Dove in his deep gravelly voice. "I believe that would suit me fine."

Chapter 6

Walking on the opposite side of the street from the Even Odds Saloon with Delbert Watts right beside him, the ranger noted the pensive look on the new sheriff's face as he cast a quick glance at the saloon doors. Then he noted the look of relief on Delbert's face when they both saw that none of the Rio Sagrado Gang stepped out onto the boardwalk as they passed by. The two didn't stop until they stood outside of the big ragged tent where the stranded travelers from Nicodemus, Kansas, had taken up temporary lodging.

"We're not going inside, are we?" Delbert asked as Sam pulled back the tent flap. On a short pole stuck in the ground beside the tent flap, a faded wooden sign read: BEER, WHISKEY, CIGARS SOLD CHEAP. A big red hound lay in the dirt beside the pole. The animal only lifted its drooping face up to Sam and Delbert for a second, as if looking them over before expelling a breath and dropping its sleepy head back to the ground.

"We haven't even been invited in yet, Sheriff," Sam said, offering a thin smile. "Hello, the tent," he said through the open fly. Taking a look around the crowded tent, Sam saw two small children playing on a quilt pallet in a rear corner. Faces turned to him from the bar and from one battered wooden table in the middle of the dirt floor. Bundles of blanket-wrapped belongings lay piled along both sides of the tent. Noting the ranger badge on Sam's chest, a short stocky man stepped from behind a makeshift bar and walked to the front of the tent, drying his hands on a bar apron around his waist.

"Can I help you, Ranger?" the man asked, wiping his hand across his sweaty forehead.

"I've brought the new sheriff with me," said Sam. "Can we come in?"

"Sure enough," said the man, "this is a public facility." He smiled and added, "I'm Earnest Beavens, proprietor."

Stepping inside through the fly, Sam took off his sombrero and moved to the side, allowing Delbert to enter. "I'm Ranger Sam Burrack, Mr. Beavens," he said, "and this is Redemption's new acting sheriff, Delbert Watts."

Beavens looked Watts up and down, his eyes and expression revealing nothing. "I'm familiar with Mr. Watts." He turned his eyes back to the ranger. "What brings you here, Ranger?"

"I'm helping the new sheriff look into Henry Dove's claim that he was robbed of sixty dollars the night Sheriff Dolan got killed. I'm told the fellows who that money belonged to are staying here until they get their animals and get back on the trail?"

"Yes, they are," said Earnest Beavens. "But I think everybody's got a pretty good idea who took that money off of Henry Dove."

"Is that a fact?" said Sam. He looked back and forth between Beavens and Delbert Watts, noting how Beavens' eyes stayed fixed on Watts, but Watts seemed to have difficulty facing the man. "Hear that, Sheriff?" Sam said to Watts. "Looks like we came to the right place. Maybe we can get this thing straightened out."

Beavens and Watts both gave the ranger a curious look. Upon hearing part of the conversation, two men stood up from the wooden table, one of them handing a baby to a woman before pulling his wide suspenders up onto his shoulders and walking toward the ranger. "Ranger, I believe we're the folks you ought to be talking to," the man said. He and the man beside him looked enough alike to be twins. "I'm Raymond Beck. This is my younger brother, LJ Beck. We're the ones that money belonged to." As he spoke, his eyes fixed on Delbert Watts. "And it wasn't *sixty* dollars. It was sixty-*four* dollars to be exact."

The ranger looked at Watts. "Do you hear that, Sheriff? It wasn't sixty dollars, it was sixty-four dollars."

Without looking the ranger in the eyes, Watts said, "Yeah, I heard him."

Now the Beck brothers both gave the ranger a curious look. "What is this all about, Ranger?" asked Raymond Beck. Even as he spoke to the ranger, his eyes turned to Watts and stayed there. Watts wouldn't return his gaze. "Everybody knows who took that money off of Henry Dove."

"Then why didn't any of you say anything?" Sam asked flatly.

"You *know* damn well why we didn't say anything, Ranger," LJ Beck cut in. "We'd have to be fools to open our mouths in a—"

"What my brother means is—" Raymond raised his voice, cutting LJ off as he gave him a stern look. "We didn't want to falsely accuse anybody here in Redemption, Ranger. We realize we're strangers here . . . Kansas is a long ways from here. Right, brother?"

"Yeah, that's what I was going to say," LJ murmured grudgingly.

"We didn't want to falsely accuse anybody, then," said Raymond, his eyes going back to Watts, almost nodding at the sheriff's badge on his chest, "and we for sure don't want to go blaming nobody now."

"I see," said the ranger. "What's the chance that Henry Dove might have spent that money drinking, then made up the part about somebody robbing him?"

Raymond Beck's eyes smoldered with rage. But he kept himself under control. "That *ain't* what happened, Ranger," he said in a clipped tone. "Henry Dove wouldn't leave us stranded here, with our womenfolk, with these children . . . one of them sick anyways and needing to get home to Nicodemus."

"But Henry said himself that he was drinking," said the ranger, "enough that he passed out in the alley. If he was that drunk, how'd he pay for his drinking? He didn't have that much money of his own."

"I don't know," said Raymond Beck. "But he ain't the kind of man would leave another man and his family stranded this way. No kind of man I ever known would do something like that."

"I agree with you," said the ranger. "Only the lowest kind of snake would do a fellow that way. But a lawman has to look at all the possibilities, no matter how slim they are, right, Sheriff Watts?"

"Uh, yeah," Watts murmured under his breath. "Henry is a drinking man," he said quietly.

"Henry Dove is no low-down sneak thief. He's a *good* man," said Raymond. "He didn't rob us!"

"Easy, Raymond," said the ranger, seeing the young man's fist ball at his side. "I believe Henry's a good man myself. I've known him awhile, and I never heard of him doing something like this." The ranger passed a glance to Watts, then said to Raymond and his brother, "But let's just suppose for a minute that he might have gotten a little drunk and wasn't thinking clearly. What if he used the money, then realized what a terrible spot he'd put you in and was sorry for what he done. What if he only made up the story about getting robbed because he couldn't face you and tell you the truth? I've seen people do things like that, haven't you?"

"Yes, I suppose I have," Raymond Beck said grudgingly. "But I don't think that was what happened." His dark eyes went back to Watts and stayed there. Watts looked down at the dirt floor.

"But let's say it did happen that way," said the ranger, "and now Henry is sorry for what he did, the way any decent man would be after he had time to think about it. Then all he would have to do to clear himself with you is get the sixty dollars back to you and let you get on your way, is that right?"

"Sixty-*four* dollars," Raymond corrected him. "Of course that would be all there is to it. I'd be so happy to get on my way, I'd forgive Henry Dove, or anybody else if they were to bring our money back to us."

"I bet you would," said the ranger. As he spoke he began to walk around the tent, looking at the children on the floor, the baby in the woman's arms, the piles of belongings stacked up the sides of the tent. "Sometimes even a good decent man like Henry Dove can run out of money, get desperate, not know which way to turn, all of sudden he sees an opportunity present itself, and he jumps without thinking. Then his circumstances change, and things get a little better for him, but he doesn't know how to go back and change the wrong thing he did." Sam looked down at the woman and the baby in her arms. Walking back to the front of the tent, he said, "Seldom in life does a man get the chance to make things right before it's too late. If Henry did something like this, he's lucky he can still step forward and make amends." Sam stopped and let a silent pause hang in the air for a second. "That is, if he's really the decent man we all think he is . . . right, Sheriff?" he said finally.

"Yes, right," said Watts without raising his eyes from the dirt floor. "Are we going to be here much longer?" he asked, backing a step closer to the tent flap.

Seeing how uncomfortable Watts had become, the ranger stepped to the side and said, "Why don't you wait outside, Sheriff? I'll only be a minute or two longer."

Watts wasted no time stepping out through the tent fly. He walked a few feet from the tent and stood with his thumbs hooked down into his belt, scraping his boot toe back and forth in the dirt. Looking out at Sheriff Watts, LJ Beck said with a tone of contempt, "*Sheriff*, my ass. He's the thief and we all know it!"

"Hush up, Brother LJ!" said Raymond. "We just said we don't want to go accusing nobody! So let's don't!"

LJ turned to face his brother and the ranger. "Why not," he said, "just because this ranger came here to make us feel like the law is going to do something for us? Is that supposed to make us feel better? We still got our money stolen . . . we still don't have mules to take us home." He singled his words to the ranger saying, "Does any of this get us any closer to Kansas, Ranger?"

"LJ, keep quiet!" Raymond warned him.

The ranger said, "Start looking for a team of mules. When you find some, have the owner hold them for you."

"Wait a minute, Ranger," said Raymond. "I know we're in a fix here, but we don't take charity from no man."

"I'm not offering charity," said the ranger. "I've just got a feeling your money is going to show up in the next couple of days." He turned and started to walk out of the tent. "Go find yourselves some mules."

"What about Henry Dove?" Raymond asked. "What's going to become of that man? He did nothing wrong. Even the sheriff's daughter doesn't believe Henry killed her father."

"I know it," said the ranger. "Let me worry about Henry Dove."

When Sam had stepped out of the tent and the Beck brothers watched him join Watts and watched the two walk away, LJ said, "Think this ranger means anything he says, or is he just blowing hot air?"

"I don't know," said Raymond. "But right now we best trust him. He's the best chance we got at getting our money back . . . best chance Henry Dove's got at not getting his neck stretched."

"So, what are we going to do now, Brother?" LJ asked, letting the tent fly fall shut.

"We're going to go look for some mules," said Raymond.

On their way back to the sheriff's office the ranger and Watts crossed the street to the boardwalk out front of the Even Odds Saloon. Before they reached the saloon, Delbert Watts saw Charlie Floose rise from a chair and stand facing them, his palm resting on his pistol butt. Watts grew fidgety and said, "Ranger, do you see what you're walking us into up ahead?"

"He's a friend of yours, isn't he?" Sam replied without taking his eyes off of the gunman.

"Friend of mine? No!" said Watts. "He's no friend of mine!"

"He's one of Giles Capp's gunmen," said Sam. "The Capps have gotten real friendly with Andrew Swain. Since Swain is real friendly with the councilmen who appointed you, I figure that makes you one of them."

"Ranger, I was legally appointed to this job . . . and I need this job bad," said Watts. "The fact is I was about to go bust running the blacksmith shop here. I took the shop over, and there was too much debt against it for me to make a living. The bank's going to take it from me any day. That's one reason I took this badge. You can think what you want about me, but I ain't a part of any outlaw gang."

"Suit yourself, Sheriff," said Sam. "The way I see it, if you work for that kind of people, you're one of them."

"That's all just politics, Ranger," said Watts. "I had to go along with Avondale and Meaker . . . how else would I have gotten this job?"

"Like I said, Sheriff, suit yourself," Sam repeated.

When they started to turn into the Even Odds Saloon, Charlie Floose stepped in front of the ranger as if to block his way. "Hold it right there!" said Floose, holding his arm out in front of Sam and Watts.

Sam grabbed Floose by his wrist, gave it a vicious twist, then slung the helpless gunman forward, slamming him face-first into the front of the building as he and Watts stepped through the bat-wing doors. Inside the saloon, faces turned toward the loud crash, followed by a heavy thump as Floose pitched backward onto the boardwalk. Watts looked back over his shoulder through the swinging doors, stunned by what he'd just seen. "Is he all right?" Watts whispered.

"I'm sure he is," Sam said without taking a glance. He crossed the floor quickly toward Swain's private table, drawing his big Colt on his way. "Don't get up, gentlemen," he said cordially, holding the Colt down his thigh, but cocking it as Bo Altero, Danny Boy and Giles Capp rose halfway from their chairs. "I'm only here to ask you all a couple of questions."

Seeing the ranger's cocked Colt, the three gunmen stood suspended. "Go on, now, sit down," Sam said, raising the Colt an inch, letting them know he meant business. He had gotten the drop on them, and he could tell by the accusing look on Giles Capp's face that Capp wasn't pleased with his men for letting it happen.

Giving each man a hard stare, Giles Capp lowered himself into his chair. Altero and Danny Boy did the same. Across the table sat Swain, having made no attempt to stand up when the ranger entered the saloon. Near Swain, Snake sat holding a wet bar towel to his swollen face with both hands. He raised his pain-filled eyes enough to see the ranger. "Jesus," he rasped.

"The hell do you want, lawdog?" said Giles Capp, having to talk tough to make up for the fact that the ranger had taken charge so quickly and easily.

"Like I said"—Sam uncocked the Colt but kept his thumb over the hammer—"I've got a couple of questions to ask about Sheriff Dolan's death." He tossed a glance at Swain and said, "You're free to leave, Mr. Swain. This has nothing to do with you."

Swain started to get up from his chair.

"Sit down, Swain!" Giles Capp growled at him. "I say who goes or stays."

The tone of Capp's voice caused Swain to drop like a rock.

Sam gave Swain a curious look, making sure that both Swain and Capp saw it and drew their own interpretation from it. "Looks like you *are* the one in charge here, Giles," the ranger said.

"That's right, Ranger," Capp said in the same inhospitable tone, cutting a passing glance at Swain. "Has anybody told you different?"

After a slight pause, Sam said, "No, nobody told me different." He stepped closer to the table. "It doesn't matter to me who's in charge of this bunch anyway. As far as I know, your gang is not wanted for anything on this side of the border. If you were, we wouldn't be talking."

"Yeah?" said Giles Capp menacingly. "What *would* we be doing?"

Sam didn't answer. Instead he gave a look at the faces one at a time and said, "I want to know where each of you were the night Sheriff Dolan got shot."

Danny Boy Wright said, "I was on my way to—"

"Shut the hell up, Danny Boy," said Giles Capp, cutting him off. "Nobody is answering anything this lawdog asks, unless it's me." He turned his eyes from Danny Boy back to the ranger. "I answer for all of us, lawdog." He thumbed himself on the chest.

"Good enough," said the ranger. "Where were all of you?"

"That's a stupid question, lawdog," said Capp, spreading a mirthless grin. "What do you think I'm going to say, that we were out hiding in the shadows along the street? Waiting to bushwhack Sheriff Dolan?"

"If that's where you were," said the ranger, "then, yes, go ahead and say it." His thumb cocked the Colt's hammer again, raising the barrel slightly.

"Wait a minute," said Giles Capp. "I didn't say we were *really* doing that . . . all I was doing is pointing out how stupid your question is!"

"Oh, I see," said Sam, lowering the barrel, "That was just a little joke?"

"Yeah, something like that," said Giles. "I thought you could tell I was only joking." He cocked his head slightly, turning his gaze to Delbert Watts, who stood as if dumbstruck by the thought of even being there. "What about you, *temporary* sheriff? Couldn't you tell I was only joking?"

"Yeah, I suppose so," Delbert said in a weak voice. He lowered his face.

Sam gave Delbert a look of disappointment and shook his head slightly. Then he raised his voice a bit and said to Giles Capp and his men, "Everybody listen up. I came here to talk to all of you at once. But since Giles doesn't want to go along with that, I'm going to come see each of you one at a time. Do yourself and me both a favor and have your story straight when I get there."

"Have our *stories* straight?" Danny Boy said, looking around at the others.

"That's right," said the ranger, "be able to tell me where you were that night." He looked at Swain and said, "All except for you, Mr. Swain. "We've already talked about it. You're in the clear."

Giles and the men turned a harsh stare at Swain. But only for a moment. As soon as the ranger spoke again, all eyes turned back to him. "I don't know why Giles doesn't want us talking all together like this. You'll have to ask him. But I'll be around to see each of you. Be prepared."

Giles Capp took on a wizened expression. "I see what you're doing, lawdog. You're wanting to get these men to wonder about me. But it ain't going to work. We all stick together. So you can come see any of us anytime. You might be surprised what you find waiting for you." He looked Sam up and down, then said, "You shouldn't have come to Redemption by yourself, Ranger. This ain't one of those *one town, one ranger* kind of deals."

"I'll do the best I can," Sam said in quiet tone. He took a step back, ready to turn and leave, having done exactly what he'd come there to do. "Are you ready to go, Sheriff Watts," he said respectfully.

"Yes, I'm ready," said Watts, looking a little sheepish, keeping his head lowered.

"Sheriff, ha!" said Giles Capp. He looked at Swain and said, "Maybe you better warn the new *temporary* sheriff here about the kind of company he keeps, Swain."

Swain fidgeted and looked away. "I have no say-so in such matters," he said almost under his breath.

Sam turned, smiling slightly to himself, and said, "Come on, Sheriff. I think we both see where we stand with these men."

Walking out of the saloon, the ranger and Watts stepped around Charlie Floose, who had just sat up and rubbed his swollen forehead. "You can't go in there," he said in a groggy voice. Watts looked down at him as he hurried along behind the ranger.

A few yards away from the saloon, Sam stopped and turned facing Watts. "All right, Sheriff, you saw how they treated you. Is your new job worth being looked at that way?"

"All right," said Watts, "maybe I did tell Avondale I'd go along with things, maybe give Swain and his saloon some special attention. But I want to be a good lawman. You can believe that or not. But it's the truth. I've been watching you today. I want to handle my job the way you handle yours."

Sam looked him up and down. "I don't *know* if I believe you or not, Watts. But if you really want to be a good lawman, the first thing you better do is purge yourself of any wrongdoing you've got on your conscience and start with a clean slate."

Watts' face reddened. "Are you a preacher, or a lawman?"

"I'm a man who believes you can't be half right when it comes to law work," said Sam, "you've got to be all the way right. If you're not, you'll end up destroying yourself."

"Well, it doesn't matter anyway," said Watts. "I've got nothing bothering my conscience. I've got nothing to be ashamed of."

"Then I reckon we're wasting time discussing the matter," said Sam, turning back toward the sheriff's office.

"I know what you're getting at, Ranger," said Watts, hurrying along beside him. "You think I took that money off of Henry Dove."

"Whatever gave you that idea?" Sam asked, dismissing the matter.

"What business did a man like Henry Dove have carrying around that much money anyway?"

Sam cast him a glance now. "He had the money on him in order to help some travelers on their journey home, the way any decent man would do. What difference would it make anyway? What do you mean by 'A man like that'? Do you think because of his color he shouldn't have money in his pocket?"

"That ain't what I meant," said Watts.

"Yes, I believe it is what you meant, Watts," said Sam.

"No! What I meant was, he never worked for it! For all I know neither did those other two. They probably stole it themselves."

Again the ranger stopped and looked at him. "That's the second time you've said these folks probably stole the money themselves. What's gnawing your belly, Watts? I think you better tell me and get it out of your system."

"Nothing," Watts said flatly. "I just wish I had never gone to that tent with you!" He stomped on toward the sheriff's office in front of the ranger. Sam smiled to himself and followed.

Chapter 7

No sooner than the ranger and Watts had left the Even Odds Saloon, Giles Capp said to the rest of the men, "Everybody clear out of here! I want to talk to Swain alone!"

Swain started to stand up, but Capp clamped a hand on his shoulder and forced him down as the rest of the men walked away, some going to the bar, others to the boardwalk out front. "You heard me, Swain!" said Capp. "We've got some things to talk over between us."

"I was just going over to get the bourbon from behind the bar!" said Swain, his eyes widening in fear.

"That's what bartenders are for," said Capp. He raised a hand and called out to the bartender, "Dick, bring us both a fresh glass and that bottle of Kentucky bourbon."

Dick ignored Giles Capp and looked to Swain for approval. As soon as Swain gave him a nod, Dick Norton quickly snatched up two shot glasses, pulled the bottle from under the bar, and hurried to Swain's table.

Capp eyed the bartender narrowly as he set up the glasses and pulled the cork from the bottle. "Listen to me, Dick," said Capp. "The next time I tell you to do something and you act like I ain't here . . . I'll put a bullet in you, in the worst place I think of."

"I work for Mr. Swain," Dick said cordially but firmly. "I take orders from him only when it comes to doing my job."

"Is that so?" said Capp. "Then let me put it to you this way. The next time I tell you to do something and you act like I ain't here, I'll put a bullet in *Mr.* Swain. We'll see how you both like that."

Dick Norton started to say something, but Swain cut in, saying, "Dick, from now on, do like he asks you . . . consider it an order from me."

"Yes, sir, Mr. Swain," said the bartender, finishing what he was doing and disappearing back to the bar.

Giles Capp remained standing for a moment. He picked up the bottle of bourbon and filled Swain's glass, then his own. "Now, you sip your bourbon, Swain, and clear you mind . . . and tell me just what the hell you and that ranger talked about that has him treating you so damn special!"

"Nothing, Giles!" said Swain. "I swear we never talked about a thing that would cause him to single me out that way! I think he's just doing it to turn us against one another!"

"Yeah? Well, he's starting to do a damn good job of it," said Capp. "If I find out you told him something about me or my men just to save your own ass, you won't believe how many bullets I'll put into you!"

Swain only stared in silence for a moment, realizing that what the ranger said might be true, how these kind of men would turn on him like wild dogs. Finally he said in a quiet tone, "Giles, I haven't said anything *about* anything to the ranger. He slipped in here while you and your men went to get Snake off of the boardwalk. I think he planned it that way. I think he's dangerous to what we're trying to do here."

Giles gave him a smug grin. "I think you've let him buffalo you. He's not that smart. He's just one more lawdog hiding behind a badge. But I mean what I said." He pointed a finger in Swain's face. "If I get the slightest notion that you're jackpotting me and my men, I'll kill you." He turned and stomped away. Swain sat staring after him, a sheen of sweat on his forehead. He felt his world growing smaller and tighter around him. Giles Capp couldn't see what he was saying about the ranger playing them against one another. If Capp was already threatening to kill him at the *slightest notion* that he'd said something to the ranger, then maybe it was time he started making some moves on his own behalf. He didn't want to be facing the Rio Sagrado Gang alone. He'd better start thinking about getting the ranger on his side, he told himself, raising the shot glass to his lips and tossing back a drink.

Out front on the boardwalk, Giles Capp joined Danny Boy, Charlie Floose and Bo Altero. Giving a guarded glance in the direction of the sheriff's office, he said, "We're going to start meeting some place beside out front here where the whole damn world sees us."

The three men looked at one another. Floose said, "I thought you said the other day that we had nothing to worry about, we could show our faces anywhere . . . 'Redemption is *our* town,' you told us."

Giles Capp gave him a hard stare for a moment. "Things have changed," he said finally. "This ranger is getting down our shirts. We've got to pull back out of sight a little. Let things cool off while he runs in a circle chasing his own tail. He'll soon leave, once he sees that he ain't going to get nobody here to jackpot one another."

"I say we all get our bark on and face him down in the street," said Altero.

Giles gave him the same hard stare for a moment. "That might be exactly what we'll do. But for now, everybody quit congregating out front here. It makes us too damn noticeable."

"Where we supposed to go to talk things over?" said Danny Boy.

"Yeah . . . and how are we going to keep an eye on the sheriff's office except from right here?" asked Floose.

"Damn it to hell! Just stop hanging around right here in front of the saloon!" said Giles Capp. "Can't you understand what I'm saying? Are you all idiots?" He stared from one to the other. "If we need to meet to discuss things, we'll do it behind the livery barn!"

"Behind the livery barn," said Altero, sounding a bit disgusted at the prospect. "That sounds like some sort of chid's punishment for being naughty."

Capp's face reddened. "It was good enough meeting there before we gained our toehold here . . . it'll be good enough until we get settled with that ranger one way or the other!" He fanned everybody away with his hands. "Now, break it up! Get out of here! Everybody find something to do! Danny Boy, you and Snake go on to the livery barn and check on our horses!"

Snake Bentell walked out of the saloon just as the men began to disperse. He fell in alongside Danny Boy and said in his muffled voice, "Where are we going?"

Danny Boy continued walking as he looked back over his shoulder and saw Giles Capp disappear through the swinging doors. "Giles just told us to break it up and stay off the boardwalk out front of the saloon. Me and you are supposed to go check on our horses."

"Check on our horses? For what?" Snake asked through his bruised cheeks.

"I don't know," Danny Boy shrugged. "That ranger has stuck a burr under everybody's blanket, if you ask me."

Touching a hand carefully to his swollen purple jaw, Snake said, "He sure got the drop on me." Looking Danny Boy up and down, noting his holster with a small pistol he'd borrowed from Charlie Floose sticking up from the big holster. "He got the drop on you too for that matter."

"Yeah, I know," Danny Boy grumbled under his breath.

"If we can't stand around on the boardwalk, just where are we supposed to stand around?" Snake asked. He adjusted the spare gun he'd gotten out of his saddlebags and shoved it down into his holster.

Danny Boy gave him a flat expression. "Behind the livery barn, Giles said."

"Jesus," said Snake, "I thought we'd risen above that kind of meeting place. I thought this was *our town* now."

"That might be what we thought," said Danny Boy, "but the ranger must be thinking different. If Giles ain't careful, we're going to lose everything we've gained here."

"Do you think he'll really leave once he sees none of us is going to tell him anything about Sheriff Dolan's death?" Snake asked.

"I don't know what I think anymore," said Danny

Boy. "All I know is things ain't been going right ever since the ranger got here."

Turning the corner, the two saw Raymond and LJ Beck enter the livery barn and close the door behind themselves. "You see what I see?" said Snake, giving Danny Boy a flat grin.

"Yeah, I see them. That's the two who said they gave Henry Dove money to buy them a fresh team of mules."

"Yep," said Snake. "They also said they couldn't buy any mules afterward because that was all the money they had to their names."

"So, what are you getting at, Snake?" asked Danny Boy, both of them stopping for a moment.

"I'm just wondering what they're doing at the livery barn," said Snake, "if they own no animals and they can't afford to buy any." He raised a knowing brow. "Think we might be walking upon a crime in the making?"

Danny Boy returned Snake's grin. "I believe it's our duty as citizens to go see." He raised the small pistol from his holster as he spoke.

"I agree completely," said Snake, also drawing his pistol as they approached the barn door.

Snake reached out and quietly shoved the door open. The two stepped inside and slipped into the shadows, watching and listening to the Beck brothers, who stood at the rear door and looked out into the corral attached to the building.

"Let's go," Raymond said to LJ. "I don't like being in here when there's nobody minding the place." He started to turn and walk to the front door, but LJ wasn't ready to leave yet.

"What's your hurry, Raymond?" said LJ. "Folks

come here all the time when nobody's here. We're just looking for mules, like anybody would."

"If you don't know the difference between those folks and us by now, you're never going to, little brother," Raymond replied. "Now, let's get going before we get accused of something the way Henry Dove got accused."

"You go on if you want to," said LJ, "but I ain't through looking just yet." He stubbornly shoved his hands down into his pockets and stepped out into the wide corral.

"Don't go getting hardheaded on me," said Raymond. "You know how things are here. There's men in this town just looking for a reason to hang somebody, or shoot somebody, or God knows what."

"So what? We ain't doing no wrong," said LJ. "Anybody wants to say something about us being here, I'll tell them straight to their face, we got as much right to be here as they do!" He thumbed himself on the chest. "If that ain't enough, I'll tell them something else, you bet I will. I'm tired of being told where I can and can't go."

Hearing LJ, the two gunmen stepped out of the shadows and walked forward with their guns cocked and aimed. "What have we here, Danny Boy," said Snake. "Sounds like this young man is looking to be taught some manners."

"Yeah," said Danny Boy, "not to mention what they were both about to do if we hadn't showed up when we did." He wagged his pistol back and forth, saying, "All right, both of yas, get your hands against that door. We saw what you were about to do here."

"We were about to do *what?*" LJ asked, taking a wide stance in defiance of Danny Boy's orders.

"Come on, LJ, don't argue!" said Raymond, who

had already turned and put both of his hands flat up against the open barn door. Then without pause he said to the two gunmen, "We came here looking for mules! That's all! We weren't doing nothing we shouldn't be doing!"

"We'll decide what you *should* or shouldn't be doing," said Danny Boy, giving Snake a wink. He said to LJ, "I ain't going to tell you again. Get your hands out against that door!"

"You got no right coming here accusing us of anything," said LJ. "We come here as customers!"

"LJ, get your hand on this door!" Raymond demanded. LJ did so, grudgingly.

"Oh, yeah?" said Snake, raising his pistol and pointing it in LJ's face as the man stared over his shoulder at him. "What business have you boys got looking for mules? We heard Henry Dove drank up all your traveling money." Both Snake and Danny Boy chuckled under their breath. Snake nudged LJ's face away with the tip of his pistol barrel.

"The ranger told us to go pick us out some mules," said LJ, staring straight ahead at the rough wooden door. "Go ask him if you don't believe us."

Danny Boy chuckled, looking at the two men's humble, patched field clothes. "Oh? So you two scarecrows are friends of the ranger, eh?"

"He never said we were the ranger's friends," said Raymond. "He told you the ranger told us to go pick out some mules."

"You speak when you're spoken to, boy!" said Snake. He jammed the gun barrel solidly into Raymond's ribs from the side, causing Raymond to buckle and clasp an arm around himself. When he did so, he lost balance and fell against the rough wooden door and down to the dirt floor.

"What's wrong with you, boy, can't you stand up?" Snake shouted. "Get up from there and grab that door!" He gave Raymond a kick to hurry him to his feet.

Seeing the gunman kick his brother was more than LJ could take. He spun around from the wooden door and flew into Snake with a flurry of solid punches, the first one knocking Snake's cocked gun from his hand, causing it to go off when it hit the floor.

Snake staggered backward, with LJ's punches coming so fast and furious that the hapless gunman couldn't even get his guard up to protect himself. From the floor Raymond saw Danny Boy trying to get a clear shot at LJ. Without hesitation he flung himself up from the dirt floor and onto Danny Boy.

The elderly livery hostler had heard the gunshot as he stepped in through the front door. "Oh, Lord!" he shouted, seeing the four men fight their way out the back door and into the corral. Hurrying back through the front door, he turned and ran toward the street, yelling for the sheriff at the top of his lungs.

In the corral Snake Bentell managed to get both arms around LJ in spite of the smaller faster man's flurry of sharp punches. Raising LJ high in the air, Snake slammed him to the ground with enough force to knock the breath out of him. LJ was stunned for only a moment, but a moment was all it took for Snake to land a couple of hard boots to his ribs.

"Son of a bitch!" Snake shouted, blood flying from fresh cuts on his already battered face. Looking around, he saw his pistol lying on the floor inside the barn door. He hurried toward it, staggering a bit from the beating he'd taken. But seeing where Snake was headed and seeing that his brother LJ was struggling to catch his breath, Raymond Beck slung Danny Boy away from him and ran for Snake, tackling him just outside the barn door.

In the dirt LJ tried hard to recover from the kicking Snake had dealt him. He struggled up to his knees and looked around at Danny Boy, who had drawn his pistol now that he wasn't too busy defending himself from Raymond's punches. Seeing Danny Boy try to focus on aiming his gun at Raymond without hitting Snake, LJ glanced around desperately looking for something to hurl at him. There were no sticks or rocks, only a pile of crusted-over horse manure lying near his hand. With no time to lose, LJ scooped it up in his hand and flung it at Danny Boy with all his strength.

The heavy pile of waste matter made a loud slapping sound as it struck Danny Boy in the side of his face. The impact caused the gunman to stagger sideways, his gun going off wildly and thumping into the barn above the rear door. He threw his free hand to his face and felt the clamminess. "Ayiieee!" he shrieked, slinging it from his hand, turning his attention to LJ, swinging the pistol toward him. "I'll kill you! You son of a—"

LJ had not hesitated for a second. As soon as the manure had hit Danny Boy, he'd raked his hand through the remaining pile and rushed forward, quickly covering the fifteen feet between them. Danny Boy's words had cut short as LJ jammed the handful of dung into his face. Danny Boy shrieked again, spluttering and spitting, dropping his gun and wiping his face frantically with both hands. LJ bounced around on the balls of his feet, his fists poised, timing himself, looking for that just right second. It came when Danny Boy lowered his hands and batted his dung-filled eyes. "Fight fair! You lousy—"

His words stopped short again, this time because of
the hard right cross LJ delivered to his exposed left
jaw. Danny Boy staggered backward, still blinded by
the thick wet horse manure. He hit the ground with
LJ on his chest, unleashing punch after punch, batting
his head back and forth, horse dung flying with each
blow.

Chapter 8

As soon as the first shot rang out, Delbert Watts gave the ranger a questioning look, saying, "Was that from the livery barn?"

"That's what it sounded like," Sam replied, already headed for the door. "Better grab yourself a shotgun, Sheriff. This could be your first call to duty."

Watts looked worried, but hurried to the gun cabinet and jerked a shotgun down from the rack. He started toward the door. "Whoa, Sheriff," said Sam, "better check it first."

"Oh, right!" said Watts, his hands nervously opening the double-barrel. Seeing the two loads in the chambers, he clicked it shut. "Thanks, Ranger," he said.

Sam only nodded and headed for the door with him, Julie Ann walking with them. Before the three had gone twenty yards, they heard the elderly livery hostler shouting for the sheriff as he rounded the corner and nearly ran into them.

Watts caught the elderly hostler by the shoulders and steadied him. "What's going on, Earl?" he asked.

"They're killing one another!" the old man shouted, pointing a trembling knurled finger back toward the big sun-weathered barn. "Hurry, there's a bunch of them! They're armed and fighting like mad dogs!"

Giving the ranger a look, Watts said, "Ranger! How should I do this?"

"Take the front door," said Sam, "I'll circle around the barn and cover you. Don't jump in the midst if you can keep from it." As Sam spoke, he gave a glance toward the Even Odds Saloon and saw Giles Capp and his men walking along the boardwalk at a quick pace. "The trick will be to stop it without it getting worse out of hand," he said, loosening his Colt in its holster. Other townsfolk had been drawn toward the sound of gunfire and hurried along from all directions.

As Watts hurried away toward the front door of the barn, Sam ran ahead, taking a shortcut around a small woodshed toward the rear. Julie Ann followed, but stayed a few feet back for safety. Reaching the corral, Sam saw the four men paired off, rolling and fighting on the ground. Raymond and Snake scrambled and fought and rolled their way beneath a fence rail and into a smaller corral where mules worked and horses moved about nervously to keep themselves out of the melee. Seeing LJ sitting atop Danny Boy, his fists flying like blades on a windmill, Sam stepped over, drawing his Colt. "All right, break it up," he said in a raised voice.

But LJ would have none of it. He only gave Sam a quick glance without slowing down his punches. "They started it!" he shouted.

Without another word, Sam gave LJ a swipe of the barrel on the back of his head and watched him slump forward, not out cold, but slightly dazed. His punches ceased. Sam grabbed him by the back of his shirt and dragged him off of Danny Boy, who groaned and rolled over onto his side, his face bloody and covered with rising welts and streaks of fresh horse manure. Sam caught the smell of it as he dragged LJ a few feet away and dropped him at the rail of the smaller corral. "Stay right here," he said. LJ nodded, weaving back and forth on his knees.

Sam stepped into the smaller corral and watched Raymond and Snake roll back and forth, fighting among nervous hoofs. From the rear barn door, Watts came carrying the shotgun, pointing it back and forth, then lowering it when he saw LJ weaving in place on his knees and Danny Boy struggling to sit up in the dirt. Joining Sam at the corral, he nodded at Raymond and Snake, saying, "Are we going in there and break them up?"

"Not now," said Sam. "Those animals are spooked enough as it is. These two are winding down anyway. Let them play it on out." In the smaller corral, the punches had slowed down and lost most of their strength. Both men's clothes were torn and bloody, as were their faces.

Behind the ranger, Julie Ann said in a lowered voice, "Sam, here comes Giles Capp and his men."

Sam and Watts both turned, facing Giles Capp as he stopped and stared at Danny Boy, then at LJ, who sat slumped and wobbly on the ground beside the ranger. Pointing at LJ, Capp said, "Did he do that to Danny?"

Without answering the gunman, Sam said to Watts, "I believe he's talking to you, Sheriff."

Looking down at LJ Beck, then back at Giles Capp, Watts said, "They did this to each other, Mr. Capp." He gestured over his shoulder at Raymond and Snake in the small corral. The two men were on their knees and had collapsed against one another, holding each other up. Blood and caked dirt covered their sweaty faces. The lower half of Snake's right ear lay flapping down on his jaw. "We got here in time to see it winding down."

Seeing Snake's dangling ear, Capp turned enraged. "That cheating bastard has cut Snake! Look at his ear!" He took a step toward the smaller corral with his hand on his gun butt. "I'll kill him!"

But the ranger stepped in sideways, blocking his way. He calmly lay his thumb over his gun hammer and kept the big Colt pointed down his thigh. "Nobody has done any cutting," the ranger said, "and nobody's *doing* any killing." He stood firmly between Capp and the corral gate.

"Like hell!" said Capp. "I'm going in there!"

"I said, '*Nobody's* going in there.'" The ranger cocked the hammer, letting Capp hear it and think about it.

Capp stopped. Behind him Bo Altero and Charlie Floose also stopped. But they spread out a few feet staring coldly at the ranger.

"I thought the sheriff is in charge here," said Capp without taking his eyes off of the ranger.

"That's right, he is," said Sam, standing poised.

"Sheriff," said Capp, "I'm going in there . . . any objections?" From the growing crowd of onlookers came Councilmen Avondale and Meaker, both of them watching closely as if anxious to see what Watts' answer would be.

Watts gave the ranger a look, then faced Capp saying, "No, you're not. It's been a fair fight. Everybody stay back until I say otherwise."

Giles Capp gave Avondale a hard stare. "Did you hear the *temporary* sheriff, Councilman? He says I can't go in there and help my friend Snake."

"Sheriff Watts," said Avondale, controling his rage,

in order to keep the onlookers from hearing him side with Giles Capps. "Let this man go get his friend out of there this instant! Do you hear me?"

"I hear you, Councilman," said Watts, his hands growing sweaty on the shotgun stock as he held it firmly, "but I'm the man in charge here, and nobody is going in that corral until I say so."

The ranger kept his Colt cocked and listened, a bit surprised at Watts' response. He watched Avondale's face turn red with rage. "Either do as I say, or you can damn well take that badge off and hand it over, Watts!" said Avondale.

Watts stood his ground. "Sorry, Councilman." He reached up and started to take off the badge.

"Keep the badge on, Sheriff Watts," said the ranger. "This man can't fire you without the whole town council sitting down and voting on it. Ask Mr. Meaker here."

Watts looked back and forth between Sam and the two councilmen. "Is that true, Mr. Meaker?" he asked.

"Uh, well . . . yes, I believe it," Meaker spluttered, unaccustomed to anybody asking his opinion on any matter when Avondale was around.

"Then rest assured I'll call an emergency meeting of the council and have you thrown out of office so fast you won't know what hit you!" Avondale raged, still trying to keep his angry voice lowered.

Meaker cut in, saying, "As soon as the other two councilmen get back to town, that is."

Avondale shot Meaker a sour look. "What are you talking about, Horace?"

Meaker continued in a quieter tone, saying, "Halbert and McNutt are both down in Texas, speculating on some cattle."

"I know that, damn it!" said Avondale. "It has nothing to do with—"

"Do what you need to do," said Watts, cutting Avondale off. "Until the *whole* council says otherwise, I'm doing the job I swore an oath to do, upholding the law."

Avondale pointed a warning finger at him. "Don't let this ranger fill your head with nonsense, Watts!"

Delbert Watts ignored the councilman and turned his gaze to the smaller corral where the two combatants had spent their last drop of energy and collapsed backward onto the dirt. "Ranger Burrack, will you help me drag them out of there? It looks like they've both had enough."

Without a word the ranger reached out and lifted the latch on the corral gate. He stepped inside, took Raymond by his collar and dragged him out of the corral while Watts stepped in and did the same thing with Snake Bentell. Outside of the small corral, Floose and Altero had dragged Danny Boy to his feet and helped him walk over to where Giles Capp stood with Avondale and Meaker. Floose walked away for a moment and gathered the two gunmen's hats for them. "All right, Danny Boy," said Capp, "tell us what this was all about!"

Danny spoke in a gasping tone through bloody swollen lips. "Giles, me and Snake come upon these two snooping around the barn. They attacked us!"

"We was looking for mules," LJ murmured, still out of breath himself.

"Yeah, that's what they told us," said Danny Boy. "But we knew they had no money for mules! We heard what happened to them!"

"There you have it, *Sheriff* Watts," said Giles Capp, giving a nod down at LJ and Raymond Beck. "Throw those two in jail. Lucky for everybody that my men came along and saw them." He formed a flat grin, raising his voice for everyone to hear and said, "Maybe it's time the new sheriff here rids Redemption of this bad element that has set in here."

"They were looking for mules," said the ranger, "just like LJ here said."

"*LJ* is it?" said Giles. "Looks like the ranger is on a first-name basis with these two *barn* burglers."

"How do you know they were looking for mules, Ranger?" Avondale asked in a skeptical tone of voice.

"I know because I told them to go ahead and start locating some mules for themselves." His eyes went to Watts as he spoke. "In case the sheriff and I happen to find their money."

"Oh, I see," said Avondale, haughtily sticking a hand on his hip, "and just how likely is that to happen?"

"We're working on it," said the ranger, taking his eyes from Watts back to Avondale with a cold stare. "Now, all of you break it up . . . go on about your business," he said loud enough for all of the onlookers to hear. "Sheriff Watts has everything under control here."

"What about my men?" said Capp, still wanting to agitate. "Can people like this just ride into Redemption and start beating on folks who are only looking out for one another's property?"

"It's not the first time your men have taken a beating, Capp," said Sam, "and I doubt it'll be the last. Either call this a draw, or sheriff Watts and I will throw all four of them in jail and sort it out when the territorial judge comes through here."

"You ain't throwing any of my men in jail, lawdog," said Giles Capp. He spread his feet shoulder width apart, taking a stand. Avondale and Meaker took a step back, seeing a gunfight coming.

But the ranger didn't seem impressed. Without raising the Colt still in his hand, he recocked it and said, "Don't start talking too tough, Giles, your brother Axel's not here to wipe your nose for you. I'll throw you in jail face-first, then throw your men in right behind you . . . show them what a coward you are."

Avondale and Meaker looked stunned. Nobody, including Capp himself, had anticipated such a statement from the ranger. A slight gasp went up from the onlookers. At the rear of the gathering of townsfolk stood Andrew Swain, looking on with sharp interest at how Giles Capp responded to the ranger's threat. He had no idea that the ranger had spotted him there and had thrown out the threat at just the right time to give him a good close look at Giles Capp.

Giles Capp couldn't allow himself to be called a coward in front of the world and let it go unchallenged. But before he could make a move, he saw a look come to the ranger's eyes that he hadn't seen before. The ranger's eyes had lost all expression, as if inside his mind the conversation had suddenly stopped. The ranger looked at him the way a person might look at a dead man. The look unnerved the young gunman for just a second. But in the dark world of blood and killing, a second was all it took to show both himself and the ranger that there was a weakness in him. In the second when he should have responded, he'd allowed himself to hesitate. Now the ranger had seen his hesitation and seized upon it. Sam raised his Colt an inch and watched Capp raise his hand away from his gun butt altogether.

"You just wait, Ranger!" Capp bellowed. "Your

time is coming!" He turned the act of raising his hand away from his gun into a pointing gesture. But the ranger saw it, and Capp knew he'd seen it. He clenched his teeth in rage, but took a slight step backward, knowing that the ranger had just beaten him without firing a shot.

There were many responses the ranger could have made, many things he could have said. But he'd made his point, both to Capp and to the onlooking Swain. Now he lowered the Colt an inch, laid his thumb over the hammer and deftly uncocked it. "Get your men and get out of my sight, Capp," he said in almost a whisper. "If I keep seeing any of you on the street, I'll figure you're looking for a fight with me."

Jesus . . . Swain said to himself, backing away from the gathered townsfolk and slipping out of sight before Capp and his men noticed him there.

"All right, Floose, Altero!" said Capp, still staring hard at the ranger, but showing no sign of wanting to lock horns with him, "help these two bummers get back to the saloon!" He looked at Avondale and Meaker with poison in his eyes, not about to say anything to them in public, but letting them both know that they had let him down. The two councilmen backed farther away.

"Get your hands off of me! I can walk!" Snake Bentell bellowed through split bleeding lips once Floose and Altero had raised him to his feet.

"Then walk, you sorry-ass wretch!" said Altero, stepping back and dusting his hands of the matter.

Snake staggered over to Danny Boy and fell against him. The two held one another up. "We showed them, Danny Boy," Snake gasped. The two turned and staggered away behind Giles Capp and the others. Watching them leave, Sam noted that Charlie Floose cut away from the others and headed inside the big livery barn.

As the onlookers broke up and moved away, Watts started to reach a hand down to help the Beck brothers to their feet, but the ranger stopped him and shook his head slightly. They watched LJ and Raymond help one another to their feet. "Well, Ranger," said LJ in a rasping voice, "this is what listening to you got us. Got any more good advice for us?"

"Don't blame the ranger," said Raymond. "He had nothing to do with this."

LJ dusted his sleeve and touched his fingertips to his lips. "Whatever you say, brother. Anyways, we didn't take anything off them poltroons." He spit blood to the ground.

"Yeah," said Raymond, "but we still don't have any mules." He stared at the ranger and Watts. "Any word yet on our money?"

The ranger looked at Watts, who turned his eyes away. "We're working on it," Sam said.

While the men had collected themselves, Julie Ann had walked about the corral and the rear door of the barn and gathered Raymond and LJ's floppy hats. She came back and handed the men their hats. "Good luck," said Raymond, sounding skeptical as he gave a cool gaze toward Delbert Watts. Taking both of the hats from Julie Ann, Raymond passed LJ's along to him. "Much obliged, ma'am," he said to Julie Ann. He dusted his hat against his leg and placed it atop his head carefully, avoiding a fist-size lump on his sweaty forehead. He turned to his brother and said, "Let's go, LJ, before the womenfolk hear about this and get worried about us."

But as the two turned to walk away, unexpectedly

Delbert Watts said, "The ranger is right, fellows, we might have some good news about your money any time. You'll be hearing from us."

The Beck brothers walked away, both of them looking back at Watts with puzzled expressions. "Do you mean that, Sheriff?" said the ranger.

Instead of answering Sam right away, Watts said, "Tell me something, Ranger, were you all set to kill Giles Capp?"

Sam studied his face for a moment, then replied, "What do you think?"

"If I thought I knew I wouldn't ask," said Watts. "You sure looked like you were ready to shoot him . . . Capp must've seen it that way too."

Sam didn't answer directly. He looked away toward the livery barn and saw Charlie Floose ride out on a big roan and take a back trail out of town in the direction of the border. Sam smiled to himself, then said to Watts, "There's times when wearing a badge means you've got to be the one who makes the strongest move, just to see what it causes to happen."

"I have no idea what that means, Ranger," said Watts.

Sam turned his slight smile to Watts, saying, "It means this. If Giles Capp wants his men to have any respect at all for him, he can't let me get away with calling him a coward, and he knows it. He's got to do something about it. It might take him an hour, it might take him a week. But he'll strike back at me, then we'll see some things start happening around here."

"What will any of this mean in regards to who killed my father?" said Julie Ann Dolan.

"Be patient, Julie, we'll uncover your father's killers before it's over," Sam said. "Swain and the Rio Sagrado Gang have had everything going their way long enough. Now they're going to have to start stepping aside for the law. There's no telling what it will cause them to do." He looked at Watts, saying, "Sheriff, we've got to get things straightened out with the Beck brothers. Think you can handle that?" He gave Watts a deep stare.

"Yes, I believe I can," Watts said quietly.

PART 2

PART 2

Chapter 9

Axel Capp sat in his saddle with his wrists crossed on his saddle horn, undaunted by the searing hot wind off the Mexican desert. In the large holding corral before him, three of his men kept a steady pace, downing the dusty steers one at a time and changing their brands with the glowing hot tip of one of the running irons that lay in the coals of a fire. Next to Axel Capp sat Denton Spears, who had just ridden up and stopped his horse beside him. Lifting his wide hat brim and wiping his forehead with a damp bandanna, Spears said, "Axel, we're working for nothing, wasting our time cross branding and running cattle back and forth across the border."

"Money is money, is how I look at it," said Axel, without turning to face him.

"Me too," said Spears, lowering the damp bandanna from his brow and looking at the dirt and grit on it, "but some money is harder earned than other money. Cattle rustling is the hardest dollar a man ever earned. I'd damn near as soon take a job and work for a living."

"Watch your language," said Axel, allowing himself a slight grin.

"It's the truth," said Spears. He nodded toward the three men working in the wavering heat. "Look at these two. They're half dead on their feet." He nodded toward the third man, saying, "Even Hector ain't acting real spry, and he's used to this godforsaken furnace."

"It ain't for much longer," said Axel. "Any day now Giles is going to be giving us a signal. We'll move across that border and never look back." He gazed back and forth in the wavering heat, then spit and said, "Meanwhile, we're going to run any Mexican cattle that's got four legs and more than a pound of meat on its bones. Don't forget, they're wanting to string me up over there . . . every court from Oregon to Texas."

A moment of silence passed, then Spears asked, "Are you sure Giles has everything under control over there?"

Axel turned a cold stare to him. "I'm sure he's doing what I told him to do. I'm sure he's got our best interest in mind. I'm sure I'm obliged to shoot any sonsabitch that tries to say otherwise!" With each word his voice raised.

"No offense, Axel," said Spears. "You know me . . . hell, I worry myself about everything."

"Worrying is bad for your health, Spears," said Axel with a trace of a warning in his voice. He turned his attention back to the cattle branding.

"I know it, Axel," said Spears. "All this waiting around is driving me crazy. I can't stand it much longer."

"You're like a hound who's been too long away from the hunt," said Axel. "I think maybe it's time we take you out somewhere and rob a bank or two, maybe shoot up a town. What do you say?"

Spears' eyes lit up. "Do you mean it, Axel?"

"Didn't I say it?" said Axel, calmly.

"Yee-hiiii!" Spears shouted, spinning his horse in a circle. He jerked his Colt from his holster and started to fire it in the air. But Axel grabbed it out of his hand, chastising him soundly. "Damn it, Spears! You want to spend the night chasing these flea-bitten steers all over Mexico? Settle down!"

In the holding corral Curly Barnes and Rod Sealey looked over at Spears as he tried to control his sudden excitement. "Listen up, boys!" Spears shouted at the two sweaty cowhands, "We're going to rob us a bank!" He turned his gaze to the Mexican who rode forward on his horse from amid the milling steers. "Hector! We're going to *rob-o el banco*!"

Hector Ruiz nodded with a smile but continued to coil the rope in his hands and prepare to cut out another steer for branding. "Didn't you hear what I said, Hector?" Spears shouted. "We're getting ready to—"

"Let it go, Spears," said Axel Capp, cutting him off. "He hears you. He knows he's got work to do. Whatever Hector does, he takes seriously. He ain't like you," Axel grinned. "That's why I took him on. Somebody has to work around here."

"He damned sure ain't like me," said Spears. "The minute I heard the word *bank*, my interest in cutting and branding cattle just dropped below the horizon."

Axel looked him up and down. "Yeah, I noticed that," he said. "But I want to let you know something, Spears. Once we hit these banks, we're going to have to cross back over the border for a while until things settle down here."

Spears rubbed his chin as if in contemplation. "Let's see now . . . we robbed and killed all over the territories, so we had to come here for things to cool down.

Now we're going to rob and kill here, so we'll have to go back to the territories until Mexico cools down?"

Axel nodded with a thin smile. "Yep, something like that," he said.

Denton Spears nodded with him. "Suits the hell out of me, Axel. I hope that someday we have to go to France or somewhere because this whole side of the world is too hot for us. It means we're good at what we're doing."

As Axel and Spears talked back and forth, Hector Ruiz rode up on his horse, followed closely by Barnes and Sealey. "I hope you are not toying with me, Spears," said Hector Ruiz. "I have been having dreams about robbing a nice juicy *Americano* bank."

"He's not toying with you, Hector," said Axel. "But you can stop dreaming about an American bank for a while."

"Oh?" Ruiz looked at him curiously.

"Yeah," said Axel. "We're hitting that big new bank in Sonora. The one at *Ciudad Del Centro*."

"The bank at Center City!" Hector's expression turned troubled. "But it is the bank that handles the pay for all the *federales*! The *Banco Nacional*!" He stared in disbelief.

"Sure, why not?" said Axel. "Somebody's got to rob it sooner or later. I'd hate for it to have be some local *bandito*, doesn't know his ass from a saddle blanket." His grin widened as he looked from face to face.

Hector still looked troubled. "But there is no bank more heavily guarded in all of Mexico!"

Still grinning, Axel replied, "Did I say it was going to be *easy*?"

"No, you did not," said Hector Ruiz with a shrug, giving in a little, allowing himself a slight smile.

"All right, then," said Axel, "who's all for it?"

"I'm all for it," said Denton Spears, getting edgy just thinking about the prospect of robbing a large brand-new bank run by the Mexican government. He looked at Barnes and Sealey. "What about you boys?"

"Damn right, I'm all for it!" said Curley Barnes. He gave Rod Sealey a look, saying, "What about you, Sealey?"

"Anything it takes to get this running iron pulled loose from my arm," said Sealey, jiggling the branding iron in his gloved hand.

"Don't pull it loose just yet," said Axel. "We've got to finish up this herd of cattle and get them ready for market. We're going to run this herd into Center City in front of us." He looked all around at them again. "Another thing . . . I want everybody to take some time the next few days getting used to riding and shooting again. Center City is full of both Mexican army and German troops. This is no light piece of work we're going into. Everybody better be at his best."

Barnes and Sealey stood watching as Axel and Spears backed their horses and turned them back toward the adobe hacienda a mile away. "Is that it?" Sealey asked just between Barnes and himself. "That's all he's going to tell us?"

"Yep, for now it is," said Barnes, adjusting his gloves as he turned back toward the corral of cattle. "He'll tell us more when he figures we need to know it. Let's finish sticking these doggies."

But Hector did not return to cutting out the steers right away. Instead, he galloped his horse alongside Axel and Spears. "Axel, tell me, *por favor* . . . how are we going to handle what could be a hundred armed soldiers in Center City?"

"I'll let you know when the time comes, Hector,"

said Axel. "You threw in with me because you wanted to go after the big money, right?"

"Yes, of course," said Hector.

"Well, *mi amigo*," said Axel. Big money is exactly what we're going after." He looked the Mexican up and down, and asked, "Tell me, Hector, what's the first thing you thought of when I said the bank in *Ciudad Del Centro*?"

Hector shrugged. "The *federale* payroll of course. It is what anyone would think of first. Center City is a *nacional* town. It belongs to Mexico but is supported by the czar of Germany."

"There, you see?" said Axel. He gave Spears a smile of satisfaction. "Everybody always thinks about that big ole government payroll first thing."

"Is the payroll not what we are going there for?" Hector asked.

"Stop asking so many questions, Hector," said Axel. "You're starting to get on my nerves." He jerked his head back toward the corral. "We've still got to get those beeves ready to go."

"I understand," said Hector, backing his horse a step, turning it and heading back toward the corral fifteen yards away.

Looking back as Hector arrived at the corral, Spears asked in a guarded tone, "*Is* the payroll what we're going after?"

Axel stopped his horse, turned it and stared back at the corral as he said, "That payroll is a big piece of change, isn't it?"

"Damn right it is," said Spears, "bigger than anything we've ever done, if I've heard right about it."

"Oh, you've heard right about it," said Axel. "It's so big that all of us will need some more men helping us out."

"We will, sure enough." said Spears, looking a bit stunned at the size of such an undertaking. "How many more will we need? Who are you going to get?"

"I'm bringing in six extra men, nobody you ever heard of. These boys are all on the run, same as me. But they're mostly horse thieves and saddle tramps."

"Are they going to be any good in a fight?" Spears asked.

"I doubt it," said Axel. "But they'll do well enough for our purposes."

Spears thought about it for a second, then said, "Hold on, Axel. You tell me and the others to sharpen up our riding and shooting, then you say you doubt if these men you're bringing are any good in a fight?"

"Yep, that's what I said all right," Axel grinned, staring straight ahead toward the hacienda.

"You're up to something, Axel," said Spears, grinning. "I can hear it in your voice."

"You're not worried about it, though, are you?" said Axel.

"Hell, no," said Spears, "I know where you and I stand with one another. Whatever you're fixing to do, I know I'm in on it, right?"

"That's right, Spears," said Axel. "So, sit tight and be ready to do what I tell you. As soon as we hear from Giles that everything's all set for us to move back into the territory, we'll be ready to go."

"I love stealing payroll money," said Spears.

"Forget the payroll money," said Axel. "The payroll money is small stuff compared to what we're getting ready to take out of Center City."

Spears looked at him. "What are you talking about? You said yourself the first thing that comes to mind is the government payroll that comes there."

"It is," said Axel, "but that's not what we're after." He stopped his horse and looked at Spears. "This is just between you and me for now. There's going to be a bank full of German gold lying in Center City next week. Nobody is supposed to know anything about it, but I put some money in the right hands and found out. It'll only be there a few days, so we've got to make our move quick."

"Gold . . ." Spears let his words trail. Then, as if snapping out of a trance, he asked greedily, "How much gold are we talking about?"

"Enough that I'm having a couple of the boys put bigger wheels and supports under the wagon bed, just to be able to carry it. The fact is we'll still have to leave a lot of it behind." He looked at Spears closely. "I'm guessing your part of it should come close to a hundred thousand dollars."

"A hundred thou—" Spears' voice failed him. He swallowed hard and said, "No! That can't be right, can it?"

"Oh, yes, it's right," said Axel, his grin widening, seeing the stunned look on Spears' face. "We pull this off just right, and none of us will ever have to smell burnt cowhide ever again."

Spears looked ahead of them at the hacienda, where four men stood looking in their direction. "So, everybody already knows about it?"

"Yep, I told them before I rode out to the corral, so they can get started working on the wagon. But they don't know it's gold we're after. I told them we needed a heavier wagon to haul some goods across the border afterward."

"What about any of the others?" asked Spears.

"I told them. But as far as anybody knows, we're

stealing the payroll. You're the only one I've told about the gold."

"I'm the only one who knows . . ." Spears thought about it for a moment. "Damn, I almost wished you hadn't told me."

"What's the matter, pal," asked Axel. "You can still manage to keep a secret, can't you?"

"Hell, yes! You know damn well I can keep a secret," said Denton Spears. "Just like my life depended on it!"

"That's good . . . because it does," Axel said flatly, heeling his horse forward toward the hacienda. "This is the sweetest deal of a lifetime. I'd have to kill anybody who messed this up for me."

Late afternoon shadows had begun to stretch long across the desert floor when the five new men stopped their horses and sat abreast overlooking Axel Capp's hacienda. The five were raggedly dressed, riding unkept horses. In the center of the riders, Bobby Combs pushed his frayed hat brim up and gazed all around, taking in the corral far to the left and the smoke curling up from a *chimenea* in the side yard, where they saw men gathering beneath a canvas canopy. "Ten to one says they're cooking us up a bunch of steaks right now," he said, offering a slight smile.

"How would they know we're coming tonight?" asked one of the riders, a gaunt dull-eyed man named Mose Winton.

"Jesus . . ." a young gunman named Ulie Saggs groaned under his breath. "He was only making conversation, old-timer," Saggs said with a low scornful laugh. "I hope you ain't this ignorant all the time."

"Who are you calling ignorant?" Mose Winton asked in a harsh tone.

Saggs shook his head and sighed, gazing down at the hacienda. "Never mind, old-timer . . . you'll figure it out sooner or later."

Ignoring the two's bickering, Bobby Combs said, "They might not have been expecting us tonight, but they for damn sure know we're here." He looked all around the desert land for places a guard might be watching them down the length of a rifle barrel. "From what I've always heard about the Rio Sagrado Gang, you never catch them off guard."

"Yeah, well, that's real impressive," Saggs said in a bored tone, casting a skeptical look at the two men on his other side. "How about it, are you boys as impressed as I am?"

The two looked at one another, then back at the hacienda without answering Saggs. One of them, an old gunman and drifter known as Doc Cain, wore a dusty ragged swallowtail dress coat and a tall battered top hat. He leaned slightly and said to the man beside him, a horse thief named Parker Stiles, "Only thing troubles me is that the Sagrado boys are even taking in any new blood. I always heard they're a hard bunch to hook up with."

"Me too," Stiles replied. He gave Combs a trace of a crooked smile and said, "But if they're cooking steaks for us, I already feel right at home."

"Before we ride down there," Combs said to the other four, "I think we all ought to get something straight between us."

"Yeah? What's that?" Saggs asked, lifting his pistol from his well-worn holster and twirling it idly, paying more attention to the gun than to Combs.

Combs looked from one face to the next and said, "I know we haven't ridden together before, and we don't owe one another a thing. But, since Axel Capp rounded us up at the same time and we're all newcomers, maybe we ought to think about watching out for one another for a while . . . at least till we all know where we stand with this bunch."

Saggs gave a haughty tilt of his head. "You boys look after one another all you want to. I've always looked out for myself. I wouldn't have it no other way."

"I've always been a loner myself," said Combs. "But none of us knows the Capps or any of the Rio Sagrado Gang . . . hell, none of us even knows one another, except since Axel Capp brought us together. "Don't anybody here think it might be a good idea to stick together for a while?" He looked from one face to the next. No one offered a response.

Saggs chuckled, "Well, there's your answer I reckon.

"Yeah, I reckon," said Combs. He gave his horse a tap with his boot heels and rode off toward the hacienda.

"Damn, fellows!" said Saggs, "looks like we've all hurt the man's feelings."

Without acknowledging Saggs, the rest of the men heeled their horses forward and rode along a few yards behind Combs. After a moment Saggs shook his head and said to himself, "Damn, what a God-awful string of dead-weight." Then he grinned and gigged his horse forward.

The riders were within ten yards of the hacienda before they realized that horsemen had slipped in around them from behind and formed a half circle following them the rest of the way. Saggs caught a glimpse of the riders coming up behind him, but looking forward and realizing that Combs and the other three hadn't seemed to notice, Saggs shook his head again. "What the hell did Axel Capp have in mind hiring this ragged-assed bunch?" he grumbled under his breath.

In the yard of the hacienda, Axel Capp looked out across the looming evening darkness as the five riders came in and stopped. Behind them four of his regular men stopped their horses as well. They sat silently with their rifles drawn and ready. Combs and the new men gave a look around at the riders and sat still, waiting for Capp to call the riflemen down. He did, with the toss of a hand. Then he grinned at Combs, noting that he didn't seem too surprised when he saw the riflemen. "Welcome, Combs. I've been expecting you boys all day."

"We spotted an army patrol yesterday evening, and swung wide of it," said Combs. "It cost us a few hours, but I remember you said to keep ourselves out of sight as much as possible."

"Yes, I did say that. Good man," said Axel. He puffed a cigar and looked around at the other new men. "Where's Al Decker? He was supposed to met up with you in El Paso."

"Al Decker's dead," said Combs. "He got himself stuck to death in a knife fight in a cantina the night before we got there."

"Too bad," said Axel. "But that's the life he lived." He shrugged. "We'll just have to get by with the five of yas. Step down, get yourself fed and rested, meet the rest of this outfit. Tomorrow we'll talk about the job we're going to do."

As soon as Bobby Combs and the others stepped down from their saddles, Axel Capp pointed at the men standing around him, saying to the newcomers, "Boys, these fellows are the Rio Sagrado Gang in person. Meet Curly Barnes, Rod Sealey, Hector Ruiz and

Denton Spears." He grinned proudly and pointed at the four riflemen on horseback behind them. "That's Dallas Ryan, his cousin, Joe Murphy, Millard Trent and Ace Tinsdale."

The four horsemen nodded. Axel Capp pointed at the new members one at a time and said to the men around him, "Fellows, this is Bobby Combs, Ulie Saggs, Mose Winton, Parker Stiles and Doc Cain. I want you to make them feel at home. They're going to be riding with us on the big job I told yas about."

Combs and the other newcomers nodded. Axel stepped forward and said to the four horsemen, "All right, you four, back to guarding. First thing in the morning everybody starts practice shooting! I want everybody in top form for this job."

The four horsemen turned and rode away silently, shoving their rifles back down into their saddle boots. When Axel turned back to Bobby Combs, he said, "Of course you five don't need to practice unless you just feel like it."

"Why not?" Combs asked, giving him a curious look. "If we're going to be riding into trouble, I'd like to know I'm ready for it."

"Well, yes, you're right," said Axel, as if it had just then dawned on him. He raised his voice to the other four newcomers, saying, "Everybody gets in some practice come morning. We don't want nobody riding unprepared!" He threw his arm across Combs' shoulder and walked him toward the *chimenea*, where the sound of sizzling meat rose through a haze of mesquite smoke. "Now, come with me, let's eat and drink!"

"Damn Combs," Saggs said under his breath to the others as they all followed along behind Combs and Axel. "He had no right speaking up for me. I don't need no practice. What about the rest of you?"

Doc Cain took off his dusty top hat and shook it back and forth. "You wasn't hearing what was being said, was you, Saggs?"

"Yeah, I heard," said Saggs defensively. "We wasn't going to have any shooting practice until Combs butted in."

"And that was all you heard?" said Doc Cain.

"Yeah, what else was there to hear?" said Saggs.

Doc Cain smiled, placing his battered top hat back onto his head. "Nothing, Saggs," he said. "Nothing at all."

Chapter 10

Bobby Combs awoke the next morning to the quiet clicking sound of metal on metal and looked across a low smoldering campfire at Doc Cain, who sat idly cleaning his big Walker Colt. Combs noted that Doc's eyes were upon him as if the trail-weary gunman had been watching him sleep.

Seeing Combs' eyes open, Doc Cain stood up slowly, the big Walker hanging loosely in his hand, and stepped around the fire toward him. Doc stooped down beside Combs, clicked the revolver shut and shoved it down behind his belt. He looked around cautiously, then said in a lowered voice, "I've been thinking about what you said, about watching one another's back. Count me in on that."

Combs raised up on an elbow, his own Colt coming up from beneath his blanket and slipping into his holster. "As I recall, that offer didn't get many takers yesterday, Doc. Maybe it wasn't such a good idea after all." He too spoke in a guarded tone, casting a glance around at the blanket-wrapped sleepers in the grainy predawn light.

"Maybe the others don't see it, but I do," said Cain. "As far as I'm concerned, you and I can watch out for one another. If the others ain't up for it, let them suit themselves."

As Doc Cain spoke, the two stood up. Bobby Combs stepped into his boots and turned facing him. "What changed your mind, Doc?" he asked.

"Oh, I was for it all along," said Doc, gesturing a hand away from the fire and the circle of sleeping men. The two drifted a few steps away, then stopped. He continued quietly, "But I didn't feel like declaring myself in front of the others." He gave a nod toward the dark hacienda, where only a single lamp glowed dimly in a window. "Call it just a hunch, but I don't think Axel Capp has our best interest in mind."

Combs nodded. "I started getting the same hunch riding in here yesterday. Nothing against any of us newcomers, but Capp could have done better."

"Nothing cuts sharper than an honest opinion," said Cain.

"I didn't mean you, Doc," said Combs.

"Sure you did." Doc Cain gave a tired smile. "You meant every one of us. And I hate to admit it about myself," he said, "but it's the truth. We wouldn't none of us be my first pick for a big bank robbery. "

"All right," Combs nodded. "You and I have ourselves a deal. We watch each other's back and keep each other informed. The minute it looks like we're about to get put in a jackpot, we'll be prepared to back one another's play."

Doc Cain smiled thinly, tugging a tight-fitting glove onto his hand. "I'm thinking that just coming here has already put us in a jackpot, so we might as well start looking for the best way out."

"But I still want that bank money," said Combs.

"Oh, absolutely so," said Cain. "As far as I'm concerned, I'd just as soon die on the bank floor as to have to leave here broke with my tail between my legs."

"That's the way I feel," said Combs. "I might have been brought here to be jackpotted, but if there's money to be made, I'll still take my chances."

"Me too," said Doc Cain. Rubbing his beard-stubbled chin in contemplation, he asked, "Just how good are you at riding and shooting from horseback?"

"Better than most, Doc," said Combs. "Fact is, I can knock apples off a tree at full gallop."

"Good," said Doc Cain, "so can I. But let's not do that today when we're practicing, all right?"

"You mean why show our hand before all the bets are in the pot," Combs said, already catching on.

"Exactly," said Cain. "It will be interesting to see how Capp acts when he sees we're not the sort of gunmen he needs on this kind of job."

Bobby Combs nodded and returned the gunman's crafty smile. "I believe you and me might do all right sticking together, Doc."

As they turned and stepped back in closer to the fire, Hector Ruiz walked in from the direction of a small shed, his arms loaded with wood for the fire. "You are up early, ahead of the others I see," said Hector. He tossed the wood onto the smoldering campfire and stepped back as sparks, ashes and smoke billowed skyward. "I too am an early riser." He looked the two up and down. "My best thinking comes in the hour before dawn."

"Is that a fact?" said Doc, showing only polite cordial interest.

"*Sí*, that is a fact." Hector's dark eyes seemed to study the two even closer for a moment. Then he

turned and picked up the coffeepot sitting near the
fire. "I will go get some water and make us a pot
of coffee."

"Yeah, you do that, *más rápido*," came the mocking
voice of Ulie Saggs as he tossed his blanket to the
side and stood up. Stretching his back, he looked at
Hector and said, "I don't like being kept waiting for
my coffee. While you're at it, I could use a stack of
hot cakes and some beans. I expect you know how to
cook beans better than anybody here."

Hector's eyes flared hot with anger. His free hand
almost went for his gun. But looking at Saggs and
seeing that the man was not even aware of the insult
he'd made, let alone prepared to back it up, Hector
seemed to expel his anger. He even managed to force
himself to smile. "Ah, I see! You make a joke. That's
pretty funny, what you say." His gun hand seemed to
ease away from his holster. Looking away from Saggs
and over at Combs and Doc Cain, he said, "So now
I go to make some coffee."

"Gracias," said Doc Cain in a humble tone of voice.

No sooner than Hector Ruiz was out of sight, Saggs
said to Bobby Combs and Doc Cain, "What are you
boys doing up so early?"

Combs and Doc Cain stared at him for a moment.
Without answering him, Combs said, "Are you all
ready for shooting practice today?"

"I was born ready," said Saggs. "The way I figure
it, this is going to be more than just practice. This is
Axel Capp's way of seeing if we've got what it takes
to ride with the Rio Sagrado boys."

"Yeah?" said Doc Cain. "You know, come to think
of it, you just might be right."

"Are you going to be up to it, Saggs?" asked Combs.

"Hell, yes, I'm up to it," said Saggs. He looked

Combs up and down. "Are *you*?" he asked with a twist of sarcasm.

"I'll sure give it my best try," said Combs, turning his gaze from Saggs to Doc Cain as he spoke. "What about you, Doc?"

"You know it," said the trail-worn gunman.

When Hector Ruiz returned, carrying the big pot full of water and ground-up coffee beans, he placed the pot on a blackened iron rack above the licking flames. In moments the aroma of coffee seemed to draw the rest of the sleeping men from their blankets and position them around the glowing fire, their tin cups in hand. They filled their cups in turn and drank steaming coffee in silence until Axel Capp, Denton Spears, and a man in a black business suit and a white goatee who had arrived in the middle of the night, walked out of the hacienda toward the campfire. The man in the business suit split away from Spears and Capp and trotted toward the barn. In a moment he came out of the barn on horseback and rode away in the grainy morning light.

As soon as Spears stopped beside the campfire, he reached down, looped the loose rawhide strip around his leg and tied his holster down. Standing beside Spears, Axel Capp said, "All right, men, the sun's coming up. Before breakfast, we're going to get some leather under us and go out back of the corral, where Hector set us up some whiskey bottle targets. We're going to be shooting from our saddles at a flat-out run. I want to see nothing but gun smoke and broken glass when we're finished."

He looked at the men one at a time, then added, "Make this shooting count; it's all the practice you're going to get. Soon as we get back here and get our-selves fed, we're riding out. I got word that bank is just sitting there waiting on us to rob it!" His face broke into a wide grin. A loud cheer rose from the men.

"You heard him, boys!" said Denton Spears. "Let's get some horses twixt our knees and get busy!"

Axel Capp and Spears stood watching the men move from the campfire to the barn in the breaking morning light. Nodding in the direction the man in the business suit had just taken across the desert floor, he said, "It was kind of unexpected, him showing up last night, wasn't it? I thought you said it would be at least another week before we heard from him."

"Yes, that is what I said," Axel replied, "but he said the gold is arriving ahead of schedule. To tell the truth I'm glad of it. The sooner we get this done the better, as far as I'm concerned."

"Me too," said Spears. "But once that gold is stolen, this strip of ground is going to be swarming with Germans and *federales*, every one of them madder than a nest of smoked hornets."

"Don't worry about it," said Axel. "I've got Giles over there setting things up for us in the territory." Axel grinned. "I figure by now he's got the town ready to string up some welcoming banners for us."

"Yeah, that's what I figure too," said Spears. He gave Axel a quick sidelong glance then looked away, hoping Axel could not see the look of uncertainty that came into his eyes at the mention of Giles' name.

Charlie Floose's horse was winded, covered with froth and streaked with sweat and dirt when Floose finally stopped on the rise looking down on the hacienda. Staring past the hacienda into the dusty haze past the corral where the sounds of pistol shots came from, he saw the gathering of men watching as a horseman rode, firing at a row of bottles. "What the hell is this?" Floose whispered aloud to himself.

"It's target practice, Floose," said the voice behind him.

Floose, caught by surprise, turned suddenly in his saddle. His hand went instinctively to the gun on his hip. But he checked himself down at the sight of Ace Tinsdale sitting atop a big dun with his rifle pointed loosely at him. "Damn it, Tinsdale," Floose growled halfheartedly. "Make your presence known before you say something that way. You're lucky I didn't shoot a hole in your belly."

"Oh, yeah? You're telling me who's lucky?" Tinsdale offered a smug grin, jiggling the rifle in his hand.

Dismissing the matter, Floose gestured toward the pistol shots. "Practice must mean Axel's getting ready to make a move?"

"Yep," said Ace Tinsdale. "I was one of the first to shoot. So, I'm riding lookout for the rest of them." His grin widened. "I hit everything I shot at."

"Good for you," said Floose, grudgingly. "I best get on over there. I've got news for Axel that he needs to hear."

"Go on then," said Tinsdale, lifting his rifle barrel slightly. "You better rest that horse and water it before it drops dead beneath you."

Floose only grunted sourly in reply and heeled the exhausted animal forward, having to hammer his boot heels to the dun's sides to get it moving again. The horse struggled forward past the corral and stopped where the men stood shouting and cheering as Denton Spears sped along on his horse, raising a boiling wake of dust. Spears lay low on his horse's neck, firing shot after shot at a long row of bottles standing along a fence rail twenty-five yards away. The empty bottles exploded one after another in a spray of shattered glass.

"Floose, here I am," said Axel Capp. Having seen Floose ride in, Axel stepped his horse forward from the thin shade of a cottonwood tree and said, "Come on over here." Then he backed the horse into the shade and said to Dallas Ryan and Joe Murphy, who stood leaning against the tree trunk, "You two go over there with the others. Me and Charlie needs to talk."

Ryan and Murphy gave Floose a nod as they walked past him to join the rest of the men. Axel looked Floose up and down, noting the condition of his horse. "You must have something awfully important to say, riding an animal down that bad."

"Yeah, I do, Axel," said Floose. He stepped down from the horse and dropped the saddle from its back as he spoke. "I'm glad I caught you before you headed over to Redemption." He slipped the bridle from the horse's mouth and gave the wet worn-out animal a shove. The horse turned and plodded off toward a water trough at the corral gate. "Things ain't going the way you wanted them to in that town."

"Come on, out with it, Floose," said Axel impatiently. "Can't you see I'm getting these men ready to make a raid?"

"Giles is got some big trouble in Redemption," said Floose. "You told me to keep you informed, so I came just as quick as I could. I don't want him jumping all over me for telling on him."

"You're just doing what I told you to, so don't worry, I'll square it with Giles," said Axel, sounding more impatient. "Has Giles and Swain done what I wanted done there?"

"Well, they've got the town leaders in our hip

pocket, the way you wanted them. The sheriff's been replaced by a man who don't know spit about law work. All in all, things was going pretty good," said Floose. "Except that no sooner than we got back there this last trip, Giles and Swain wanted to rob the bank."

"Damn it to hell!" said Axel. "I told Giles I want that town as a friendly spot on that side of the border! I don't want no robbing going on there! Hell, he's got the whole damn western frontier to rob! Why Redemption?"

"To tell the truth, Axel," said Floose, "I believe dealing with us Rio Sagrado boys has gone straight to Swain's head. I think he just wants to know he was in on a robbery. You know, to sort of make him think he's a member? He likes to think he's one of the bulls of the woods."

"Bull of the woods?" Axel sneered. "I'll nut him with a pair of wire cutters, that son of a bitch!" he raged, then settled a bit and gave Floose a hard stare. "You weren't influencing my brother on robbing the bank there, were you?"

"Why, hell, no, Axel!" Floose lied, acting shocked at such a suggestion. "The fact is, I tried every way in the world to change his mind. But you know how Giles can be."

"Yeah, I know," said Axel, seeming to calm down, watching Doc Cain race along firing at a fresh row of empty bottles. Axel grinned slightly, seeing only two bottles explode. "Giles sure loves robbing banks. I reckon that's a family trait. Is there still time to stop him?"

"Yeah, I believe so," said Floose. He gestured a hand toward the gathering of men who stood watching

Doc Cain check his horse down to a walk, looking disappointed with himself. "But there's another problem." He hesitated.

"Yeah? What's that?" said Axel.

"There's a ranger in town," said Floose.

"So," Axel shrugged, "shoot him."

"I wish it was that simple," said Floose, "but it ain't."

"Oh?" Axel's interest piqued. "I've never seen a problem with a lawman that a bullet won't stop."

"I know," said Floose. "But this one had already beat the living hell out of Snake Bentell and buffaloed everybody else so bad they can't seem to get the upper hand on him!"

"What about Giles?" said Axel. "I never known of anybody, lawdog or otherwise, to get the upper hand on him."

"Me neither," said Floose, "that is not until now."

Axel snapped a sharp stare at him. "What are you saying?"

Floose held his hands up chest-high in a show of peace. "Don't get mad at me for telling you, Axel, but this ranger has backed Giles down . . . right in front of all of us and the whole damned town."

"Backed him down?" Axel looked stunned. "What the hell has gotten into my brother?"

"I ain't blaming Giles for backing down," said Floose. "This is that ranger everybody's been talking about. The one who killed Junior Lake and his bunch? The one that rides Sazes' big Bear-claw Appaloosa stud?"

"I've heard of him . . ." Axel Capp fell silent for a moment, watching Bobby Combs ride along firing at a fresh row of bottles, doing no better than Doc Cain had. But this time he didn't smile as he watched. His thoughts had turned to the ranger he'd heard so much about. "What's he doing in Redemption?"

"That sheriff's daughter had him sent there, is what I heard," said Floose. "And you know how a lawdog is when it comes to one of their own getting killed. It seems like they just won't turn loose till somebody pays for it."

"And my brother has let himself get bulldogged by this man . . ." Axel said in contemplation, shaking his head slowly.

"Well, luckily I got the word to you before you did something here and needed Redemption as a cooling-off spot, huh?" said Floose, gesturing a hand toward the gathered gunmen. "Now you can put things off here for a while until we get Redemption back under control."

Axel sat in silence for a moment, watching Combs and Doc Cain stand beside their horses, looking at their pistol as if the big Colts had something wrong with them. "No, Floose," he said finally, "what I've got planned can't be stopped. It's a once in a lifetime deal. I've got to go on with it. There's too much at stake."

"Damn, Axel," said Floose, getting interested, "what is it? Am I going to be a part of it? I've done everything just like you asked me to, keeping an eye on Giles and reporting back to you and all."

"We're all in it," said Axel, watching Bobby Combs and Doc Cain as he spoke to Floose. "Those of us that matters anyway."

"Huh? What does that mean?" Floose asked, looking puzzled.

"Never mind," said Axel. "All you need to know

right now is that you're in on it. We get it done, we're going to have to go to Redemption. There won't be a place on this side of the border safe enough for us."

"All right, then," said Floose, "at least you won't be riding into Redemption not knowing what to expect. I'm thinking once we all hit town, that ranger won't be as hard to handle."

"That ranger is dead right now," said Axel, "he just ain't aware of it." He booted his horse from the shade and rode in closer to watch the shooting.

At the end of the shooting practice as Doc Cain and Bobby Combs walked along leading their horse by their reins, Saggs, Mose Winton and Parker Stiles came riding by them slowly. Stopping his horse in front of the two and turning sideways, blocking their way, Saggs said with a flat nasty smile, "Well, well, if it ain't that famous couple of sharpshooters we've heard so much about . . . Bobby Combs and Doc Cain!"

"Get out of the way, Saggs," said Bobby Combs.

Saggs made a show out of backing his horse out of the way. "Begging your pardon, I'm sure!" he said in a grand gesture of sweeping his ragged hat from his head and motioning for them to walk past him. "I wouldn't want to do or say anything to cause you two to get your bark on. Not after seeing that dazzling shooting you both did!" He looked at Winton and Stiles, saying, "Did you boys happen to see these men shoot? Between them, they made twelve shots and hit four bottles!" Taunting Combs and Doc Cain, he held up four gloved fingers for emphasis. "I'm talking *four* whiskey bottles, *twelve* shots!"

Some of the passing gunmen saw Saggs goading Combs and Cain, but they only smiled to themselves and went on. "You've had your fun, Saggs," Doc Cain said in a lowered voice, "now, go on and leave us be."

"Leave you be?" Saggs grinned. "Is that a warning there, Doc?"

"Call it what you like, Saggs," said Doc Cain. "Just get on away from me. You've said what you wanted to say."

Saggs turned harsh; his flat smile disappeared. "No, I ain't said everything I want to say. I want to say that you two bummers have no business riding with a gang like this. You made fools of yourselves shooting. No damn wonder you wanted us five new men to stick together. Neither one of you can shoot worth a damn." He said to Mose Winton and Parker Stiles, "Am I right, boys? Have you ever seen such a poor showing in your lives?"

"I got to say, it wasn't much of a showing," said Mose Winton. "But maybe you both would do better if we did it over."

"Oh, a second chance?" said Saggs. "Is that what you're saying, Mose? Give these two another try at hitting what they shoot at?"

"Yeah." Winton shrugged. "Why not? It ain't like we was shooting at somebody who was shooting back."

"That's the whole damn point, fool," said Saggs, acting put out by Stiles' mental dullness. "What if it had been people shooting back?" He gave a sarcastic nod toward Combs and Cain. "These two would be dead . . . so might we be, as bad as they shoot." He looked Winton up and down in disgust. "What the hell kind of idiots am I riding with?"

"Leave Mose alone," said Parker Stiles, staring hard at Saggs. "You asked him, he told you. What more do you want?"

Saggs pointed his finger at Parker Stiles. "You keep

your mouth shut, Stiles. I'm sick of all four of you barn-yard plugs! I think I best separate myself from all of yas. You're all making me look bad." He looked back at Doc Cain and Bobby Combs. "If I was either one of you, I wouldn't show my sorry face around here any longer than it took for me to saddle up and—"

"That's enough, Saggs!" said Doc Cain, taking a step away from Combs and turning loose of his horse's reins. "If it's a fight you're spoiling for, you don't have to go through all this bad-mouthing. Just step down off that horse and we'll have at it, just the two of us."

"I'm obliged to take you up on it, you old broken-down saloon swamper," said Ulie Saggs. He rose slightly in his saddle, ready to throw his leg over and step down.

But Axel Capp came riding in quickly and shouted, "Hold it right there! We're having none of that!"

"I'd be doing us all a favor," said Saggs, stopping, but still poised to step to the ground. "Are you sure you don't want me to put this old dog out of his mis-ery?" His eyes went from Doc Cain to Combs, then back to Axel Capp.

"Did you not hear him plainly, Saggs?" said Denton Spears, stepping his horse in closer than Axel's. "He told you we're not having any fighting among our-selves. Guess what that means?"

Saggs looked at Spears' hand poised an inch from his gun butt. He eased back down into his saddle. "All right then. I understand. I won't kill him." He looked at Axel and said, "But I'm a man to be taken seri-ously. You've got to realize how bad it makes me feel. These two scarecrows rode in here with me. I don't want nobody thinking they're pals of mine."

"Duly noted," said Axel Capp. He gave a nod toward

the hacienda. "Now, get on over to the yard. We've got a lot to get done. I need all the men I've got."

Saggs turned in his saddle and booted his horse toward the yard. Combs and Doc Cain started to step up into their saddles and do the same, but Axel stopped them, saying, "You two hold up a minute." The four sat atop their horses watching as Saggs caught up to Stiles and Winton, who had already ridden away.

"What the hell did happen back there?" Denton Spears asked Bobby Combs. "I never seen any worse shooting from two men who make their living with a gun."

Combs and Doc Cain looked at one another, both of them seeming to be at a loss for an answer.

"Let's not go making a big deal of it," said Axel Capp, speaking up for the two gunmen. "Anybody can miss now and then. They'll both do better when we get into some action. Right, men?" He looked at Combs and Doc Cain.

"You bet we will," Combs said flatly.

"You can count on it," said Cain, tipping the frayed brim of his top hat. The two waited a second longer as Spears turned his horse and followed Axel Capp toward the yard. "There's our answer," he said quietly to Bobby Combs. "We're being jackpotted sure enough. Would you rob a bank with two men who shot as poorly as we did?"

"Nope," said Bobby, "not unless I just needed them to draw somebody's attention."

A slight smile came to Doc Cain's face. "We'll sure keep that in mind once we get inside that bank."

"Do you suppose he'll let us get *inside* that bank?" Bobby Combs asked.

"It'll be up to us to see to that he does," said Cain.

Chapter 11

The ranger stood looking out the window beneath the big wooden star, watching the reflections of Danny Boy, Snake and Bo Altero walk toward the Even Odds Saloon. From the opposite direction he saw Councilmen Avondale and Meaker walking his way. Sam turned away from the window and faced Sheriff Watts, saying calmly, "Looks like we've got company coming, Sheriff."

Delbert Watts looked up from his desk, where he sat writing a report with a short pencil stub. "You said we'd be hearing from them after all that shooting the other night. You called it about right."

"Yep," said Sam, "too many things have gotten out of control for them. It's time they talk to the sheriff, see if you'll straighten their mistakes out for them."

Watts folded the piece of paper over on itself, opened the desk drawer and put it away. From another drawer he took out a spare pistol that he had broken apart and wrapped in a cleaning cloth. He quickly unwrapped the cloth atop his desk. The ranger smiled slightly to himself, watching Watts spread the parts of the pistol out on the soft cotton cloth. Seeing the look on the ranger's face, Watts stopped for a second and said, "This is what you said, isn't it? Keep them at arm's length while you clean your gun?"

"That's right," said the ranger, glad to see that Watts had been listening when he'd told him. "It lets them know right off that they've stepped into your world. No matter what they've got to say, it's not as important as keeping a clean firearm."

"I understand," said Watts, picking up the gun frame with the barrel attached to it as the sound of the two sets of footsteps moved up from the street onto the boardwalk out front. He held the gun barrel up pointed at the door as the two councilmen walked in without knocking.

"Whoa!" said Councilman Avondale, stopping abruptly, his eyes widening at the sight of a gun pointed at his chest. Meaker bumped into him from behind.

"Come in, gentlemen, nothing to fear," Watts said respectfully, lowering the pistol frame, letting the two men see that the pistol was in pieces on his desk. "I'm only cleaning a gun."

Avondale tugged down on the front corners of his vest. "Well, you might at least lower it when a person comes in!"

"Had you knocked first, I would have," said Watts, again with respect. Turning his attention back to the pistol, he asked as he blew a speck of dust from the frame, "What can I do for you, Councilmen?"

Avondale composed himself, cleared his throat and stepped aside enough for Meaker to stand beside him. "Sheriff, we're here to talk about the shooting that went on out in the street night before last."

Watts picked up a corner of the cleaning cloth and rubbed it back and forth along the gun barrel, giving the gun most of his attention as he said, "You mean when Giles Capp got drunk and emptied his pistol into the sky? I saw the whole thing through the window."

"You were here?" said Avondale, looking surprised. "You watched it happen and didn't try to stop it?"

"When you offered me this job, didn't you tell me to leave the Capps and their friends alone?"

Avondale's face reddened. He gave the ranger a nervous glance, then looked back at Watts as the ranger turned away and looked out the window. "Well, I did ask you to show some consideration for those who support this community."

"Yes, that's what I meant." Watts smiled, still looking at the gun as he began putting the pieces of it back together, taking his time. "So, I felt like one thing you wouldn't want me to do is go out there and get into a shoot-out with Giles Capp."

"No, of course we wouldn't want you getting into a shoot-out with the man," said Avondale. "But you could have talked him down, taken his gun away from him."

"I don't think a person can take Giles Capp's gun away from him without shooting him first," said Watts. "And I know you don't want me shooting him, do you?"

"Well, no!" said Avondale, getting frustrated, unsure of exactly what he did want Watts to do. I expect you to look for other options, other than shooting him."

"Like what for instance?" said Watts.

"I don't know what!" Avondale barked. "That's your job! You come up with some alternatives! Do you know he shot out my office window?"

"Yes, I saw that," said Watts, still attending the gun. "Do you want to file a complaint and bring him up on a charge?" He shrugged a shoulder. "Because that's the only way I can do anything about it."

Avondale looked shocked. "I'm not going to file a complaint! But something will have to be done. You'll have to talk to him! Let him know that we can't have this sort of thing in Redemption! If he goes unchecked, he'll only get worse!"

"I can talk to him," said Watts, "if you're sure that's what you want done."

"Yes, talk to him," said Avondale. "Just be diplomatic about it."

"I don't know if I can be diplomatic," said Watts. "Would it be better if you spoke to him yourself? That way you wouldn't have to worry about me saying the wrong thing."

Avondale turned to the ranger, too frustrated to talk to Watts anymore. "What about you, Ranger? Will you talk to Giles Capp? I mean in words he'll understand? I saw how you handled him the other day."

"After the other day I'm afraid if I tried to talk to him, I would just have to shoot him," said Sam. "I'd have to kill him." The ranger shook his head. "No, I better not go sticking my nose into town business. Besides, I'm about to solve my robbery case. I'll be ready to leave Redemption most any time now." He picked his hat up off a peg and set it atop his head. "You're right about one thing, though."

"Oh? What's that?" said Avondale.

"He's going to just keep getting worse," Sam said matter-of-factly. Then to Watts he said, "I'm going to the barn and check on my mount." He turned and walked to the back door, taking his time. But once out the back door, he hurried along the larger alley to the small alley running alongside the Even Odds

Saloon. In the shadows he waited, peeping around the corner every now and then, keeping watch on the boardwalk and the bat-wing doors, waiting for the gunmen to come out.

Inside the saloon, Andrew Swain sat at his personal table and watched Bo Altero, Danny Boy Wright and Snake Bentell lift Giles Capp to his feet from where he'd fallen to the floor. They half-carried, half-dragged him to Swain's table and plopped him down into a chair. Swain sat up straight, snatching his bottle of expensive bourbon from atop the table. "Why don't you lay him on the cot in the back room? Let him sleep it off awhile," said Swain.

"He ain't sleeping in no back room like some drunken barfly," said Bo Altero. He'd picked Giles' hat up off the floor. He dusted it against his leg and shoved it onto Giles' head. "I'll tell him what you said when he wakes up. I'll also tell him how you left him lying on the dirty floor while you sent for us to come get him."

Swain gave a shrug. "What was I supposed to do? You boys have been making yourselves pretty damned scarce the past week, ever since that ranger faced Giles down in the corral." He gestured with his cigar toward Giles. "Look at him. He's been coming in here drinking more and more . . . getting drunker and harder to handle every day!"

"He's still the boss, far as we're concerned!" Altero said in a menacing tone.

"Of course he's still the boss," said Swain, realizing he'd better tread a little easier around these men. "I just want things to be back like they were before that ranger came here. Axel Capp wants this town whipped into shape for when he gets here." Again, he gestured his cigar at the drunken passed-out gunman. "Does this look like we've got the town under control to you?"

"Poke that cigar at him again, see if I don't break a chair across your mustache," said Bo Altero. He took a step toward Swain.

"I'm sorry," said Swain, taking a step back, drawing his cigar hand in close to his chest. "But the fact remains, Axel isn't going to like how things are going here. We're starting to lose the councilmen. Last night Giles shot a window out of Avondale's office. Much more of that and we can kiss our political support good-bye." He nodded at a long crack in a large mirror behind the bar. "Look at that. That's where he started cussing his own reflection and threw a shot glass into my mirror. Night before last, he stood in the middle of the street shouting and cursing . . . fired every shot in his pistol straight up in the air, woke up half the town."

"I came and got him, didn't I?" said Altero, giving Swain a hard stare.

"Yes, you did," said Swain. "Our so-called sheriff wasn't about to do anything. Why would he? He knows how he got that badge. He can't do anything against the Rio Sagrado Gang."

"He better not," said Altero.

"But somebody's got to do something," said Swain. "I'm telling you, we can lose what we've started here."

"Ah-hell." Altero brushed it aside. "We ain't going to lose nothing here. Giles will sober up. That ranger belittled him really bad," Altero said defensively. "Giles has got a lot on his mind."

"Yeah, it looks like it," said Swain, this time carefully keeping his cigar out of the conversation. "What was he mumbling yesterday about sending a wire to Humbly, bringing Crazy Man Lewis here?"

"ManMack Lewis owes Giles a favor or two," said Bo Altero. "I'd be careful calling him Crazy Man if I was you."

"I thought everybody called him Crazy Man," said Swain.

"Not to his face they don't," said Altero. "Not if they want to live long enough to say good morning."

Swain looked worried. "Then let's forget I ever called him that," he said. "It was simply a mistake on my part."

"I'll say it was," Altero replied. "ManMack is one hell of a gunman. He might just walk that ranger out into the street and shoot the hell out of him."

"A gunman, huh?" Swain looked back and forth between the men, his eyes going to the tied-down holsters on their hips. "Is that what we need, another gunman?"

Noting the look of disgust on Swain's face, Altero said, "Careful what you say, barkeep. We ain't in the mood for it."

Snake Bentell finally stepped forward and spoke up through swollen lips and battered jaws. "He's right about one thing . . . we don't need no more gunmen! We've got plenty." Turning his puffy bloodshot eyes to Swain, he continued in a thick, barely understandable voice, "That ranger don't impress me."

"Man, oh, man!" Bo Altero gave a short laugh and shook his head. "Look at you, Snake! I keep hearing you say he don't impress you, but every time you get close to him you get the living hell beat out of you. Either take him on or shut your mouth about him."

"I'll take him on," Snake mumbled, patting his holster where a small revolver stood in place of the second gun the ranger had taken away from him. "Soon as I get me a better gun somewhere."

"You both better stay away from the ranger," Altero warned both Snake and Danny Boy, "everybody's starting to run out of *guns* to lend you."

Snake and Danny Boy both looked embarrassed, their faces still recovering from the beating Raymond and LJ Beck had given them. Danny Boy absently reached down, touched his empty holster, then rested his hand near the small borrowed pistol in his belt.

"I'll still take him on," said Snake.

"Sure you will," said Altero, dismissing the idea.

Danny Boy Wright cut in, saying, "Ain't neither one of us afraid of the ranger. It's just that there's something spooky about the man."

"*Spooky . . .*" Altero shook his head again. "Now, that just about rips it for me. He's got you both so buffaloed, you're starting to imagine things! Boys, there is nothing *supernatural* about this ranger. He's not a damn ghost!"

Danny Boy said boldly. "I ain't saying he's a ghost. I ain't saying he's supernatural! Alls I'm saying is that there is something damn spooky about him! It seems like he knows every move we're going to make before we make it! It's like he's one of them *mind readers* or something!"

"Oh, I see," said Altero. "He's not a ghost . . . he just reads minds."

Danny Boy said, "Then you tell me how the hell he always seems to know what we're up to!"

"Maybe it's because he's dealt with enough idiots that he knows what you two *are* thinking," said Altero. He reached down to lift Giles Capp up from the chair. "Now, give me a hand here, help me get him up over my shoulder. I'm taking him out of here."

"Don't you want us to help you carry him too?" Danny Boy asked, helping him stand Giles up on wobbly legs.

"No, just help me load him up, I'll take it from there."

"Oh, I get it," said Snake. "This is just your way of showing Giles he can depend on you more than he can us."

"Hell, he already knows that," said Altero, walking toward the back door with Giles hanging limply over his shoulder.

"Sonsabitch," Snake growled under his breath, starting to follow Altero.

"Hold it, Snake," said Danny Boy. "Let him go. I don't know about you, but I could use a good tall mug of beer." He looked all around. "It's been a whole week since we've been here. I'm sick of doing all my drinking behind the livery barn like some low-class slug."

Snake let out a breath, looking all around. "Hell, come to think of it so am I. Let's get us a mug and stand out front like we did before." He looked at Andrew Swain and asked, "What's the harm in it?"

"You heard what the ranger said," Swain replied. "If he sees any of you on the street, he'll figure you want to fight him."

"To hell with the ranger," said Snake. "What's one damn little mug of beer going to hurt? We've got a right to be on the street same as anybody else. Right, Danny Boy?"

Danny Boy looked dubious. "I don't know, Snake. He seems to always know what we're up to. Maybe we better go on back to the barn."

"I ain't going back to that damned barn!" said Snake. "I want to drink one beer without smelling horse shit! We'll have it drunk and be gone before the ranger even knows we're here. Now, are you going to drink one with me or not?"

Danny Boy considered it, licking his lips. "Yeah, I'll drink one with you. What's the harm? We'll stand right out front, in *our* spot, just like before. The ranger won't even know it."

"Jesus," Swain whispered to himself, wiping a hand across his beaded brow as the two swaggered boldly to the bar and ordered two shots of whiskey and two mugs of beer. Swain collapsed back down into his chair, opened the bottle of bourbon he'd tucked up under his arm and filled a shot glass with a shaking hand. "These sonsabitches are driving me crazy." He sipped his bourbon and watched the two gunmen toss back their shots of whiskey and chase it with long swigs of beer. He breathed a little easier when they took their mugs and walked out onto the boardwalk.

Out front, Snake Bentell raised his mug in a mock toast toward the big wooden star hanging above the sheriff's office. "To hell with the lawdog, I'd like to see him stop me from drinking this—"

Snake's words stopped as the ranger straight-armed him from behind, causing the beer to slosh out of the mug into his face. As Snake stumbled forward and fell to his knees, Danny Boy spun around facing the ranger from less than a foot away. The ranger cocked his Colt in Danny Boy's face only inches from his nose. "I told all of you to stay off the street," Sam hissed. He cocked the colt.

"Pl-Please!" said Danny Boy, stunned nearly speechless. "We-We're just having a be-beer! How did you kno-know?"

Sam gestured with his pistol barrel toward the boardwalk. "Set them down," he said flatly.

Snake Bentell, on his knees, reached out, defeated, and set his beer mug on the boardwalk. Danny Boy stooped down without taking his eyes off the ranger's gun and set his mug down beside Snake's. "Please don't shoot us," Danny Boy said in a trembling voice.

Sam reached out with his boot and swiped it sideways, knocking both mugs off into the dirt street. "One," he said firmly, giving a nod toward the small guns on Danny Boy and Snake.

"How did you know we was here?" Snake asked, struggling to his feet, his hands chest-high. "That's all I want to know!"

Instead of answering him, the ranger said, "Two."

"Damn it, Snake, come on!" said Danny Boy, stepping back, grabbing Snake by his arm and jerking him along the boardwalk until they both hurried away in a run, looking back over their shoulder.

Sam smiled slightly to himself and walked inside the Even Odds Saloon, looking back and forth before stepping all the way through the bat-wing doors. Seeing Swain at his table, the ranger walked toward him. Swain's shot glass stopped halfway to his lips at the sight of the ranger. "Are you doing all right, Mr. Swain?" Sam asked in a concerned tone of voice.

Swain just stared, unable to answer. Finally he set the glass down and nodded his head slowly.

"That's good," said Sam. "I've been worried about you. These boys are starting to break apart on one another. Are you needing my help yet?"

"I'm all right," Swain said softly, staring intently at the ranger, wondering how he always seemed to know everybody's comings and goings at the saloon. "Danny

Boy thinks you're a ghost or something. I'm starting to wonder myself."

Sam just shook his head slowly, staring into Swain's eyes. "I'm just a lawman, Swain. One who's trying to make sure you don't get caught up with these men when it comes time for them to die."

"I told you I'm innocent, Ranger," said Swain, "and that I don't know a thing about the sheriff's death."

"I know that's what you said," Sam replied. "But your story is getting ready to change. I can feel that change coming."

Chapter 12

Only moments after the ranger had left the Even Odds Saloon, Swain stood up, sweating profusely, picked his bottle of bourbon up with a trembling hand and hurried to a dark stockroom back behind the bar. He loosened his necktie, opened his collar and turned up a swig of bourbon straight from the bottle. *Jesus!* What was happening to him. He'd allowed the ranger to get under his skin. Giles Capp had fallen apart on him. All he could do now was sit tight and hope everything turned out all right. Surely to goodness none of the Rio Sagrado boys were going to give in and tell the ranger anything about Sheriff Dolan's death. *Or were they . . . ?* He started to raise the bottle to his lips again, but then he stopped in contemplation. Maybe it *was* time he confided in the ranger.

Sitting in the small stockroom atop a wooden whiskey crate, amid stacks of other half-empty crates with straw packing hanging over their edges, Swain heard the ring of spurs and heavy boots step into the saloon from the boardwalk and walk slowly across the plank floor. He heard them stop at the empty bar, and he heard the bartender say, "Yes, sir, what can I get for you?"

"Not very busy, are you?" said a gruff voice.

"No, sir, not at this time of day. I suppose most folks are just now—"

"I didn't ask you for a explanation," the voice said, cutting him off. "I don't care why the place is empty, so long as it ain't because you serve snake-head whiskey."

"No, sir," said the bartender, "no snake-head whiskey here. Only the best is served here at the Even Odds."

"Even Odds my aching ass," the voice chuckled in a dark tone. "Where's the owner of this lousy dump? I need to talk to him."

"He's in the stockroom, sir," said the bartender. "I'll just get him for you."

"Stay right there," said the gruff voice. "I'll fetch him myself."

"But, sir, you're not allowed—"

In the stockroom, Swain heard a loud jarring thump and the single ring of both spurs as the man hefted himself over the bar top and landed behind the bar. "Right in there, you say?" the voice asked.

Startled, Swain jumped up quickly from the whiskey crate and hurried for the door. But in his hurry to get out of the stockroom, he ran full into the owner of the gruff voice. The impact caused him to stagger back a step.

"Easy there, barkeep," said the gruff voice. "You must be Andrew Swain?"

Swain steadied himself, holding his bourbon bottle by the neck. "Yes, I am. And who might you be?"

"Manifred K. Lewis," the voice said flatly as its owner looked all about the small dark stockroom. "What the hell are you doing in here, Swain? This looks like a place to raise pigeons and rats."

"Ma-Manifred Lewis?" said Swain. "Why are you looking for me?" His voice sounded tight and worried.

"I don't know," said the tall thin gunman, wearing a slight smile behind his drooping mustache, "have you done something you shouldn't have done to somebody?" He wore a long black trail duster over a black vest, shirt and trousers, and a pair of knee-high black Spanish boots.

"No, no indeed," said Swain. "Can we please step out of here where there's more light?"

"Naw, I like it in here, nice and dark. What the hell did you say you were doing in here? Having a quiet drink, I bet?" Looking at the bottle of bourbon in Swain's hand, he took it, raised it to his thick red lips and guzzled it. He let out a belch and handed Swain the empty bottle. "Damn, that was smooth," he said, running his black-gloved finger and thumb along his mustache.

"You don't *know why* you're looking for me?" Swain asked, setting the empty bottle aside.

"I was told by Giles Capp that you'd know where I can find him," said Lewis.

"Oh, I see . . ." Swain let out a tense breath, and felt his heart slow down a full beat inside his trembling chest. "Well, I can tell you that right now you'll find him in the livery barn. He left here over Bo Altero's shoulder."

"In the *livery* barn?" Lewis chuckled. "Damn, he is in need of my services if he's stooped to sleeping with livestock."

"There have been some things happening here, Mr. Lewis," said Swain. "But I'll let Giles tell you all about it."

Lewis grinned darkly. "I can't wait to hear it."

"Oh," said Swain, "then I'm sure it's all right that I tell you."

"That was only a figure of speech, Swain," said Lewis, stopping him. He looked Swain up and down appraisingly. "I believe you are the most perspirant man I've ever seen in my life."

"The most what?" Swain asked.

"Perspirant," said Lewis. "It means *perspiration*, you know . . . sweating? You're the most *sweating* man I've ever seen?"

"Oh, I see," said Swain, not certain if there really was such a word. He ran a hand across his wet forehead. "Well, like I said, there's been a lot going on. I've had a lot on my mind lately."

"Most people who are so greatly *perspirant* have something they are trying to hide," said Lewis. He bored his gaze into Swain's wide watery eyes. "Have you been unnecessarily naughty, Swain? Are there things in the works that you don't want known? Have you double-crossed a friend, or a partner? Or, are you perhaps on the verge of doing such a thing?"

"No, no, of course not," said Swain, ducking his eyes away from Lewis' penetrating gaze and taking a step toward the doorway. "I'm not about to double-cross anybody. I resent your saying—"

"Whoa now," said Manifred Lewis, placing a black-gloved hand flat on Swain's damp chest, stopping him from leaving the stockroom. "You *resent*?" He chuckled. "My, but I must have truly struck a nerve! I hope whoever you're about to do dirt to is not a friend of mine . . . else I feel obliged to tell them."

"Please, Mr. Lewis," said Swain. "I have no such thing in mind for anyone. I've been under a lot of pressure here, running a business, trying to make ends meet."

"There, there now," said Lewis, patting Swain's chest, then smoothing down Swain's loosened necktie.

"I understand. I am always in sympathy with the plight of the small businessman. Sometimes you probably feel like the weight of the entire world is on your shoulders."

"That's the truth," said Swain. "I hope you won't mention this to Giles. The way things have been going here, he might take it the wrong way. Believe me, Giles and I are the best of friends . . . like brothers you might even say."

"Oh, then I certainly wouldn't say anything to cause trouble," said Lewis, still keeping his hand on Swain's chest.

"Good," said Swain, trying to take a step forward. "Then I'll just show you the way to the livery barn."

"No, you stay here, Swain, with your pigeons and rats," said Lewis, grinning, giving him a slight push backward into the stockroom. "I bet I can find the livery barn all by myself. In fact, I bet it's the *very same* livery barn all the signs along the street have been pointing me to . . . isn't it?"

Swain looked a bit embarrassed. "Well, yes . . ."

"Then off I go," said Lewis. He turned and left the stockroom, hefted himself back over the bar, landed with another loud ring of spurs and walked out the door without looking back.

"My God almighty!" Again, Swain wiped a hand across his wet forehead. He said to the bartender, "Dick, get me another bottle of my private bourbon . . . this situation is getting worse by the minute!"

"Anything I can do to help, Mr. Swain?" asked the bartender, already on his way to get a fresh bottle of bourbon.

"No, thanks, Dick," said Swain. "I'm going to have to deal with these people on my own. *Jesus!* They're driving me out of my mind."

Out front of the Even Odds Saloon, Manifred Lewis walked along the dirt street. His spurs rang out with each step, drawing curious eyes from both sides of the street as he led his big silver-gray gelding toward the livery barn.

From inside the sheriff's office the ranger watched the reflection of both man and horse through the window. "Crazy Man Lewis," he whispered to himself, recognizing the gunman's face from an old wanted poster. "Wears black clothes, knee-high boots and silver spurs," Sam continued under his breath. "Wanted for the theft of an undertaker's hearse in Yuma." He studied Lewis, checking out the gun hanging low on his hip behind the long riding duster. "So long ago I bet you've forgotten all about it."

He watched Lewis turn onto the narrow street leading back to the livery barn. Across the street Sam watched Sheriff Watts step out of the bank shoving a thin stack of dollar bills into a brown envelope. Then Watts folded the envelope and shoved it down into his shirt pocket.

Sam's eyes followed Watts along the boardwalk as he walked farther away from the office. "Good man, Delbert," Sam whispered to himself when Watts finally stepped off the boardwalk and cut across in the direction of the ragged tent at the far end of the street.

Sam stepped back from the window and walked to the desk where Julie sat with her head on her arm, asleep. He shook her gently by her shoulder. "Julie Ann, why don't you go to the hotel. You'd be more comfortable in your room," he said.

"Huh?" She looked all around, bleary-eyed. "Oh, was I asleep? I must've just dozed off."

Sam smiled. "You've got to get some rest. Don't worry, this place will still be here when you wake up."

She stood up, and in her half-asleep state put her arms around him and rested her head against his chest, saying, "Sam you've been so kind. What would I have done without you?"

The ranger blushed slightly. "Come on, now," the ranger replied softly, "go get yourself some rest."

"Will you come check on me later?" Julie Ann whispered. She looked up into his eyes, expecting a reply.

After a pause the ranger said, "Yes, I'll come by. Now, go get some rest."

As Julie Ann turned and walked out the door, Sam gave a look back toward Henry Dove's cell and saw Henry watching with a knowing look on his face. "Do you need some water back there, Henry?" he asked.

"I could drink some," Henry replied.

Sam walked back to the cell, took the dipper from a peg, dipped it into the water bucket sitting on a shelf and passed it between the bars to the man. "Much obliged, Ranger Sam," said Henry. He kept his eyes on Sam as he drank from the dipper. Blotting his wet lips on his shirtsleeve, Henry handed the empty dipper back to him and said, "Ranger Sam, it ain't my place to say anything, but I believe that young woman has taken a liking to you."

Sam only stared at him.

"I know!" said Henry, raised his large hands chest-high. "I ought to keep my mouth shut. But somebody needs to tell you . . . you don't *seem* to know it."

"I know it, Henry," said Sam. "But I've got a job to do here."

"Oh, you're one of those men, the job comes before everything else?" Henry asked.

"When I don't attend my job closely, people die because of it, Henry," said the ranger, without wondering why he was having such a conversation with a man behind bars. "I uphold the law, and I have little time for anything else."

"Um-um," said Henry, shaking his head. "Maybe you better *take* time for something else," said Henry. "If you're not real careful you won't *have* the job, the job will *have* you."

Sam started to say something more, but he stopped himself and looked at the empty water dipper in his hand. "Do you want more water, Henry?"

"No," said Henry, clasping his big hands around the bars. He just looked at the ranger.

Hanging the dipper back on the wall peg, Sam said, "I've got a feeling the Beck brothers are about to get some good news."

"What news is that?" Henry asked. "Are they about to get their money back?"

"Yes, I believe they are," said Sam. "I offered them money last week to buy their mules, but they wouldn't take it."

"They's proud young men," said Henry. "All they want is what's rightfully theirs; you can't blame them."

"No, I can't fault them for that," said Sam. "I respect them for it. But I believe we're about to find their lost money."

"*Lost* money. Ha!" said Henry with a wizened grin. "I notice it's turned from being *stolen* to being *lost.*"

The ranger smiled slightly in response. "Sometimes the right word is all it takes to make things happen. If it gets the Becks' money back, you don't care what we call it do you?"

Henry thought about it. "Well, I don't like thinking Watts is going to get away with stealing just because he's the sheriff."

"I know," said Sam. "But the fact is, he wasn't sher-

iff the night he took the money off you. He was just
a broke, desperate man about to lose his business. It
caused him to do something he shouldn't have. If his
heart wasn't in the right place, I reckon he wouldn't
be trying to do anything to make up for it."

Henry nodded. "If he wanted to keep denying it,
there wouldn't be a thing anybody could do about it,
that's for sure."

"I'm not sticking up for him in the *wrong* he's
done," said Sam. "But I am sticking up for him in the
right he's trying to do."

Henry cocked his head curiously. "How do you
know that he's getting ready to do the right thing
about the Becks' mule money?"

"Today's the sheriff's payday," said Sam. "I think
that's what he's been waiting for. He didn't have the
money, so he couldn't have come up with it before
now no matter how bad his conscience bothered him."

"His conscience . . ." Henry Dove grinned again.
"Whatever you say, Ranger Sam. "I'll believe it when
I see it. But if the Becks get their mules and head back
to Nicodemus, Kansas, I want to go with them . . . if
they'll have me, that is."

"You know Giles Capp and his men are still in
town," said Sam. "If I let you out, you'll stay out of
their sight until you and the Becks leave, won't you?"

"I'll try my best to," said Henry. "All I want is to
get out of here and go. I don't want no trouble with
the Rio Sagrado Gang, or anybody else."

Sam considered it, then said, "All right, Henry. If
things go the way I said with the mule money, I'll let
you out of there. I've been holding you for your own
good anyway, waiting for things to cool down."

Henry gave him a flat stare. "I know that. Can't say
I like it, but I understand it. I'm tired of folks all the

time shoving me back and forth for *any* reason, even for my own good."

"I know you're tired of it, Henry," said the ranger. "The problem is, I can only do what I think is best, whether it's for you or anybody else."

"I know," said Henry, still clasping the bars. He watched the ranger walk back to the front window and look off along the boardwalk on the other side of the street.

Sam saw the sheriff's reflection coming back from the tent, this time walking in the dirt street past the front of the Even Odds Saloon, so he stepped back from the window again and seated himself in a chair beside the battered desk. When Watts walked in, Sam sat leafing idly through a stack of wanted posters he'd picked up off the edge of the desk. He looked up as Watts walked over to a line of pegs on the wall, hung his hat up and walked to the desk. Watts cleared his throat and said quietly, "I squared things with the Beck brothers, Ranger."

Sam nodded and stood up. "I'm glad to hear it, Sheriff," he said matter-of-factly. Adjusting his holster belt, he walked over to the same line of wall pegs, took down his pearl-gray sombrero and sat it atop his head. "I'm going to take a walk past the livery barn, make sure our Rio Sagrado boys are behaving themselves. Want to grab a shotgun and come along?"

"I sure do!" said Sheriff Watts. He hurried to the gun rack, took down one of the double-barrels, checked it, made sure it was loaded and clicked it shut. "Ready when you are, Ranger," he said.

Standing near the rear door, Sam said, "I see no reason to keep Henry Dove in custody any longer, do you?"

Watts looked back at Henry, who stood clasping the

bars in his big hands. "Well, no, not really," he said. "I can turn him loose right now."

"Why don't you do that, Sheriff," said Sam, "just in case something were to happen to us."

"Huh?" It took a second for what the ranger had said to sink in. Then Watts seemed to consider it and said, "Yes, you're right."

Seeing the look of consternation on Watts' face, the ranger said, "Not that anything is going to happen to us." He looked back at Dove. "But I think Henry's got some traveling plans he needs to take care of."

"Well, Henry," said Watts, picking up the cell key from his desk, "looks like you're ready to get out there and get yourself some fresh air. I hope there's no hard feelings between us. I just spoke to the Beck brothers. Everything is square with them."

"I've no time for hard feelings, Sheriff," said Henry. "I just want to get on down the road." He watched patiently as the key turned and the cell door creaked open. "If Raymond and LJ will take me to Nicodemus with them, you'll never see my tired hide again." He looked at the ranger, and his expression turned dark and serious. "Ranger Sam, you be careful with them boys. They are a dangerous bunch."

"Thanks, Henry," said Sam, "I know they are."

Henry looked even closer at him, saying, "You intend to have it out with them in the street, don't you, Ranger Sam?"

"That's very possible, Henry," the ranger replied.

"Um-um, then I feel bad leaving you this way," said Henry, shaking his head.

"Go on, Henry," said Sam. "Go to Nicodemus with the Beck brothers. I'll be all right. I've got a job to do here."

"All right, then," he sighed, turning to the door. As

soon as Henry walked out and closed the door behind him, Sam turned to Watts and said, "Are you ready to go?"

"Yes, I'm ready," said Watts. "What is it you think is going on at the livery barn, anyway? I know you've seen something, or else you wouldn't ask me to grab a shotgun."

Sam grinned. "You're learning fast, Sheriff," he said. Reaching down and turning the rear doorknob, he said, "Come on, I'll tell you on the way."

Chapter 13

Manifred Lewis had walked straight to an empty water bucket sitting in the corner of the livery barn. While Altero, Danny Boy and Snake Bentell stood watching dumbly, Lewis carried the bucket out the back door, scooped it through the gray filmy water in the watering trough and carried it back inside the barn. Seeing him walk over to where Giles Capp lay sprawled unconscious in a pile of hay, Bo Altero raised a hand toward him, saying, "Uh—Mr. Lewis, I don' think that's a good id—"

Lewis slung the bucket of water down into Giles' face, causing Altero's words to cut short.

"Sweet Jesus . . . !" Altero whispered in disbelief, cutting a nervous glance to Danny Boy and Snake.

"Wake up! Wake up! You sleeping pole cat!" Lewis shouted as Giles sprang up into a sitting position, spluttering and strangling on the dirty tepid water. Lewis laughed hysterically, jumped astraddle of the stunned outlaw, stuck the empty bucket down over his head and pounded on the side of it with the palm of his hand. "Wake up! Wake up, you drunken sot!"

Even with his head inside the bucket, Giles snatched

his gun, shouting in a distant sounding voice, "I'll kill you! You son of—"

Lewis screamed with laughter, clamped a boot down onto Giles' gun hand and pounded the side of the bucket even harder. "What was that? What say you? Speak up, speak up! We can't hear you!"

Altero, Snake and Danny Boy stared wide-eyed at one another.

Giles shrieked with rage. He struggled to free up his gun hand and jerk the bucket from his head. Manifred Lewis allowed him to pull off the bucket, but he kept his boot planted firmly on Giles' gun hand. "Surprise! It's me! It's me! I'm here, Giles! Came just as soon as I got your telegraph!"

Seeing who it was standing over him, Giles settled down a little, wiping his free hand over his wet face, blowing the dirty water from his lips. "God almighty, Manifred!" he said, shooting his men an angry look. "Will you step off of my hand, before you break all my fingers?"

"Why, sure!" Manifred stooped down, took his boot off of Giles' hand, but scooped up the pistol before Giles could get a good grip on it. With a black-gloved hand he pulled Giles to his feet, jammed the pistol down into his holster and brushed wet hay off the front of Giles' shirt. "Look at you, how wet you are! We're going to have to get you a bib to drink with." He cackled aloud.

"No wonder everybody calls him *Crazy Man* Lewis," Snake whispered to Danny Boy and Bo Altero.

"Shhh!" whispered Danny Boy, "you don't want him to hear you say that."

Giles rubbed the side of his pounding head. "I—I wasn't expecting you this soon, Manifred," he said.

"Of course you weren't," said Lewis, "else you wouldn't be lying passed-out blind drunk."

"I've had lots on my mind," Giles said weakly.

"No kidding? So has the barkeep back there," said Manifred, nodding in the direction of the saloon. "I sort of hoped it might be him you wanted killed." He grinned and stepped over just inside the open back doorway.

"It might be him too, before this is over," said Capp. "He knows too much about my business lately."

"I can kill more than one person while I'm here," said Lewis, spreading his arms in a grand gesture.

"We'll see," said Giles, still groggy and half drunk. "Right now I've got a problem with a damn lawdog sticking his nose into our business here."

"Well, your problem is over now," said Lewis. "Just point me at the unfortunate soul you wish to see dead, and I'll make it so!"

"I've heard Lewis is pretty damn good," Danny Boy whispered near Snake's bruised swollen ear.

"Just shut up, Danny," Snake hissed in reply.

Hearing only a trace of their whispers, Lewis turned facing the three. Looking them over, seeing the cuts, lumps and bruises on Danny Boy and Snake, he said to Giles, "I see some of your men have been out stealing wildcat eggs."

Bo Altero stifled a laugh. Danny Boy and Snake gave him a hard look. Then Snake said to Lewis, "The fact is, this lawdog never gave us a chance. He whipped me with a hammer handle . . . he allowed two wild Negros to attack us!"

"My, my!" said Lewis, "it sounds like you boys have certainly been through hell! But don't worry, now that I'm here, I won't let any big bad sheriff manhandle any of you, no, sir!"

"He ain't a sheriff," Danny Boy said sullenly, "and he ain't the kind of lawman to be taken lightly."

"Well, of course he's not," said Lewis, unconcerned, idly adjusting his tight black leather gloves as he spoke. "Pray tell, just what kind of lawdog is this we're talking about?"

"He's a ranger," said Giles. "He mostly rides the badlands. I don't want you to just kill him, I want you to kill him *reeeeeal slow,* take all day if you want to!"

"Oh, a ranger, how exciting," said Lewis. He drew his big Colt from his holster, twirled it, checked it, then twirled it dazzlingly back into his holster.

Giles and the others watched in fascination. "My God!" said Giles, "I almost forgot how fast you are, Manifred!"

"Please," said Lewis with a confident grin, "don't ever forget that!" He looked around from face to face, then asked Giles Capp, "Now, then, where will I find this ranger of yours?"

"I'm right here, Crazy Man," said Sam, his shadow falling in through the back door. Lewis jerked around quickly, his hand going to his gun. But his hand stopped as if frozen when he stared into the barrel of the ranger's big Colt, raised, pointed and cocked, less than a foot from his forehead. The others froze as well. Danny Boy gasped as if he'd seen a ghost. "You're under arrest, Crazy Man Lewis," said Sam. "Raise your hands in the air." Past the gunmen he saw a sliver of light from the front door opening quickly and quietly.

"Arrest? For what?" said Lewis in disbelief. He only raised his hands halfheartedly, still looking confident, still wearing a trace of a bemused smile.

"For stealing a hearse in Yuma, three years ago,"

said the ranger. "Now, either raise those hands like you mean it, or I'll drop you dead where you stand."

Seeing the look in the ranger's eyes, Lewis' hands went higher. "You're making a mistake, Ranger," Lewis said in a low growl. "That was so long ago, I forgot about it. Besides, I only took it to get home in. I was going to take it back. It just slipped my mind."

"Save it for the judge in Yuma," said Sam. He spoke to Danny Boy, saying, "You, step over with one finger, hook his gun butt, raise it and let it fall."

"Fall! In all this horse shit?" said Lewis. "You must be joking."

"You'll find I don't do a whole lot of joking, Crazy Man," said Sam. He said to Danny Boy, "Do it, now!"

"Wait a minute!" Lewis said to Danny Boy, causing him to stop. "This is only one man here! He can't handle all of us, can you, Ranger." His hands dropped halfway; a smile widened on his thin face. "Did you honestly think you could outgun all five of us?"

"No," said the ranger, bluntly, "that's why I asked the sheriff to come along." He spoke over the gunmens' shoulders. "Say hello, Sheriff."

Watts cocked both hammers on the shotgun, doing it just slow enough for everybody to hear it. "Howdy, fellows," he said quietly, standing behind them to one side in the dark shadows.

"Uh-oh! Is that a shotgun I hear cocking?" Lewis said playfully.

"That's what it is, all right," said the ranger. Reaching behind his back, he lifted a pair of handcuffs from his belt and held them out to Danny Boy. "Stand to the side and cuff him," he said.

"Me?" said Danny Boy. "Why me?"

"Because I figure you'd rather cuff Crazy Man than get a bullet in your leg," said the ranger.

Danny Boy snatched the cuffs and fumbled with them nervously. "Lower your wrists together, Crazy Man," said Sam. The others watched tensely as Lewis lowered his wrists and Danny Boy fastened the cuffs around them. "Make sure they're on good and tight," said Sam. "We wouldn't want Crazy Man making a grab for that hideout belly gun under his duster and cause me to have to kill him."

"I've got no belly gun, Ranger, see?" said Lewis as Danny Boy snugged the cuffs and stepped back out of the way. Lewis started to reach his cuffed hands inside his duster. "And I might as well tell you, I don't allow anybody to call me Crazy Man! It offends me!" he roared.

The ranger saw his move, stepped in quickly, grabbed him by the four inches of chain connecting the handcuffs and jerked him forward hard. "Is that a fact?" he said, stepping to the side as Lewis slammed headfirst into the thick door post. Dust billowed from the barn frame as Lewis sank to his knees and fell backward. "I'll keep that in mind," said Sam to the knocked-out gunman. "I wouldn't want to offend you, Mr. Lewis." Keeping his Colt pointed at the others, Sam planted a boot on Lewis' chest, bent down and jerked out the small hideout gun from under his duster. Raising up, shoving the small gun behind his belt, he looked past Giles and said to Danny Boy and Snake, "I'm taking Crazy Man and Giles to jail."

"Me?" said Giles, looking at Sam wide-eyed. "What did I do?"

"How about conspiring to kill a lawman?" said Sam. "Is that enough? If not, there's more charges coming."

"We were just talking about it, Ranger!" Giles pleaded, wanting to go for his gun but ever mindful of the shotgun leveled on him six feet away.

"You can talk about it some more while you wait for the circuit judge," said Sam, reaching behind his back again, pulling out another pair of handcuffs. "Here, cuff him for me," he told Danny Boy. He pitched the cuffs to Danny Boy, the outlaw having to catch them or let them hit him in the face. "You and Snake give me your guns too, for safe keeping."

"Ranger, this ain't right, making me handcuff my pal!" Danny Boy protested, raising his small gun with one finger and handing it over. Snake let out a defeated sigh and did the same.

"He'll be understanding about it, won't you, Giles?" Sam asked.

"I don't give a damn!" Giles growled in anger and disgust, shoving his wrists out for Danny Boy to cuff.

"What about us, Ranger?" asked Snake, watching Danny close the cuffs around Giles' wrists.

"You boys never stole a hearse, did you?" the ranger asked.

The two just looked at him. Giles spit on the floor and cursed under his breath at the unconscious gunman.

"Then you two are free to go," said Sam. "I never heard either of you say anything about killing me *reeeal slow.*" He spoke in a mocking voice, cutting a sharp glance at Giles Capp. "So I've nothing to hold you two on. But you better both keep your noses clean."

Giving Giles a sheepish look, Snake asked the ranger, "Can we start going back to the saloon?"

"No, not just yet," said the ranger. "I think it's best you two keep out of my sight for a while. Let things settle down some. We'll talk more about it later on." He looked at Watts. "Ready to go, Sheriff?"

"Ready and waiting," said Watts, stepping back as the ranger raised Manifred Lewis to his feet and gave both prisoners a slight shove to get them started.

They filed out of the livery barn and walked to the main street, leaving Danny Boy and Snake looking dumbfounded and staring blankly as they left. "What the hell do we do now for guns?" said Snake.

"Beats me," Danny Boy replied. "What do we do about letting Axel know what's happened here?"

"Don't worry about that," said Snake. "You can bet Floose went running to him the day we got in the fight in the corral. I just hope Floose didn't paint too bad a picture of you and me to Axel. I don't want to be on Axel's bad side when he rides in here ready to spill blood."

Danny Boy said with a worried look on his battered, healing face, "I ain't sure we ought to even stay around here, the way things are starting to shape up."

"Oh, we're staying all right," said Snake. "Leastwise I am! I can't wait to see Axel whittle that ranger down to his rightful size."

Watching the ranger and Watts guide the prisoners out of sight around the corner of a building and on toward the jail, Danny Boy replied, "Everything I've seen tells me that ranger is already his rightful size. Maybe it's *us* who's overrating ourselves."

"Danny Boy," said Snake, staring along with him, "there's times I think you still have a hell of a lot to learn about life."

No sooner than the ranger and Watts turned the corner with their prisoners and proceeded on to the sheriff's office, Julie Ann came running up to the ranger and Watts from the direction of the hotel. "Sam, what happened? Are you all right!"

Sam nodded. "I'm fine, Julie Ann." He guided her away from the prisoners, keeping her from getting too close.

She looked quickly from the ranger to Watts, who walked directly behind the prisoners, his shotgun only inches from their backs. "Sheriff, are you all right?"

"Yes, ma'am, we're both all right," said Watts. In front of him Manifred Lewis staggered along like a drunkard, mumbling incoherently, a trickle of blood running down from a large knot on his forehead.

Looking back at the ranger, Julie asked again, "What happened, Sam?"

"I caught these two making plans to kill me," he replied, not wanting to get into the whole story on the street as passersby began slowing down for a look. "Lucky for me, Sheriff Watts was along with his shotgun."

"Oh, my," said Julie Ann. "Lucky indeed!"

Even from behind, Sam could see Watts stiffen with pride. "I didn't really do anything, ma'am," he said, "but I was glad to get to help out."

Sam looked at Julie closely as they walked on to the front door of the office. "I thought you went to get some sleep," he said quietly, for only her to hear.

"I did," she replied just as quietly. "I thought you were coming to join me." Her voice took on a slight sharpness.

"I meant to," Sam said. "But I saw a chance to bag these two, so I took it. I know how anxious you are to get the men who killed your father." He stepped around in front of Watts and the prisoners, and opened the door to the office. Then he stood back beside Julie Ann as the prisoners and Sheriff Watts filed inside.

"Yes, I understand," Julie said under her breath.

"Catching my father's killers is far more important than anything else to me." She looked at him closely. "Another time, perhaps?"

"Yes, another time," Sam replied. They stepped inside and Sam closed the door behind them.

The ranger stood close by, his hand on his Colt until Watts had both men inside separate cells. He watched as Watts reached through the bars and uncuffed Giles Capp. But when Watts walked to the other cell to do the same with Manifred Lewis, he saw that Lewis had stumbled to the wooden cot against the wall and collapsed on it, blood still trickling from his knotted forehead. "Is he going to be all right, Ranger?" Watts asked.

"Yes, he'll be fine," said Sam. "As soon as I get back, we'll get a wet rag and clean him up some. If he needs a stitch or two, we'll send for the doctor. No matter what either of them say or do, don't open the doors for anything until I get back, all right?"

"Anything you say, Ranger," said Watts. "Where are you going?"

"I'm going to get Andrew Swain. I think it's time I bring him here and find out exactly *who* killed Sheriff Dolan."

Chapter 14

Councilmen Avondale and Meaker sat uncomfortably in wooden chairs at Andrew Swain's table and sipped their whiskey sparingly. Having seen the ranger and Sheriff Watts escorting Giles Capps and Manifred Lewis toward the jail, Swain had decided he'd better hold back any money he was supposed to pay out until he saw where everybody stood in Redemption. Giles Capp was supposed to be the one keeping a tight hand on things. But Giles hadn't been showing him much promise lately, not since the ranger had come to town. Swain wasn't letting go of another cent until he had to.

"Our arrangement is that you bring an envelope to me at the start of each month, Mr. Swain," said Avondale. "I'm responsible for making disbursements to other parties, you know."

"Yeah, I know," said Swain, a bit sarcastic, "like our new sheriff, Delbert Watts. Now, that has certainly been some money well spent, hasn't it?"

"Granted, Watts hasn't been as favorable to us as we had hoped he would be," said Avondale, "but the ranger has had a strong influence on his attitude. Once the ranger is out of here, I think we can count on things getting back to normal." He turned a quick glance around the empty saloon, then looked back at Swain, saying, "Meanwhile, I must have the envelope. I have certain expenses that are pressing me."

"You'll have to wait, Avondale," said Swain. "You're paid to see to it the Rio Sagrado Gang has a free hand in this town." He nodded in the direction of the jail. "I don't think you can call what's happened here having a *free hand.*"

"Keeping the ranger in line is outside of our services, Mr. Swain," said Meaker, cutting in on Avondale's behalf. The ranger has been an unexpected problem that no one seems able to take care of."

"We assured Giles Capp that if something happened to the ranger, no one on Redemption's town board would be interested in pursuing the matter."

"I figured you knew Giles was bringing in a hired gun like Lewis," said Swain. Again, he nodded in the direction of the jail. "We see how well that turned out."

"Come now, Mister Swain," said Avondale, "you can't blame us for how Giles Capp has been running things!"

"No," Swain replied, "and you can't blame me for not putting any more money into the pot until I see what cards are held and how they're being played."

"What is that supposed to mean, sir!" said Avondale. "You're not speaking to a couple of common gamblers!"

"I know," said Swain, "it would be better if I was." He finished the last sip of his bourbon and said with resolve, "Gentlemen, I'll see you with the envelope in hand as soon as it looks like things get back on track."

He grinned, adding, "Since you're not *common rail-road men* either, that means as soon as things get headed back in the right direction."

"I believe we both know what it means, Mr. Swain," said Avondale, rising to his feet, Meaker doing the same. "May I say, you are making a mistake not living up to our agreement!"

"You may say it," said Swain, liking the idea that he was able to talk this way to somebody for a change instead of always being on the receiving end. "But it ain't changing a damn thing. Nobody gets any more money until I hear something from Giles. Now, both of yas get out of my sight." Swain also stood up, scooting his chair back roughly across the plank floor, giving the two a dark scowl.

Avondale and Meaker walked away in a huff, but stopped at the bat-wing doors long enough to turn and look back at Swain. "You haven't heard the last of this, Mr. Swain," said Avondale. "This will be a mistake of grave consequence."

Facing Swain, the two councilmen didn't see the ranger coming in through the bat-wing doors. Sam stopped and looked them up and down from behind. As the two turned to leave, they were stricken by his cold stare. "Gentlemen," Sam said, stepping slightly to the side, keeping his eyes bored into them as he let them pass.

Without response, the two slunk past him and hurried out, leaving the doors flapping on their spring hinges. Sam looked over at Swain and gave him a flat smile. "He always says stuff like that. If I were you, I wouldn't let it bother me."

"Ranger Burrack," said Swain, getting a troubled look on his face as Sam walked forward and stopped on the other side of his table. "I was just on my way out. If you came to talk to me, I'm afraid I don't have time right now."

"I had a feeling you'd say something thing like that, Mr. Swain," said the ranger, politely. "But I thought I'd better get over here anyway and try one more time to help you out of this mess you're in."

Swain wiped a hand across his sweaty brow. "What are you talking about, Ranger, I'm not in any mess. I saw you take Giles and Cra—I mean, Manifred Lewis to jail. But that has nothing to do with me."

"The thing is," said Sam, "I'm getting ready to start questioning Giles about Sheriff Dolan's murder. I thought I'd let you know . . . see if you wanted to go over and listen to him, maybe get some things said before he does."

"I've already told you, Ranger," said Swain, "I have nothing to say about Dolan's death."

The ranger nodded with resolve. "All right then. If that's your last word on it, I won't take up any more of your time." He turned and started back toward the bat-wing doors. "But don't make the mistake of thinking Giles brought Manifred Lewis here just to kill me."

"What are you saying, Ranger?" said Swain.

Sam stopped and looked back at him. "Do you really think Giles wants a living witness around who can put a noose around his neck? Crazy Man Lewis might have been brought here to kill me, but I wasn't the only one being discussed in that livery barn."

"Wait a minute. Are you saying you heard my name mentioned?"

"Would it make a difference if I said I did?" Sam asked, ready to walk away, but hesitating almost mid-step.

Swain ran his hand across his forehead twice, considering what to do. "Damn it, all right," he said at length, "I'll walk over to the jail with you. I can't see the harm in that."

"After you," the ranger said, stepping to the side for Swain.

On their way along the boardwalk, Sam said, "Just do me a favor, Mr. Swain. If you have anything to say once we get there, make sure we walk outside first. I don't want Giles Capp hearing anything you've got to say to me. He knows I'm out to charge him with killing the sheriff. I don't want to give him any way to try to pin it on you."

Swain gave Sam a curious look, unsure if he believed him or not. "Just for the sake of argument, Ranger, what if he did kill the sheriff, and the only way he could be brought to justice is with someone who was with him coming forward and testifying against him. Would the person who was with him also face charges?"

"Not if that person came forward first," said the ranger. "But if Giles suspected something like that was about to happen and he testified first against the person who was with him, then it would be the other way around. Giles could manage to get away with murder while the person with him hanged." He studied Swain's troubled face as the two walked along side by side. "But don't worry about something like that happening, Mr. Swain," Sam said quietly, wondering how Swain was going to respond. "My job is to see to it that only the innocent go free."

Swain stared straight ahead without a response.

They walked the rest of the way to the sheriff's office in silence, the ranger opening the door for Andrew Swain and stepping quietly behind him. Julie Ann and Sheriff Watts stood aside as if to give Swain a good unobstructed view of the two prisoners in the cells. In one cell Giles Capp stood holding onto the bars, staring out, his face piquing in surprise at the sight of Swain. In the other cell, Manifred Lewis sat on the edge of his cot, his head lowered in a wet rag Julie Ann had brought him.

The Ranger gave Swain a coax forward. "Don't be afraid, Mr. Swain. These men can't harm anybody now."

"What?" said Swain, giving the ranger a look over his shoulder.

"What?" Giles also said, only his voice raised and quickly filling with anger. "Afraid? Him? Of who?" said Giles. His grip tightened on the bars.

Looking up from the wet rag and seeing Swain, Manifred Lewis said groggily, "Well, well, if it isn't the sweaty barkeep. I told you I should have shot him for you too."

"You didn't shoot anybody, Manifred!" said Giles, quickly. "The ranger was lying about what he heard. I never said anything about having you shoot him, or Swain either! *Please* shut up!"

Manifred shook his swollen head and lowered his face back into the wet cloth, grumbling under his breath.

Swain had taken a few steps closer to the cells, but he stopped short upon hearing Giles' words. "You were talking to Lewis about shooting me?"

"Hell, no!" said Giles, "didn't you just hear me say the ranger is lying? He claims he heard me and Lewis talking about killing him! It was a lie! Then he claims I talked to Lewis about killing you—another damn lie!"

But it was enough for Swain. He knew it was true about Giles wanting Lewis to kill the ranger. Why would the ranger lie about the rest of it? He looked around at Sam as if for guidance. But Sam only gave him an I-told-you-so look.

"It's every man for himself now, Mr. Swain," Sam said quietly. "I told you the kind of men you're dealing with. Now you have to decide if he's worth dying for."

"What's that?" Giles said, straining his face against the bars to hear better. "What are you two saying?" He shook the bars with both hands.

"Settle down, Capp," Watts warned him.

"I'll settle you down, you back-stabbing sonsabitch! he shouted at the sheriff. "It was Rio Sagrado who got you this job! It was *our* money and influence that pinned the badge to your chest! It'll be our influence that rips it off of there!" He shook the bars even harder.

"Hold it, Sheriff," said Sam, seeing Watts start to take a step toward the bars. "That's what he wants you to do, come back there and fight with him. He doesn't want everybody getting together on him and figuring out what a murdering piece of work he is. Ain't that right, Giles?" The ranger raised his voice enough for the enraged gunman to hear more clearly. "It scares you, seeing Swain here, knowing he's the one man who saw enough to make you swing for the murder of Sheriff Dolan?"

Giles looked stunned, so did Swain. Watts and Julie Ann watched in hushed silence. Sam knew he was putting his own twist on things. He had no idea who had been there the night Sheriff Dolan was killed. But he'd said enough to Swain and heard enough from him that he was certain Giles Capp was the killer. He knew he'd just thrown a big card out onto the table. He waited in the tense silence that followed, hoping neither Swain nor Giles Capp could see through him.

Finally, it was Giles who broke the silence, shouting, "Swain, you son of a bitch! You spilled your guts to this dirty lawdog!"

"No!" Swain shouted in reply, sweat pouring freely down his forehead, "I didn't tell him anything, I swear!"

"Then how does he know?" Giles bellowed, climbing the bars like an enraged ape.

Seeing that Swain was about to say something more on the matter, the ranger pulled him back by his arm and said, "Huh-uh, Mr. Swain, don't say anything to him. I know you were there that night. I know you saw what happened. Look at him, he's falling apart. If you've got something to say, it better be to me. Let's step outside."

"Wait a minute, lawdog!" Giles screamed. "Don't listen to him! Swain's a liar and a coward! You want to know what happened? I'll tell you what happened!"

"Shut up, Capp!" shouted the ranger, turning with Swain and hurrying him toward the door. He gave Watts a quick glance, saying to him and Julie Ann, "Go listen to every word Giles says. If Swain here doesn't come clean with me right now, I'm going to go with Giles' version of what happened, no matter who he blames it on." His eyes went back to Swain as he gave him a slight shove out the door. "It's time you pull yourself out of this thing, Swain," he said, all of sudden dropping the *mister* when he addressed him.

Out front on the boardwalk, the ranger took a deep breath, shutting the door and leaning back against it. "There, you saw it. Giles Capp is going down, and he'll take anybody with him who's stupid enough to let it happen."

"But, Ranger, I never told you anything!" said Swain, speaking as he mopped his wet brow.

"I know it and you know it," said Sam. "But Giles Capp thinks you've told me that you were with him that night. So, what's it going to be?" he added bluntly. "Is he going to hang by himself or with you beside him?"

"All right, I was there," said Swain, his words blurting out. "I saw the whole thing. But you've got to believe I had no hand in it, Ranger. I swear to God! Giles Capp shot him. I was there, but there was nothing I could do to stop it! If I could have, I would have. I wouldn't take a chance doing something like that and going to the gallows!"

"Who else was there?" Sam asked quickly, not letting Swain get a chance to shut up now that he had started talking.

"There was Giles Capp, Charlie Floose, Bo Altero and me," said Swain. "But I swear I had nothing to do—"

"Who else did any shooting?" Sam asked, cutting him off.

"Charlie Floose," said Swain.

"And what about Altero?" asked Sam. "What part did he play?"

"He lured the sheriff out and over into the dark. I didn't realize what was going on until I saw Altero walking along beside the sheriff, then he dropped back and took cover around the corner of a building, and the other two cut Dolan down! I just stood in shock, until finally Giles gave me a shove and got me started. Later, in my saloon, he told me that being there made me a part of the Rio Sagrado Gang. He warned me to keep my mouth shut; then he told me I wouldn't believe how much money we were going to make now that the sheriff was out of the way."

"And that was all it took, huh?" Sam asked.

"Ranger, what choice did I have?" Swain pleaded. "Dolan was the only man in town who could stand up to Giles Capp and his gunmen. With him dead I knew better than to say anything to anybody, or I would be next."

"So, you were happy to keep your mouth shut and take whatever money was coming your way?"

"All right, I know it was wrong," said Swain, "but, yes, that's what I was doing. I admit, it felt pretty good being able to consider myself a member of the gang. If I ever had any trouble with anybody, I knew I could count on Giles and his pals to step in and take care of it."

"I'm sure you realize that you're going to have to tell all this to the judge when he gets here," said Sam.

Swain nodded, "Yeah, I know it." He mopped his head again. "Are you going to see to it I stay alive long enough to do it?"

"That's my job, Swain," said Sam. "Now, come on, let's get Watts."

"What now?" Swain asked.

"Now you're going to tell him everything, word for word, every bloody detail, so there'll be more than just me who knows what you'll be testifying to in court."

"And you're sure Giles Capp is going to hang?" Swain gave a him a concerned look.

"That'll be up to a judge and a jury, Swain," said Sam. "He has to be found guilty first you know."

"But, what if they don't find him guilty?" said Swain, still mopping his wet brow nervously. "He'll kill me! Even if he hangs, I've still got to worry about his brother, Axel, and the rest of that bunch!"

"One thing at a time, Swain," said Sam. "First, you go in there and tell the sheriff everything you just told me. I'll take care of Axel Capp and his pals when they come calling." As Sam spoke, he caught a glimpse of Bo Altero stepping out from the street leading back to the barn and looking all around. Reaching around behind him, Sam opened the door to the office and escorted Swain inside. Standing back by Giles Capp's cell, Sheriff Watts and Julie Ann Dolan saw the look on the ranger's face and walked toward him and Swain. Sam took a moment to look out through the window and see Altero's reflection as Altero walked into the mercantile store. Sam had a pretty good idea what Altero was looking for.

From his cell Giles Capp called out, "Hey, damn it! What has that lying barkeep said? Huh? Why's everybody running to him? He's lying I tell you!"

"Swain has something to tell you, Sheriff," said the ranger as Watts and Julie Ann stopped at the battered desk.

Giles shouted, "I want out of here, Ranger! You've got no right holding me here! You're a liar the same as he is! You can't charge me for something you *think* you heard me say!"

"All right, then, Giles," said Sam, "I'll oblige you. As of now, you're not being charged with what I *think* I heard you say . . . you're being charged with the murder of Sheriff Dolan."

Giles fell stone silent for a moment. Knowing the silence wouldn't last, Sam turned to Watts as Swain sat down in a wooden chair, still wiping his hand across his wet forehead. "I'm going to leave you and Swain here to go over what he saw, Sheriff," said Sam, lifting his Colt from his holster and checking it.

Looking the ranger up and down, Watts asked, "Where are you going now?"

"I'm going after Bo Altero before he gets his knees in the wind," said Sam.

"Shouldn't I go with you?" asked Watts, already to rise out of his chair. "I can listen to Swain when we get back."

Sam said quietly, as if to keep Julie Ann or Swain from hearing, "Listen to him now, Sheriff. If I need help, you'll be hearing about it soon enough."

Chapter 15

Bo Altero handed the mercantile clerk a fistful of money and waited nervously while the pale thin young man counted it and put it into a tall ornate cash register. "I often envy those who spend a good deal of time working and living in the glorious outdoors," the clerk said, making small talk as he raked out a palm full of change and began counting it from one hand to the other.

Shoving two of the three new Colt revolvers down into his belt as he spoke, Altero said, "Yeah? Well, jerk that apron off and have at it. The trail will take you wherever you think you need to go."

"Oh"—the clerk smiled—"but I'm afraid my job with Abercombe wouldn't be waiting for me should I decide to return."

Appraising the clerk quickly and with obvious disdain, Altero said, "Take it from me, boy. If *you* ever leave here across the desert, nobody needs to worry about leaving a light on for you."

"Oh?" The clerk gave him a curious look. "What does that mean, sir? That I'm not vigorous enough to live out in the wilds on my own?

"Forget it, boy," said Altero, loading the third Colt

and checking it as he gave the clerk a glance filled with contempt. "I've got no time to explain life to you." He shoved the loaded Colt down into his empty holster, then seemed to relax. "There, now, that's more like it." He shook out his gun hand. "You want to see what it takes to live out in the wilds, I'll show you . . . count to three for me." He poised his hand near his gun butt.

Seeing the hesitant look on the clerk's face, he coaxed, "Go on, count to three!"

"All right!" said the clerk, "but please be careful."

"Careful, huh?" Altero chuckled under his breath. "I like you, boy, what's your name?" As he spoke, Altero reached across the counter and tweaked the young man's cheek roughly.

The clerk looked embarrassed. "It's Phillip Fridley, sir," he replied, rubbing the red splotch on his otherwise ivory-white cheek. "But everyone calls me Phil."

"Phil Fridley . . . ?" Altero shook his head. "Jesus," he murmured to himself. "Well, then, *Phil*," he said, taking on a mock tone of voice, "I promise I'll be as careful as can be." Catching the change as Phil dropped it into his left hand, he said, "Now, count to three, Gawdamn it!"

"Yes, sir!" said the frightened clerk. "Ready, set, *one*—" he said. Before he could say two, the new Colt was out, up and cocked in his face, Altero holding his thumb over the hammer.

"There, *Phil*," Altero said. "That's the trick to staying alive out there." He gestured with his left hand, taking in all of the rest of the world. "When a man starts to count down on you, never let him get past the first number. I can't tell you how important that is, especially when it comes to nosy rangers."

"Nosy rangers?" said Phil, his fearful expression

only changing slightly as Altero lowered the gun, uncocked it and slipped it loosely into his holster.

"Think no more about it, *Phil*," said Altero, scoop-
ing up two boxes of ammunition lying on the counter.
"I've got business to attend to."

With a box of ammunition in either hand and the
two Colts he'd purchased for Danny Boy and Snake,
Altero left the mercantile store and looked warily
toward the sheriff's office as he crossed the boardwalk
and started to step down onto the dirt street. But as
his boot touched the street, he heard the ranger's
voice as Sam stepped onto the street from the alley
alongside the mercantile store.

"I'm over here, Altero," Sam said in a level tone.

"Damn it, how?" said Altero, turning quickly to
face the ranger, both hands full and once again caught
off guard.

"Knowing your next move is part of my job," said
the ranger, stepping wide and slow around Altero
until he stood facing him in the middle of the street.

"All right, Ranger, what do you want? I'm not loi-
tering in front of the saloon. As you can see, I've been
spending money here in a local business establishment.
What are you going to do to harass an honest law-
abiding citizen now?" He deliberately raised his voice
for the benefit of any onlookers. At the same time,
his voice brought Danny Boy and Snake out of another alley on the other side of the mercantile store.
They stopped abruptly at the sight of the ranger facing
Bo Altero, but the ranger had seen them, so they froze
in place, their hands chest-high in spite of the fact that
they were unarmed.

"I'm arresting you, Bo Altero," the ranger said in
a official sounding voice, "for the murder of Sheriff
Mack Dolan."

"You've got to be joking," said Altero, offering a weak smile that looked hard for him to support. A twitch ran the length of his jawline.

"Murder's no joking matter," said the ranger, his hand hanging comfortably beside his big Colt, not poised, but appearing relaxed and ready. He drooped a bit, putting the gun butt at palm level.

"If it's a straight-up gunfight you want, Ranger, I always knew it would come down to you and me. That's why I never butted in when you were dogging these two idiots." He gave a nod toward Snake and Danny Boy. In return they gave him an offended look. "But I didn't shoot that sheriff," Altero continued, "and that's the straight-up truth."

"I know you didn't shoot him," said Sam. "I know the whole story, who did the shooting, who set the sheriff up for it." His eyes seemed to grow distant and indiscernible. "You were the setup man . . . the one who went to him pretending his help was needed. He went with you because, like any decent lawman, his job was to find trouble and put himself in harm's way. You betrayed him, led him to his death. You're no better than the ones who pulled the triggers on him."

"And you think you're taking me in for it?" said Altero, his hands full but his knuckles white and tense.

"That's up to you," said the ranger calmly. "I've made plans for it going a couple of different ways."

Altero's expression changed. "You've underestimated me, Ranger," he said. "I'm not some fool you can lead away to jail and off to a gallows. If I'm going down I'm taking you with me." Without taking his eyes off the ranger, he said to the other two men, "It's time somebody showed you two bummers what being a real gunman's all about."

"Let's get to it, Altero," said the ranger, leaving it

open as to whether he meant go to jail or go for their guns.

"Start counting, Ranger," said Altero, already planning not to wait for the count of three, but rather make his move as soon as the ranger said a word.

But he never heard the ranger say a word. Instead he saw the big Colt come up from the ranger's holster in a streak of gunmetal and sunlight; he saw the blaze explode from the barrel and felt the impact of the bullet raise him up and backward, the bullet boxes flying from his hands before he hit the ground.

Sam walked forward, his Colt pointed at arm's length, cocked and ready for the next shot. But he saw it wasn't going to be needed. Altero grappled with the two pistols shoved down into his belt. Unfortunately, he would never get one drawn, even if they were loaded. "I hate . . . being caught . . . unaware this way," Altero said in a strained voice. Then his eyes turned sideways as if some unseen event had just caught his attention. A long breath expelled from him, and the heavy flow of blood from his chest seemed to play itself out.

Sam turned facing Danny Boy and Snake, saying, "I've heard from a witness that you two weren't a part of Sheriff Dolan's murder. Lucky for you both, else that would be you laying there too." Holstering his Colt, the ranger walked over, stooped down and lifted all three brand-new guns from Altero's holster and belt.

"Damn it," Snake whispered to Danny Boy, "there goes our new guns. Lucky for him we hadn't already gotten them."

"Yeah, lucky for him," said Danny Boy, giving him a dubious look. "How the hell did he know to show

up here when he did? I'm telling you, this man gives
me the creeps."

"You two come over here and carry your pal out
of the street," said the ranger.

"What are we supposed to do with him, Ranger?"
asked Snake.

"Get a shovel, bury him," said the ranger, turning
to walk away.

"What about us?" Snake called out. "What are we
supposed to do?"

"Keep your noses clean, like I told you before,"
said the ranger without turning around.

Upon hearing the shot, Watts had come running
with the shotgun in his hands. He stopped a few yards
back when he'd seen the ranger didn't need any help.
As Sam came closer, Watts said, "Maybe I better run
those two out of town before we get worse trouble
from them."

"Ordinarily we would have thrown them out of here
first thing," said the ranger. But ordinarily I wouldn't
have fooled around so long with Giles Capp. The truth
is I want these boys here where they'll be easy for
Axel Capp to find when he gets to town."

"You must want him awfully bad, Ranger," said
Watts, falling in beside him, the two of them turning
back toward the office where Julie Ann stood looking
on from the boardwalk.

"He's at the top of my list," Sam said quietly. "I'm
hoping I've got the right bait to bring him my way."

Inside the sheriff's office, Sam poured himself a cup
of coffee and walked to the front window, sipping from
his cup and watching the reflection of the Even Odds
Saloon as Watts continued to talk with Andrew Swain.

At the rear of the office, Giles Capp had fallen silent and stood hanging onto the bars, staring at Swain with a look of pure glowing hatred in his eyes. No sooner than Danny Boy and Snake had carried Bo Altero's body out of the middle of the street and onlookers had torn themselves loose and drifted away, Sam saw Councilmen Avondale and Meaker walk hurriedly across the street and into the saloon, looking back and forth furtively as if to keep themselves from being seen.

Knowing it would only be a moment before the two councilmen came back out, Sam turned to Watts and said, "Sheriff, if you don't mind, I have a couple of questions I'd like to ask Swain in private."

"Of course I don't mind," said Watts. He looked all around. "But it's going to be hard to find any privacy . . ."

"Not at all," said Sam. "Come on, Swain, we'll go talk out front." He glanced toward Giles Capp and added, "He's heard plenty, but he doesn't have to hear everything."

Looking nervous, Swain stood up mopping his brow with a white handkerchief he'd taken from his inside coat pocket. Blotting his forehead, he too gave a glance toward Giles Capp, then with a look of resolve followed the ranger out onto the boardwalk.

"Ranger, I don't mind telling you, Giles Capp scares me. I hate to think what he'll do to me if he ever gets his hands on me."

The ranger passed it off and gestured a hand toward the wooden chair sitting against the front of the sheriff's office. "Have a seat, Swain, and take a few deep breaths." As he spoke he managed to take a quick look toward the saloon.

Swain took in a deep breath and let it out slowly, slumping a bit in the chair. "All right, Ranger, there."

He fanned himself lightly with the damp handkerchief. "Now, what else is it you want to ask me?"

Catching a glimpse of Avondale and Meaker coming out of the saloon, Sam stooped down, his hand on his knees and spoke close to Swain's face. "See those two councilmen coming out of your saloon?"

Swain turned his head in their direction. "Sure, I see them, why?"

Sam said, "Point to the one on the right and tell me his name."

"What? You're not serious," said Swain. "You know their names!"

"I'm tombstone serious," said Sam. "Now, point and tell me."

"All right!" Swain pointed a thick finger, his sweaty handkerchief hanging from his hand. "That's Councilman Avondale on the right."

Sam straightened up and stared hard in Councilman Avondale's direction, saying down to Swain, "All right, well done . . . now the other one."

"What?" said Swain.

"Just do it," Sam said in a level tone.

"All right." Swain pointed at the nervous little councilman, saying, "That one is Meaker. There, are you satisfied?"

Still staring hard at the two men and watching them come to a halt and seem to shrink under his gaze, Sam said, "Oh, yes, I'm satisfied." He stared at the two men until they turned and walked in a wide circle as they crossed back to the other side of the street, then disappeared into Avondale's office.

"What else do you want to ask me, Ranger?" asked Swain. "It's blistering hot out here."

"In that case, let's go on back inside. Anything else I have to ask you can keep for now."

Swain gave him a disbelieving look, but shrugged, got up and walked back inside the sheriff's office. Sam lingered for a moment, staring in the direction of Avondale's office, making sure the councilmen got a good look at him. He took his time, raised his Colt from his holster, checked it and lowered it loosely back into place. He started walking toward Avondale's office.

Inside Avondale's office the two councilmen gave one another a shocked look. "My God, Swain has told him everything!" said Avondale. "Here he comes!"

"What must we do now?" Horace Meaker asked, visibly shaken.

Avondale tried to compose himself. "All he knows is what he's heard from outlaws and a saloon keeper. I feel we must stand our ground and not allow ourselves to be intimidated. We are law-abiding men as far as anyone can prove. Let's try to act like it."

"I'm with you," said Meaker, his hands shaking at his sides.

But when the ranger knocked on the door, Meaker turned and started to bolt toward the rear of the office. Grabbing the frightened man by his coattail, Avondale said in a harsh whisper, "Wait, don't panic. Stick beside me on this. We're going to be all right."

The ranger knocked again, this time more persistantly.

"Yes," said Avondale, cordially, "who is it?"

Sam replied through the thick oak door, "Avondale, you know it's me, open up."

Avondale gave Meaker a cautioning glance, then stepped over, opened the door and stood blocking it. "Yes, Ranger . . . I'm very busy," he said with confidence. "What can I do for you?"

Sam stepped inside, moving Avondale aside with a polite but firm sweep of his forearm. He took off his sombrero, looked at Meaker and said, "Good, you're both here. That'll make my task easier."

The two looked pale. Avondale said, "Oh? What task is that?"

"I've been talking to Andrew Swain about the things that have been going on here in Redemption. He's told me everything." Sam stopped and stared back and forth between the two.

After a tense pause, Avondale cleared his throat and said, "And what does that have to do with us?"

"You know full well what it has to do with you, Avondale," said Sam. "You were elected to serve this *town*, not a gang of outlaws."

"How dare you!" said Avondale, as if outraged at such an accusation. "Councilman Meaker and I have both been steadfast public servants ever since we took office!"

"Here's the deal," said the ranger, cutting him off. "I've got the goods on you both. I can either hold you until the judge gets here or call you out into the street, the way I would any lawbreaker."

"We're not gunmen, Ranger!" said Avondale. "You can't handle us that way!"

Sam continued as if he hadn't heard him. "Or, I can give you twenty-four hours to get out of town and not show your faces here again."

"Indeed!" Avondale said. "Just like that? You think you can chase us out of town, like we're some sort of common criminals?"

Sam leveled his gaze on Avondale. "Why not, that's all you are. This town trusted you to support its laws and protect its interests. You've taken dirty money

from thugs and murderers in order to look the other
way while they get a stranglehold on this town. You
tell me what you think you are."

"Politicians, Ranger," said Avondale, trying not to
show his fear. "We don't always play exactly by the
rules, but we take care of business. Redemption has
prospered while I have been in office. Mr. Meaker and
I both know how to get the job done. Sure, sometimes
it might look a little underhanded to some dull-
minded officer of the law like you. But that's only
because you're not quick enough to understand either
the game or the players!"

"Twenty-four hours," Sam said, letting him know
there was not room for any further discussion. "I bet
if I sent out some paper, I'd find out you're not who
you say you are." He eyed Avondale closely just to
see his response.

Avondale's face reddened. "Like hell," he said as
the ranger reached to open the door and leave. "I'll
get my attorney! So will Meaker! We're not leaving
this town! If anybody leaves, it will be you!"

"You heard me," said the ranger, "twenty-four
hours, mister, or be in the street, armed and ready."
He walked out the door and pulled it shut behind him.

"He can't do that, can he?" Meaker asked, shakily.
"Just throw us out of town that way?"

"No!" said Avondale, "he most certainly cannot!"
He raced to his ornate burled walnut desk and slung
the bottom drawer open.

"What are you doing?" Meaker asked, seeing the
strange look come upon Avondale's face as he raised
a shiny Navy Colt from a neatly folded oilcloth.

"What does it look like I'm doing?" said Avondale.
"I'm not taking any more of this treatment! I'm not

some common street trash he can order around this way!"

"Wait, Willis! For God sakes!" shouted Meaker, running along behind him as the irate councilman cocked the hammer and headed for the door. "You can't do this!"

But Avondale ignored him. He swung open the door, bounded across the boardwalk and down into the street. "Ranger!" he shouted long and loud, raising the Colt and taking aim at Sam's back at a distance of thirty yards.

Along the boardwalk the townsfolk gasped. A buggy veered in the street. The ranger turned, recognizing the voice and understanding the threat. His Colt came up from his holster sleek and fast, startling Avondale even though the councilman had already drawn a bead on him. Two shots exploded from the Navy Colt. The first whistled past the brim of the ranger's sombrero as he made his own shot. The second explosion from the Navy Colt seemed to be swallowed up by the overpowering blast from the Ranger's big .45.

Sam lowered his smoking gun slightly, seeing Avondale turn a spinning backward flip on the dirt street. He walked back toward the spot where Avondale lay as still as stone. Then he stopped a few feet back and said to the downed councilman, "Get up, Avondale, you're not dead yet."

Avondale groaned and rolled over onto his side, his fingers seeming to crawl closer to the Navy Colt lying in the dirt. "Huh-uh," the ranger said, cocking his pistol, letting Avondale hear it. "I'm not giving any second tries today. Pull your fingers back or lose them."

Avondale's hand came away from the Navy Colt as if it were red-hot. "You . . . caused all of this, Ranger," Avondale said in a strained voice, blood flowing from his wounded shoulder. "You . . . set this up. You forced me into a corner . . . turned me into a low-life thug."

"The makings was already there, Avondale," Sam said, reaching down, taking him by his good shoulder and dragging him to his feet. "You took money. You turned your office into a criminal operation. Now you're going to jail for it."

"You can't . . . prove anything against me," said Avondale, growing stronger, getting defiant. "I don't care what that saloon keeper says, my attorney will rip his story apart."

"I hate to admit it, but you're right," said Sam. "That's why I wasn't wasting my time charging you with something that petty and hard to prove." He looked Avondale up and down before giving him a shove in the direction of the jail. "But now I've got a charge you can't deny. You just attempted to murder a peace officer." Avondale stumbled a bit in the dirt. Looking back at the ranger with dirt in his hair and down his cheek, he said to the gathering crowd, "It was all a mistake, folks! Didn't you see that? Simply a misunderstanding!"

But the look on the townsfolk's faces told him they weren't interested in what he had to say. The ranger gave him another shove. "Nice try, Avondale, but no takers."

"I need a doctor," Avondale whined, clenching his wounded shoulder. "I need treatment!"

"The doctor will make a house call to your cell," Sam replied.

From the jail, Watts and Julie Ann came running,

Watts holding the shotgun at port arms. "Ranger! What happened?" he said, his eyes scanning the crowd.

"It's over now, Sheriff," said Sam. "Willis Avondale here just tried to back-shoot me."

"My goodness," said Watts, lowering his voice just between him and the ranger, "and to think he's the one who gave me my job."

"Yep," said the ranger. He handed Watts the Navy Colt he'd picked up from the dirt. "Aren't you glad you decided to take the job seriously and become a real sheriff, instead of a flunky for somebody like this?"

Watts looked Avondale up and down from behind, his dirty clothes, bits of dirt clinging to his hair, a bloody bullet hole in his tailored pinstriped coat. "Yes, Ranger, you can believe I am." He shoved the Navy Colt down into his belt and gave Avondale a harder shove. "If I had gone along with this snake, it might have been me walking to jail right now."

"Or worse," said Julie Ann, walking along with the two.

"Yeah, or worse," Watts repeated, giving her a smile.

Sam looked all around the streets and alleyways and said as they walked along toward the jail, "Well, it looks like this town is cleaned up . . . for a while anyway."

"What now, Ranger?" asked Watts.

"Now I wait for Axel Capp and his gang," said the ranger. "Then the fireworks begin."

PART 3

PART 5

Chapter 16

The Rio Sagrado Gang had arrived in *Ciudad del Centro* in twos and threes, some of them having ridden in the night before and taken rooms in the small adobe sleeping quarters behind the cantina. Axel Capp, Denton Spears and Charlie Floose had arrived first, coming in dressed in dark business suits, Axel carrying a leather business valise. They had spent the night drinking and buying rounds in the cantina, mingling with countless other businessmen from both sides of the border. As the rest of the gang showed up, they kept their distance from one another and did their drinking, eating and gambling at separate tables. By the end of the first night in town, no one was the wiser to what the men had in mind. Near midnight Hector Ruiz arrived, riding into town aboard the wagon the gang had brought along from their hideout.

The last two to arrive were Bobby Combs and Doc Cain, who rode in together the following morning and hitched their horses at the iron rail out front. Ulie Saggs, Mose Winton and Parker Stiles stood lounging in the shade of an adobe wall beside the cantina. Walking over to join them, Bobby and Doc's eyes went to the half-full bottles of tequila and mescal hanging in their hands.

"Well, now, *buenos tardes*!" Saggs said drunkenly, seeing the two approach and noting the way they looked at the bottles of tequila. He raised the bottle to his lips, then said before taking a drink, "Don't worry, boys . . . Axel Capp said drink it while we've got it." He laughed and tossed back a drink. Lowering his voice, he said, "Hell, it could be a long time between drinks once we do what we came here to do."

Bobby and Doc Cain looked around quickly as if to make sure no one outside of their circle had heard the drunken gunman. "Relax," said Saggs, pushing the bottle toward Bobby's face. "Axel told us to have ourselves a good ole time today. So that's exactly what we're doing."

But Bobby refused the bottle, giving Doc Cain a look. "Is that what he's told everybody, or just you three?" he asked.

"What's the difference?" asked Saggs, leering at Bobby and Doc. "We're Rio Sagrado men now. We've got nothing to worry about."

"Sure," said Doc Cain, "you keep thinking that way." He and Bobby turned and walked inside the crowded cantina, into a thick gray haze of cigar smoke and the blare of lively Mexican music.

"There he is," said Bobby under his breath, nodding toward a table in the far corner where Axel Capp sat with a young woman on his lap, a bottle of tequila and two glasses standing in front of him. Across from him sat Denton Spears, also with a young woman on his lap. She held his gun in her hands, stroking the barrel playfully.

"And there are the rest of them," said Doc Cain. Without giving a nod, he directed Combs with his eyes. At one end of the bar stood Hector Ruiz and Dallas Ryan, farther down the bar from them stood Joe Murphy and Millard Trent. At the other end stood Ace Tinsdale drinking alone.

"All right, let's mix in," said Combs.

The two walked toward the middle of the crowded bar, but before they got there, Axel Capp and Denton Spears dismissed the two women and stood up. Spears walked over to them. "Axel and me are riding over to take a look at some things. He wants you to ride along."

The other members of the gang hardly gave them a glance as Combs and Doc Cain followed Axel and Spears outside to the iron hitch rail. "Is everything going as planned?" asked Combs almost in a whisper.

Axel grinned and answered in a voice a bit louder than Combs expected under the circumstance. "Oh, yes, everything is going fine. I just thought you two might want to ride along with Denton and me, look this deal over a little." He nodded toward Saggs and the other two standing beside the cantina. "Those boys would be lucky to stay in their saddles."

"They said you told them they could drink as they pleased," said Combs.

"Yeah, I did," said Axel. He shrugged. "No harm done. I sent them past the bank earlier, before daylight, just to get a look at the layout."

"So, all the others have seen the job, except for us two?" Combs asked, indicating himself and Doc Cain.

"That's right," said Axel, grinning as the four of them unhitched their horses and stepped up into their saddle, "but now you boys are going to see it too. I like for all my men to get a good look at things before we go to work."

Combs and Axel Capp rode side by side down the

middle of the dusty stone street, their horses' shoes clicking amid the bustle and noise of commerce. Doc Cain and Denton Spears rode a few feet behind them. Doc noted a good number of *federale* uniforms among the townsfolk. His eyes searched the wide stone street from one end to the other in an effort to familiarize himself with the quickest ways out of town should something go wrong. Seeing the way Doc Cain scrutinized his surroundings, Spears sidled in close to him and said, "Doc, I've heard lots about you across the panhandle and down West Texas way, but I never heard of you being so skittish."

"I like to keep track of where I am," Doc said with a half smile, "and where I might want to be."

Spears chuckled. "Well, I reckon I can't blame a man for that. I meant no offense of course."

"No offense was taken," said Doc, gigging his horse a step ahead of him.

They rode around the corner off of the main plaza and onto a smaller but equally crowded street where stone and adobe buildings stood jammed against one another in a long row. At the end the street stood the largest bank either Doc Cain or Bobby Combs had ever seen.

The two gazed as if in awe, until Axel said with a slight laugh, "Didn't I tell you this was going to be the biggest job you've ever done?"

"You sure did," said Combs, "but I never imagined something this size."

"I know," said Axel, "and after tomorrow you'll never have to imagine another bank as long as you live, if you both play your cards right." As he spoke he looked over his shoulder at Doc Cain, seeing the old gunman looking warily around over the heads of the pressing crowd. "What about you, Doc?" he said. "Does this look good to you?"

Doc managed a tight smile. "It looks grand to me."

"I thought it would," said Axel. He gave Spears a look of satisfaction. But as he turned forward in his saddle, Bobby Combs nodded ahead of them and off to one side at a railroad platform where four armed *federales* stood smoking thin black cigars out front of an express office. "What makes that express office so popular?" he asked. Inside the express office door two more *federales* stood at attention, their rifles at their sides.

"Who knows?" said Axel, playing it off as nothing. "Who cares?" He laughed and gave his horse an extra nudge. "This time tomorrow we'll be on our way to the border, richer than we ever dreamed we could be." He circled his horse among the crowd and looked at Combs and Doc Cain. "You boys ride on through here and take a good look for yourselves. Me and Denton are going to turn back now, just to make sure we ain't seen too often out front of that bank. We'll get back together tonight and go over things one more time. Tomorrow morning when that bank opens its doors, all hell breaks loose."

Combs and Doc Cain watched Axel Capp and Denton Spears push their way through the throng of people until they were almost to the corner leading over to the main plaza. "Damn, Doc," Combs said quietly, turning an admiring glance back to the large bank building, "it sure would be nice robbing something that size. Think there's any chance that Axel could be shooting straight with us?"

"Not a chance in the world," Doc said flatly. Out of sight behind a rise of green hills, the sound of a

train whistle blew long and loud. The two looked
across the crowd and out across the land and saw the
drifting plume of smoke rising up, coming closer
toward town. Doc Cain took out a pocket watch and
noted the time. Then he looked at the express office
again and said, "Let's get ourselves a cigar and light
them up out back of that express terminal. See what
that incoming train has on it."

The two walked to their horses, stepped into their
saddles and maneuvered their horses through the
pressing crowd until they saw a sign that read: TO-
BACCO SHOPPE, in both English and Spanish. They
hitched their horses in the shade in front of the shop,
walked inside, purchased cigars and made their way
back to the train station on foot, leaving their horses
where they were hitched. On their way back to the
station, as they walked past a large store whose windows exhibited a cabinet full of firearms, Doc Cain
said, "Let's remember this place on our way back."

"Will do," said Combs.

At the platform along the rear of the train station,
the laborers had begun unloading large wooden crates
from the arriving train and stacking them outside
along the building. Armed guards stood on either side
of the doors leading inside the station's freight ware-
house. The guards watched the two *Americanos* light
their cigars and stroll idly back and forth on the loading dock. When Doc Cain ventured too close to the
open doorways and leaned a bit for a peep inside, one
of the guards stepped forward with his rifle across his
chest and pushed him back.

"Whoa, easy, young fellow," Doc Cain said amiably.
He held up his cigar, smiling, saying in Spanish, *"Estoy
sólo disfruta mi humo."*

"Enjoy your smoke some other place!" the soldier said firmly.

Doc Cain nodded politely and backed off, walking over to the crates being stacked on the platform. "A bit touchy, wasn't he?" said Combs, walking up idly, puffing on his own cigar.

"Yes," said Doc. "And I can only imagine why." He puffed his cigar and inspected the crates as the laborers stacked them tediously.

"Well," said Combs, "one thing's for sure, there's nothing valuable here, else they wouldn't be leaving it outside."

"Very true," said Doc. He puffed his cigar and nodded at the shipping label on the side of a crate. In Spanish the label read: LADIES' HATS. "But it makes me think that whatever freight was already inside there must be pretty important . . . enough to make the workers leave these lady's hats sitting out here in the weather."

Combs gave him a curious look. He smiled, puffed his cigar and said, "Doc, how's your cigar?"

"Wonderful," Doc replied. "Let's stroll over to the bank, see how many guards they've got over there."

Leaving the rail platform, they made their way along the crowded street to the big brick-and-stone bank building, climbed the wide limestone stairs and walked in through the wide brass-trimmed doors. Looking around, their eyes went to the two guards and stopped in surprise. "What do you think of that?" Combs whispered.

"Well, I'll be," Doc whispered.

Whatever suspicions the two gunmen had were only strengthened when they stared at the two young *rurales* who stood with their rifles leaning against a wall while they flirted with a couple local young ladies.

"Now, that's what I like to see when I'm about to rob a bank," Combs whispered.

"It's the kind of guards I've always dreamed of," Doc whispered in reply.

They took their time walking about in the large bank lobby, as if inspecting the architecture. Then, without another word, they turned and walked back out in the heat of the day.

"So, what do you think?" Doc asked, puffing his cigar.

"I'll tell you what I think," said Combs. "I think it's big and it's fancy, but it doesn't require as many men as we've got here."

Doc gave him a questioning look. "Makes you think that maybe Axel didn't need us five new men after all?"

"Not as far as I can see," said Bobby. They looked back and forth along the intersecting streets and the crowd of businessmen and townsfolk.

Doc still puffed his cigar, saying, "Judging the layout of the place, the layout of the streets . . . and the number of soldiers hanging around this town, I'd say this whole thing only needed five or six men at the most. Five doing the job, one watching the street and holding the horses."

"Yep," said Combs. "*Six* is the exact amount of new men Capp brought in when he hired all of us, before Decker got himself killed."

"That's the way it looks," said Doc, still checking the street in both directions. His eyes went in the direction of the rail station and lingered there for a moment.

A silence passed, then Combs said, "So what do you think Capp's got up his sleeve for us?"

"I don't know," said Doc, "but whatever it is, he's

not planning on us being alive long enough to come looking for him." His eyes went back in the direction of the rail station and stopped on two high-ranking German officers who stood quietly talking among themselves. "Why was it Capp said the Mexican brought that big wagon along?"

"Said he had some goods to haul back across the border," said Combs.

"That makes no sense to me at all," said Doc. "What goods could he have here that he couldn't replace at a store over in the territory?"

"Beats me," said Combs. He gave Doc a somber look. "It ain't too late for us both to back out of this."

"I can't back out on it, Bobby, I'm desperate. If there's any chance in the world of making a stake off this deal, I've got to do it."

"Me too, I reckon," said Combs with resolve. "But as far as I'm concerned, we don't owe Saggs and the other two a thing. If things go wrong, we agree to watch each other's back. They didn't want to go along with us, so that's their problem."

"I'm glad to hear you say that, Bobby," said Doc, "because I've got an idea that just might work. Let's get back over to that store, see what kind of handy firearms and other handy items he's got for sale."

At the cantina, Axel Capp, Denton Spears and Hector Ruiz pushed their way through the sweaty, milling drinking crowd and stepped out onto the wide stone walkway. As a shapely young woman passed by and gave Hector a smile, Hector started to take a step toward her, but Denton Spears grabbed his arm, stopping him. He turned to Spears with a harsh glare and jerked his arm free. "Never try to lay your hand on me again," Hector warned him.

"Easy, Hector," said Axel. "Denton's only doing what I asked him to do. I told him that I want you close by my side until we go do our job tomorrow."

"Oh?" Hector looked offended. Jutting his chin, he asked boldly, "And why is it that you want me by your side?"

Axel gave him a flat stare. "You're questioning me?"

Hector stood his ground, his right hand near the pistol holstered across his belly beside a bandolier of bullets. "When it concerns me? *Sí!*" He thumbed himself on the chest. "I must question you, even though you are the boss."

"No you don't," said Denton Spears, ready to make a move on the Mexican.

"Hold it, Denton," said Axel Capp. He turned back to Hector, took a step closer to him and said, "All right, then, I'll give you my reason, just this once." He raised a finger for emphasis. "I want you close by because you're the one man I know I can count on if I need something done at the last minute. Does that satisfy you?" He stared into Hector's eyes with a flat cold expression.

Hector relented. He raised his hand away from his pistol butt and said, "*Sí*, that is different . . . of course I will stay close by your side."

"What's the matter, Hector?" asked Axel Capp, still wearing the same unreadable expression. "Did you think your honor was being questioned?"

Before Hector could speak, a uniformed German officer stepped onto the stone walkway. Flanking him were a half dozen young *federales,* each carrying a long rifle with a bayonet affixed to its barrel. The German officer held his black-gloved hand on the butt of

a large Smith and Wesson with a lanyard attaching it
to his gun belt by a length of golden cord. "We will
have none of this public brawling on the streets of
Center City!" he demanded as two of the *federales*
shoved Axel and Hector away from one another.

"Hold it, everybody!" said Axel, seeing that Denton
Spears was ready to draw his pistol and make his play
on the German officer. "There's no trouble here!"
Axel added quickly.

"Then what was this that I saw?" said the German.
He seemed to ease down at the sight of Spears' hand
poised on his gun butt.

"We just had a business disagreement, mister," said
Axel. "That's how us good old American boys act."
He tried a stiff grin. "We jump all over one another.
But the fact is Hector and me are good *amigos*, right,
Hector? Me and this boy have worked together for
years!"

"*Sí*, it is true," said Hector, scowling at the German
officer who stood too close to Hector. Nodding at
Axel, he said to the German, "This man is my friend.
But you are not."

The German took a step back, looking Hector up
and down. "Oh? Are you one of those who resents
my being here in your quaint little country?"

"*Sí*, I resent it, you German pig!" Hector spit at the
German's highly polished black riding boots.

"Arrest this man!" said the German to the *federales*.
"Take him to the compound where I can teach him
some respect!"

Hector stood braced, but made no move for his gun
as the *federales* closed in around him. One of them
flipped his gun from his holster.

"Whoa, fellows!" said Axel Capp. "My friend

meant no harm. He's just been drinking too much! I
was chastising him for it when you showed up! There's
no need in arresting him!"

"I am taking him to the jail," said the German. "He
can sober up in a cell with a dozen other drunks!"

"Hey, come on, now," said Axel. As he spoke he
pulled a black cigar from a pocket inside his coat and
handed it to the German. "Let me buy you and your
soldiers a drink, see if we can't talk this thing out and
forget about it. I need this man working for me first
thing in the morning, not laid up in jail." He pulled a
black wallet from inside his coat pocket. "If there's a
fine for public drunkenness, maybe I could just pay it
here and now, save us all some bother."

"Put your money away," the German demanded.
"You Americans are all alike. You think you can
wave your money and make up for all your mistakes!"

Axel just stared at him. Seeing the look in Axel's
eyes as he shrugged and put the wallet back inside his
coat, the German said to the *federales*, "Turn him
loose. Give him back his pistol." He looked back at
Axel and said, "I better hear no more from either of
you this night, or you will both go to the jail! Do
you understand?"

"You are most kind, mister," said Axel, his expression showing that his words were no more than a
formality.

Ignoring Axel, the German looked around and said
to the soldiers, "Let us get away from here, these men
are offensive." He turned on his heels and stalked off
into the crowd, the *federales* following at his heels.

Watching them disappear out of sight, Axel turned
to Hector and said, "Damn, *mi amigo*. What made
you say something like that to the German? You're

lucky you didn't end up searching for your teeth on a wet stone floor."

Hector appeared to have cooled down. "I could not help it. I hate those German pigs!"

Axel laughed aloud, giving Denton Spears a bemused look. "Hear that, he spits on the German's boots! Says he couldn't help himself!"

"Yeah, how about that." Spears smiled grudgingly, still staring at Hector Ruiz.

Axel collected himself, shook his head, then looked as Combs and Doc Cain came walking up to them along the stone walkway. "I thought you two would have been back before now," he said as the two stopped.

"We thought we better check that bank out real proper like," said Doc Cain, his eyes going in the direction the German and the *federales* had taken. "What was all that about?" he asked.

"That was nothing," said Axel, waving the incident off. "Just Hector jumping on some soldiers. So, did things check out to suit you?"

"Yeah," said Doc, "I think we've got everything cut down to bite size."

"Good," said Axel. "By the way, Hector here is going to be riding with you and the new men tomorrow."

"Me?" said Hector, looking surprised. "But, Axel, you just said you want me by your side!"

"That's today, Hector," Axel said. "Tomorrow, I want you riding with these boys, help them keep things going like clockwork so to speak."

Doc Cain said, "I think me and the others can handle everything ourselves."

"Yes," said Axel, "I'm sure you do. But if something goes wrong tomorrow, I want to make sure you've got the best of my bunch covering your backs." He gave each man a look that said there was no more discussing the matter. After a silent pause, he said, "Now, let's get something to eat . . . then we'll go over our plans, make sure everybody does what's expected of them?"

"Anything you say," Doc Cain replied.

"That's the spirit," Axel grinned, slapping Doc on his back. "Now, come, boys, the drinks are all on me." He led them back inside the cantina, into the din of music and laughter. Hector noted how close Denton Spears remained beside him as he followed Axel to the bar.

Chapter 17

"Do all of you remember the plan we laid out last night?" Axel Capp asked the six men mounted on their horses in a narrow alley a hundred yards from the bank building. Beside Axel sat Denton Spears with a rifle across his lap. Axel looked from one face to the next: Hector Ruiz, Bobby Combs, Doc Cain, Mose Winton, Parker Stiles. Then he looked at Ulie Saggs as he said to all of them, "Saggs, I want you to be the man in charge once all of you get inside that bank. You keep things going smooth until me and the rest of the boys join back up with you."

Hestor Ruiz stiffened. "*Him*? He is the *segundo* in charge? Why has nobody told me this before?"

"Because that's the way I wanted it, Hector," said Axel. He spoke with such harshness that Hector fell silent. He stared down at his saddle horn with a brooding expression as Axel continued, saying, "I decided Saggs here is the best man for the job. Any other questions?" Axel looked from face to face again.

Ulie Saggs sat with his head held high, liking what Axel had said about him. "Don't worry, Axel, I'll keep this thing going slicker than a cat's back."

"I know that, Saggs," said Axel. Looking at Hector,

he said to Bobby Combs, "I want you and Doc Cain
to stick close to Hector here. Don't let one another
out of your sight. Do you understand that?" He stared
straight at Doc Cain.

"Sure"—Doc Cain shrugged—"we understand it."

Axel studied Doc Cain's eyes for a moment. Reaching inside his long tan riding duster and lifting a
pocket watch from his vest pocket, he turned his attention to the time. "That bank opens in an hour. Everybody break up here for now, but stick close. Give
yourselves two minutes between yas as you go inside
the bank. Then wait for Saggs to make the announce-
ment. Soon as he lets them know they're being
robbed, get to doing it. But nobody leaves until they
hear us start a shooting ruckus on the next street over
toward the plaza. Once we draw the *federales* over
there to us, you've got a free ride right out the back
door of this town." He grinned. "Everybody got
that?"

A silence passed, then Mose Winton asked with a
confused look, "Am I supposed to kill a guard right
off?" He raised his gloved fingertips up under his hat
and scratched his head.

Axel just stared flatly at him for a moment. Finally
he said, "No, Winton. You're supposed to grab the
guard, make sure he doesn't fire his gun. Nobody fires
their gun unless they have to," he added, looking
around at the men. "Leave the shooting up to us.
That's the decoy." He looked back at Mose Winton.
"Did you listen to one damn word I said last night?"

Before Winton could answer, Saggs cut in, saying,
"I'll make sure he understands, Axel. Leave everything up to me."

"That I will, Saggs," said Axel. Turning to Spears
he said, "See, Denton. I told you Saggs was my pick

of the litter." He backed his horse a step and turned it toward the empty street, Spears doing the same right behind him. The two rode away slowly and turned toward the plaza where Dallas Ryan, Joe Murphy, Millard Trent, Ace Tinsdale, Charlie Floose, Curley Barnes and Rod Sealey awaited them.

Watching them ride out of sight, Saggs beamed and said to Hector and the new men around him, "Boys, you all heard the man . . . let's break up here, ride around the street a little until the bank opens." He gave Combs, Doc Cain and Hector Ruiz a smug grin. "You boys be sure and stay together, though, like Axel said." As the others pulled their horses back and drifted away, he said, "Everybody play this thing out the way we planned it."

Sitting on his big pinto horse between Doc and Combs, Hector spit at the ground and crossed his wrists on his saddle horn. "That *bastardo*! What did he have to do with the planning of this?"

Doc and Combs looked at one another. Doc said, "What did *you*?"

Hector scowled at the two. "I had *plenty* to do with this. I am the one who told Axel about the bank." He thumbed himself on the chest. "It was I who put him in contact with the man who knows when the *federale* pay comes in each month. Without my connection, he would not have known the right time to rob it!"

"The right time, huh?" said Doc Cain.

"*Sí*, the right time," said Hector.

"What date does the government pay its soldiers?" Doc asked.

"The first day of every month," said Hector. As soon as he'd spoken, a puzzled look came to his face. He turned in his saddle, facing Doc and Combs. "But the *first* will not be for another week!"

Doc Cain and Combs both gave him a flat stare. "Makes you wonder don't it?" said Doc.

Hector took on a worried look. "It is the wrong time to be here! I must tell Axel there has been a mistake!" He started to gig his horse forward, but Bobby Combs' pistol came up from his holster and cocked as he poked it into Hector's ribs. At the same time, on the other side of him, Doc reached out and grabbed his horse by its bridle.

"Sit tight, Ruiz," Combs warned him. "There's been no mistake made. Axel knows exactly what he's doing."

Hector looked back and forth between the two, his gun hand tense, fighting the urge to make a grab for the pistol across his stomach. "What is this? What is going on with you two?"

"Don't you get it, Ruiz?" said Doc. He offered the Mexican a slight smile, saying quietly, "Tell us something. Did Axel want us keeping an eye on you, or did he leave you here to keep an eye on us?"

Hector let the question sink in. Then he eased down in his saddle and said to Doc Cain, "All right, *amigos*, you tell me."

Ulie Saggs stood restlessly staring at a Mexican newspaper inside the bank while he waited for the last of the men to enter. Twice he'd caught the guards looking his way. He'd extended the two young men a nervous smile, raised the spread newspaper in front of his face and whispered sidelong to Parker Stiles, who stood nearby acting as if they were not together. "We can't keep waiting! I've got a feeling those three turned yellow on us at the last minute!"

Without nodding or turning toward him, Stiles said, "All the more money for the rest of us to split up."

"Yeah," said Saggs, "but still, if I ever cross trails with any of them, I'm killing them graveyard dead, on the spot."

"Can't blame you," said Stiles. Looking all around, he noted that Mose Winton stood at the rear of a line of people, giving him and Saggs a bewildered worried look. "We best do something quick, though," Stiles said. "Winton's drawing attention, keeps stepping to the back of the line like some damn simpleminded idiot."

Saggs looked across the bank at Mose Winton, who had just allowed two more people to get in front of him. Winton stared at Saggs and shrugged, mouthing some unheard words, as if asking Saggs what else he should do. "Good God!" said Saggs. "He's going to have everybody watching his stupid ass!" He wadded up the newspaper and dropped it to his feet. "To hell with it! Let's get it going!"

"Now you're talking!" said Stiles, stepping sidelong, drawing his pistol at the same time as Saggs.

"All right you *Mexicano* sonsabitches!" shouted Saggs, stepping into the middle of the wide marble floor, leveling his Colt toward the two young guards whose rifles stood against the wall six feet away from them, "everybody who wants to stay alive show me your hands! You guards, don't even think about making a grab for your guns. I'll cut you in half!"

"*Qué?*" one guard said to the other, stunned at the sight of the armed American shouting at them.

The other guard gave him a shove farther away from the rifles, saying to him in Spanish, "They are robbing the bank. Do as they say!"

In Spanish the other guard whispered as he stumbled awkwardly, "But why? There's not money here yet!"

"Shhh," said the first guard. "Let them find out for themselves."

At the end of the line of customers, Winton had jerked his gun from his holster and waved it back and forth, taking in everybody between himself and the teller windows.

A woman gasped as Winton reached out, snatched her to him and threw an arm around her from behind. "Don't make me kill her!" he shouted. The stunned customers raised their hands quickly.

"All right, then!" said Saggs, casting a quick glance at Stiles. "All of you line along that wall! You guards too! *Vámonos* now, Gawdamn it! We ain't got all day!"

"Want me to keep ahold of her, Saggs?" Mose Winton shouted from across the ornate lobby.

Ulie Saggs winced at the sound of Winton's voice, so did Parker Stiles. "Damn it, man!" Saggs hissed, trying to keep his voice down and at the same time give Winton a hint of what he'd just done, "That ain't my name!"

"It ain't?" Winton blurted out with a blank expression.

"No, it's not," said Saggs, trying to give him a signal with his eyes.

But Winton was having none of it. "Then what is your name?"

"Sweet Jesus!" said Parker Stiles. "Just shut up!" He looked at Saggs, saying, "Keep me covered, watch those guards! I'm going to the safe!"

"Hey, hold on!" said Saggs, "I'm in charge here!"

But Stiles had already started across the floor to the far end of the long polished wood and marble counter where a thick wooden door seperated the customers from the tellers. "Hurry up, you! *Prisa rápido!* Open the door, you sonsabitch!" he demanded, pointing his gun through the ornamental ironwork at a frightened man in a black business suit.

Saggs watched, jerking his head back and forth nervously between the guards and Stiles. "Get it all! Don't leave nothing behind!" He listened to the sound of metal against metal as the big vault door swung open. Then he heard heated words from Stiles to the nervous bank official. Finally Stiles' voice blared, echoing in the wide-open lobby. "Are you telling me that's *it*? This is all there is?" A gun hammer cocked loudly in the tense silence. "I will blow your lying head clean off!" Stiles raged.

"Señor, por favor!" came a quivering reply. "Is all the money. Is all the money! Is all the mon—!"

His words ended in a dull thump, followed by a louder thump as a swipe from Stiles' gun barrel knocked him backward onto the floor. "Son of a bitch!" Stiles shrieked in an almost hysterical voice, "I've knocked him cold!"

"What's the matter back there?" shouted Saggs.

"Wake up, Gawdamn it! Wake up!" Stiles screamed and pleaded.

Saggs heard the sound of Stiles slapping the knocked-out bank official's face back and forth. "He won't wake up!" Stiles shrieked.

"Get the money, damn it!" Saggs shouted.

"That's just it!" said Stiles, "there ain't near the money here that there's supposed to be!"

"There's not? But there has to be! Look around some!" Saggs screamed. He turned from the guards and ran toward the door to the door at the end of the counter. But on his way there, an urgent voice shouted in Spanish from the steps out front, "The bank is being robbed! Help, the bank is being robbed!"

Saggs stopped mid-step. "Damn it! We've been seen!" He stared at Winton, unsure of what to do next. Then he hurried to the open door at the end of the counter and looked in at Stiles standing over the unconscious bank officer. "Grab one of these tellers! Make him tell you—" His words stopped short at the sound of someone ringing a loud warning bell in the church a block away.

"Where's that decoy firing we're supposed to get from Axel?" Stiles asked.

"Stop using names, damn it!" shouted Saggs. "I don't know! He's probably heard all this ruckus and knows we're trapped! He'll be coming for us real quick! He'll get us out of here!" He shot a dark glance at the young tellers, who huddled cringing against the inside of the counter with their hands raised. "He'll be in a killing mood if we don't have the money gathered and ready to ride!"

One of the young tellers ventured upward into a crouch and said, "*Por favor*, mister, there is no more money here, only what you see!"

Saggs hurried to the vault, shoved Stiles away from the door and looked in. A few stacks of money lay stacked on one of the otherwise empty shelves. "This don't make sense! There's supposed to be payroll money here!"

The two tellers looked at one another, then the one still crouching said in a frightened voice, "Next week will be the payroll money, mister!"

"Next week?" Saggs looked stunned.

"*Sí*, is next week." Both tellers nodded in unison.

"I won't *be* here next week," Saggs said coldly, raising his pistol at arm's length toward the frightened young men, "and neither will you."

"*No, señor!*" the crouching teller pleaded.

Saggs squeezed the trigger, but in the split second before his gun went off, another shot resounded, this one coming from one of the guards who had inched his way to the two rifles, grabbed one and fired. Saggs' pistol shot wild as the rifle bullet ricocheted first off of the ornate iron bars, then off the steel vault door and sliced through his left ear. "Jesus!" Saggs shouted, slapping his ear as if he'd been stung by a bee. The two tellers raced past him and out the door just as Stiles turned and fired, missing them both.

Another rifle shot exploded, the other guard having also grabbed his rifle and aimed at Mose Winton. Without thinking, instead of holding the woman pressed against him for cover, Winton shoved her aside in order to get a better aim. But the second guard's shot lifted him backward and slammed him against a marble column. Customers screamed and flung themselves to the floor as shots resounded from behind the counter. But Saggs and Stiles were too late to help Mose Winton. He slid down the column leaving a smear of blood on the polished marble. "I messed up," he gasped, looking down at the gaping hole in the center of his chest.

"Drop the rifles!" Saggs shouted at the guards.

"Ha!" one of the guards replied. "*You* drop your pistols!"

"Damn it!" Saggs said, giving Stiles a sick, frightened look, "where's Axel?"

"I don't know," said Stiles, "but I ain't basing my plans for the day on the Rio Sagrado Gang showing up at all!" Rising with his pistol out at arm's length, he fired at the two guards as they backed to the front door, their rifles blazing, their bullets striking sparks and pinging off the elaborate ironwork above the counter.

"This is sure as hell smelling like a jackpot to me!" Saggs shouted amid the gunfire. He slung a bandolier of bullets off of his shoulder, taking stock of his ammunition inventory. On the other side of the counter, customers crawled instinctively toward the front door, hoping to get out of the shooting.

On the other side of the front door, the German officer who had chastised Axel Capp and his men the day before stood beside the closed door with his back flat against the stone wall. From all directions *federales* had come running at the first sound of gunshots, their rifles in hand. Now, following the waves and shouts from the German officer, the soldiers had formed into a half circle around the large bank in both the street out front and the alley behind. When the door swung open and the two guards came spilling out onto the stone front landing, the German raised a hand to keep the soldiers from firing on them. "Get out of the way, quickly!" the German officer shouted, giving the two guards a shove to the side.

Behind the soldiers came three of the eleven customers, crawling frantically on their hands and knees. The other customers pulled back to safety along the wall and behind marble columns when heavy bullets from the outlaws behind the bank counter screamed only inches above their heads. "Take cover and stay down!" the German shouted.

"*Capitán* Liebermann!" said a young Mexican sergeant beside him, "the men are in place! What is your command?"

"They are now trapped!" the German said, breathing hard in excitement. "I command we hold them this way until we can get the innocent parties out of the bank!"

"This could take some time," said the sergeant.

"Sergeant Santage," the German said with a tight smile, "time is on our side here. We will take advantage of it." He took an appraising glance back and forth along the street, seeing more and more soldiers arriving every second. "These fools do not realize what a formidable foe they have unleashed upon themselves!"

Chapter 18

Axel Capp listened to the shots coming from the bank a half mile away from the rail station. Smiling to himself, he stepped over the body of one of the three guards who lay dead on the floor, each in their own pool of blood. Stooping long enough to wipe the blade of his boot knife clean across the chest of one of the other bodies, Axel said to Charlie Floose, "Help them get these loaded, Charlie. You can admire them after we get them across the border!"

Floose snapped out of his state of awe and shook his head as if to clear it. "I've just never seen anything so damn beautiful in my life!" He'd helped Axel and Dallas Ryan kill the guards quietly a moment earlier when they'd arrived. Then, having thrown the tarpaulin back off of the first pallet, he'd stood staring down in awe at the stacks of small gold bars.

Axel gave him a cold stare until Floose reached down, scooped up two bars and hurried out onto the loading dock with them. Coming in as Floose left, Joe Murphy and Millard Trent grabbed more bars from the pallet and hurried outside with them. Ace Tinsdale and Denton spears came in, rushing past Axel toward the gold. "Denton," said Axel, giving his close friend a smile, "didn't I tell you this town would never know what hit them?" As he spoke to Spears, he walked over to the pallets of gold with him.

"You sure enough did, Axel!" They each picked up two bars of gold and walked out onto the dock with them.

Stepping down onto the bed of the wagon backed up against the dock, Spears lay the gold bars onto a stack and gave a jerk of his head in the direction of the shots coming from the bank. "Sounds like Hector and all of our new members didn't know what hit them either." He reached around and took the two bars from Axel Capp and stacked them, the two of them laughing at the fate of what they thought were the six men they'd just betrayed.

"I almost hated putting ole Hector in with that bunch," said Axel, watching the men file back and forth quickly, loading the wagon. "But my Mexican government friend said he knew too much and had to go." He grinned and gave a tip of his hat in the direction of the gunfire. "So, *adiós*, Hector!"

Two blocks away atop the clay tile roof of a powerful Spanish *hacendado*, Hector Ruiz looked through a pair of new binoculars at Axel Capp and cursed him heatedly under his breath. "He tips his hat toward the bank and laughs because he thinks he has sent us there to die!"

Lying beside him, Combs and Doc Cain looked at one another. "From this distance you can tell all that?" said Doc. "You must be a mind reader."

"I should have been a mind reader sooner and figured out what these two *bastardos were* thinking. It was I who was responsible for bringing them two together." He nodded down at the *hacienda* beneath them where he'd moments ago left the wealthy landowner lying dead, a pillow with a bullet hole in it covering the man's face. "But now it is not hard to figure . . . they decided I knew too much. So they put in with the rest of you. We were the decoys! It was us who were drawing the attention to the bank while they stole a shipment of gold!"

"Yep, that's the whole of it," said Doc Cain, reaching up and taking the binoculars as Hector lowered them from his eyes and handed them to him. "It was all so simple that none of us noticed it. We all wanted into Capp's gang, each of us for our own reasons." He raised the binoculars and looked through them as he spoke. "I don't mind telling you mine. I'm getting old. I ain't able to handle this life the way I once did. I needed one more good *raza*. I figured I could find it with the Rio Sagrado Gang." He spit in disgust. "Hell, I ought to know better."

"All of us should have," said Hector. He glanced toward the sound of shooting coming from the bank. "The fool, Saggs was too pleased with himself to be suspicious of anything." He shrugged. "He is a proud and stupid man. Men like that are easy to mislead."

Bobby Combs had been listening in silence. He took the binoculars as Doc lowered them from his eyes and passed them over to him, and said, "What about you, Hector?"

"What about me?" Hector asked, gazing at him as Combs raised the binoculars and looked out through them.

"You say Saggs was easily tricked. What about you?" he asked. "What brought you so far along without smelling a rat?" Combs saw the stack of gold growing higher as the men hurried back and forth, in and out of the rail depot.

"I do not know." Hector looked ashamed. "Perhaps

I too have been a fool, falling for Axel Capp's scheme."

Lying between the two, Doc Cain reached out with both hands and slapped them on their backs, grinning. "Don't be too hard on yourselves, boys. Look at it this way. We might've all been had. But we have managed to turn this little trick around on Axel Capp. If he gets away from here and clears the border with all that gold, all we got to do is reach down and take it from him. Then we come out on top after all."

"You make it sound awfully easy, Doc," said Combs.

"It is easy," Doc replied. "Everything in life is easy, once a man comes to reckon he's got nothing else to lose." He rose up onto his knees, listening to the gunfire from the bank. The firing suddenly grew more intense. Reaching a hand back for the binoculars, he said to Combs, "Bobby, let me take a look over there, see what's going on with them."

Combs handed him the binoculars and watched him raise them to his eyes. After a moment as the firing grew even more intense, Combs asked, "Doc what the hell *are* they doing down there?"

Doc kept the binoculars to his eyes, shaking his head slowly. "You just about have to see it to believe it," he said, watching through the narrow circle of vision.

On the street out front of the bank, the German officer and the Mexican sergeant had moved away from the door and taken aim at Parker Stiles, who came walking out slowly with his arm around the throat of one of the young tellers, keeping the frightened man pressed tight against him. Using the teller as a shield, Stiles moved slowly and warily down the stone steps and toward the iron hitch rail. But as he got to the rail and tried to unhitch a horse, the teller acted quickly. He jerked Stiles' arm away from his neck, stepped around sideways to him, giving the gunman's arm a swing over his head.

"Whoaaaa!" Stiles shrieked. His pistol flew from his hand as the young man flipped him forward, high over his shoulder, and brought him down with a heavy slapping sound onto the hard stone street.

The teller stepped back and watched Stiles stagger dumbly to his feet. From the door of the bank the remaining hostages came running free, shouting and screaming. On the street the German raised a hand, keeping all the soldiers in check until Stiles staggered away from the horses. But as soon as the half-conscious outlaw swayed back and forth in the middle of the street, with no living thing in danger on the other side of him, the officer stiffened his raised arm and bellowed, "Ready! Aim!"

"Oh, hell!" Stiles managed to turn and cast one last stunned look into the barrel of countless rifles.

"Fire!" shouted the German officer, dropping his arm with finality.

Looking on from the rooftop, Doc Cain winced, then looked back through the binoculars as a woman in a long gingham dress came racing out of the bank with a shawl pulled over her head. "Should have left the boots behind," Doc Cain said, seeing the woman was actually Ulie Saggs. The *federales* had missed noticing it at first, Saggs being partly hidden in the fleeing hostages surrounding him. He'd made it to the hitch rail and mounted his horse before a half-naked woman ran out of the bank pointing at him, screaming in Spanish, "He is one of them! He is one of them!"

"Damn you to hell, woman!" Saggs cursed. He whipped a pistol from beneath the dress and leveled it toward her, but three *federales* fired as one, two of the shots hitting him high in his chest, lifting him out of the saddle and tossing him to the street beside the bullet-riddled body of Parker Stiles. Saggs, barely alive and knowing he wouldn't last long, tried to rip the dress from himself. But a big polished black boot came down on him, clamping his hands to his bloody chest.

"Come on, now," Saggs rasped in a failing voice, looking up at the German officer, "be a sport . . . to a dying man, huh?"

As if considering it for a moment, Liebermann stared down at him dispassionately, pointing his cocked pistol at Saggs' forehead. Then a trace of a cruel smile came to the German's face, and he shrugged, saying, "No, I think not. It looks so good on you!" He squeezed the trigger.

"Oh!" said Doc Cain, taking his eyes away from the binoculars at the sight of Saggs' head snapping back, a blast of red exploding from it, "that's a bad way to go . . . shot dead wearing a woman's garment." He handed the binoculars over to Bobby Combs, who had stood up along with Hector for a better look at the distant melee.

"Part of me says we should have tried to save them," said Combs.

"Yeah? What does the other part of you say?" Doc Cain asked. He stooped down and unfolded a blanket from around a long-barreled buffalo rifle the two had purchased along with the binoculars.

"The other part says to hell with them," said Combs. He turned his attention and binoculars back to the rail platform where Axel and his men loaded the wagon with no interruptions while the rest of the town gathered out front of the bank. "As plans go, Axel could have done worse," he said.

"Sí," said Hector. "Now, let's go take the gold away
from him and have it for our own, eh?"

"That's what I say," said Doc. "Shame on the Rio
Sagrado Gang, wasting our time this way. I'll follow
them to hell if I have to." He stared with his naked
eye at the rail platform, barely seeing Axel and Denton Spears hurry out to the wagon, each with gold
bars in both of their hands. "You two go on; I'll catch
up soon as I can." He turned his attention back
toward the bank.

On the loading dock Axel waited until Spears had
laid down his load and turned to him, taking the bars
from him and stacking them on the others. When Axel
gazed off across the rooftops, unable to see Combs,
Doc and Hector for the glittering morning sunlight,
Spears asked, "What's wrong?"

Axel continued searching the roofs as he replied, "I
got a feeling like I'm being watched all of a sudden.
Feels like being in somebody's gun sight."

"Yeah?" Spears stepped up from the wagon onto
the rail platform and looked all around himself. "I
don't see nobody. If you was in somebody's gun sight,
I expect we'd heard about it by now. Anybody saw
what we're doing here, you can bet they'd be shooting,
or else shouting their heads off."

Axel shook off the feeling and looked at the now
heavily loaded wagon. "I think you're right. Besides,
another few minutes and it won't matter what they
saw, we'll be out of here and making our run for
the border."

"They're going to see these wagon tracks plain as
day," said Spears, "you can bet on that."

"I know," said Axel, "that's why we're going to
make it a *hard* run for the border." He turned to the
others as they came out carrying gold bars. "Get those

bars loaded, and that's all we're taking. We've got to save room for the big gun." He turned to Spears and said, "Denton, you and Floose go get it and set it up while we roll out of here."

"But there's almost a whole pallet load left in there, boss!" said Joe Murphy.

Axel gave him a look. "We knew we couldn't get it all. Don't start getting greedy on us. The way I figure it, we've got close to a million dollars worth of gold there." He nodded at the wagon.

"A *million* dollars!" said Ace Tinsdale. "God almighty! And my old daddy said I never would amount to nothing. That old sonsabitch ought to see me now!" He hooted with laughter.

"All right," said Axel. "Let's haul out of here." He jumped down from the platform and hurried over to the waiting horses, casting one more look back over his shoulder at the roofline, still not seeing Combs and Hector, who hurried along the clay tile in the morning sun.

At the edge of the tile roof, Hector said, "Hold it!"

Combs was ready to start climbing down, but he stopped. "What is it?" he asked. Hector stared with his naked eyes, squinting toward the rail platform. "Now I see why he can risk having the *federales* hound him to the border! Axel has gotten himself a Gatling gun!" Staring closer down into the rear of the wagon bed, he saw four small wooden kegs. "Damn it, he's got blasting powder too!"

"Figures," said Combs.

"I don't know about you," said Combs, "but I'm still going after the gold."

"*Sí*, of course, so am I," said Hector, "but it makes me wonder what else he might have acquired for this job. We must be prepared for anything." The two looked back at Doc Cain, who stood staring toward the street out front of the bank through the binoculars.

Combs called out, keeping his voice lowered. "Doc, it looks like they've got a Gatling gun and blasting powder. Does that make any difference to you?"

"I was counting on him having blasting powder, it just makes sense," said Doc.

"And the Gatling gun?" Combs asked.

"I've always wanted to own me a Gatling gun," Doc said without turning to them.

"Good enough," said Combs. He climbed down onto a lower roof, then down to the waiting horses, Hector following close behind him.

On the street in front of the bank, Captain Liebermann paced back and forth impatiently, awaiting the two men he had sent to get a French photographer who had practiced his craft in *Ciudad del Centro* after having fled Paris ahead of an army of angry debtors. While Liebermann waited for the Frenchman, the *federales* dragged the bodies of Saggs, Stiles and Winton out of the sun and propped them against the front of the bank.

At the sight of the heavy Frenchman with his camera and tripod under his arm and his dwarf helper toting a mountain of equipment on his back, Lieberman, shouted, "Hurry up for God sakes, LeBirge! Do you think I have all day to fool around waiting for you? I have reports to file! I have superiors to contact!"

"We're coming, we're coming!" said the Frenchman. He and his dwarf helper followed Liebermann up the stone steps to where the dead outlaws lay. "Why is this man wearing a dress?" LeBirge asked.

"Never mind why," said Liebermann. "Get your equipment set up."

LeBirge turned to the dwarf and issued a string of orders in French. Then he backed away a few feet and set up the tripod and camera on the flat stone landing. As he hurriedly prepared the camera and his helper measured out a load of flash powder, Sergeant Santage trotted up beside Liebermann and said, "*Capitán*, should I send all the soldiers to look around town for others who might have been with these men?"

"Not all of them, Sergeant," Liebermann said calmly, having taken matters firmly in hand. "Send only a small detail of soldiers. "I don't think we have anything to fear. But if there are others of course I want them captured, if only to make an example of them before the town."

"*Sí, Capitán*, I will send a detail right away," said Sergeant Santage, snapping a salute to the German officer. "Should I send word to the garrison and tell them everything that has happened here?"

"No, that won't be necessary," said Liebermann. "I will be sending a letter and a full report to my commandant. I will explain it to him."

"I am almost ready, Captain Liebermann," said LeBirge, finishing up with his camera preparations. "Show me how you would like to pose for 'em, please."

"These men were fools," said Liebermann. "They came here to rob the bank when there is no money in it!" Liebermann laughed as he stepped over and posed beside the dead outlaws, propping a boot on Ulie Sagg's shoulder. "How about this position?" he asked LeBirge. Then he continued talking to Sergeant Santage, saying, "Had they but waited a week longer, at least they would have died trying to steal something worth have stealing!" He looked down at the outlaws and shook his head in disgust.

"Hold that position," said LeBirge. "Be very still now."

The German officer stiffened his neck proudly, staring stoically into the camera lens as LeBirge bent down and flipped the black drape over his head. The dwarf stepped in close to the camera and raised a flash tray above his head on a long stick. Watching Liebermann through the lens, seeing his image upside down, LeBirge saw dust puff out of his chest. Then he heard the rifle shot resound along the stone street as Liebermann slammed back against the bank building and fell lifeless across the laps of the dead outlaws.

It took a second for Sergeant Santage to realize what had happened. In that moment he saw LeBirge fling the drape off of his head and stand up with his mouth agape, shouting something in French. But a rifle shot picked him up on his toes and sent him tumbling forward, taking the camera and tripod to the ground with him. Beside him, the flash tray ignited as his helper jumped away screaming and ran for cover.

"*Sante Madre!*" shouted Sergeant Santage. "Take cover! Everyone!" He shouted, he himself making a leap behind one of the large round pillars standing atop the landing. Atop the clay tile roof, Doc Cain lowered the big buffalo only an inch from his shoulder as he reloaded it. "I always hated picture takers," he said to himself. Then he raised the rifle butt into place again and took aim through the long brass-trimmed scope, searching for another target. "You'll do," he said, seeing the magnified image of Sergeant Santage as the soldier peeped out from behind the thick stone pillar.

The shot missed Santage by only an inch and struck the pillar with a loud thud, taking out a large chunk of stone.

"You son of a bitch!" Santage shouted at the unseen shooter. Jerking back, grabbing the side of his
head where a fleck of stone had left a small cut on
his forehead, he continued cursing under his breath.

On the roof, Doc Cain saw that his third shot hadn't
killed anyone, but that was all right. He had all of
them ducked down behind cover. It would be awhile
before they ventured out, not knowing if he was still
somewhere out there waiting to kill them. Smiling to
himself, he stepped down, wrapped the rifle in the
blanket and crept away along the roofline, down to
the horses and away.

Chapter 19

The Rio Sagrado Gang had raced along the trail out of Center City and across the stretch of flatlands. They'd pushed the horses and the wagon teams as quickly as they dared without taking a chance on running them into the ground or tipping the wagon over once they'd entered the line of hill country and began rounding the elbow turns.

In the early afternoon Axel Capp doubled back and searched the trail for any sign of rising dust. Smiling to himself, he could hardly believe that no one had gotten onto their trail yet. As he looked back across the trail, he heard Denton Spears yell at him from the wagon seat:

"There it is, Axel! Black Canyon! We've done it, ole hoss!"

Axel spun his horse and raced forward until he slid his horse to a halt beside the wagon where Denton Spears sat chuckling under his breath. Axel looked all around as if in awe at the steep walls of rock on either side of them. "Now, that's what I call making good time!" he said. He turned in his saddle and waved the men in around him. "But let's not stop now . . . we've got some serious work to do! Four of you get the blasting powder and ride out ahead of us. Go all the way to the last turn in the trail. Get some holes dug back into the hillsides. We're pulling this canyon shut behind us!"

Floose, Joe Murphy, Millard Trent, Dallas Ryan and Ace Tinsdale rode their horses over beside the wagon. Reaching down to Floose, each man hefted one of the kegs from him and set it on their laps. "All right, hurry it up," said Axel. "Me and Denton will come along right behind you. Get this set up and ready to go."

"How short should we make the fuse?" asked Tinsdale.

"Give us four feet," said Axel. "We don't want to be picking the hillsides out of our teeth.

"It's all going fine," Axel added quietly. He and Denton Spears watched the men ride into the canyon ahead of them, knowing it would take longer for the wagon to make it through the upcoming rockier terrain. "They'll have this canyon ready to smoke by the time we make it to the last turn. Once the *federales* get there and see they can't make it through, they'll have to circle back and ride thirty miles around these hills. By the time they get all that done, we'll be kissing the ground across the border."

"What about the things Floose was telling you, about the ranger and all?" Spears asked.

"We just stole close to a million dollars in gold right out from under the Mexican government's noses." He grinned. "Do I look like I'm going to worry about one ranger?"

The two laughed, Denton Spears shaking his head. "No, hell no! I reckon not!" He looked back and all around. "I got to admit I'm going to miss ole Mex, though. We had us some good times hiding out here."

"Good times is wherever we make them, Denton," said Axel, also looking all around the rough terrain. "Let's go spend this fortune!" He rode ahead of the wagon, Spears taking it easier now the trail had turned rougher and harder to negotiate.

Atop a ridge five hundred yards back overlooking the trail, Doc Cain looked through the binoculars, watching Spears and Axel Capp ride away cautiously into the wide canyon. "This is going just about how I had it figured," he said to Combs and Hector, without taking the field lens down from his eyes. "The others rode on ahead with the blasting powder. That gives them time to finish their work while the wagon catches up to them."

"Too bad we couldn't just put these two in the scope from here, knock them down and take the gold right now."

"Naw, that's bad planning," said Doc. He lowered the binoculars and ribbed his eyes. "We'll let them get the gold across the border, then we'll take it. Let them close off the canyon for us. Let them fight any *federales* who happen to get to them first." He smiled slightly. "Besides, I never much cared for driving a freight wagon, what about you two?"

"It always depended on what was in it," said Combs. "In a case like this, I think I could force myself to do it."

"*Sí*, I think I could too, for a wagon full of *gold*," said Hector, looking back over his shoulder along the trail, checking for any followers.

"We'll have to put these horses to task," said Doc, "if we're going to ride around the long way and not get too far behind that wagon."

"How far in do you think they'll go before they blow these walls?" Combs asked.

"A long ways," said Doc. "The farther in they go, the farther the *federales* will have to double back just to get to this point. Then they've got a long ride all the way around the hill line."

"Too bad for them," said Combs.

"Yep, and good for us . . . if we push it hard from right here. Once we get around and ahead of the *federales*, we might let Axel and his boys know we're breathing down his shirt. For all they'll know we could be a hundred soldiers on their tail. We'll give them something to worry about all the way to the border."

"I like the sound of that," said Combs, turning his horse as he spoke. "Start pushing." Taking off his hat, he used it to reach back and smack his horse's rump as he put his boot heels to its sides. Hector did the same. Doc Cain took one more look with his naked eyes, shoved the binoculars into their leather case hanging from a strap around his neck, and put his horse into a run right behind them.

At the farthest turn in the trail through Black Canyon, Charlie Floose and the others sat atop their horses awaiting Axel and the wagon. When the wagon rolled into sight Floose breathed a little easier. He and the others turned their horses sideways to the wagon as Spears slowed it to a halt, and Axel Capp stood up from the seat, stepped down and walked back to his horse hitched behind. "What's wrong with your horse, boss?" asked Dallas Ryan.

"Nothing at all," said Axel, unhitching his horse and walking it back to the front among the men.

Dallas Ryan looked at the other men, bemused at the sight of Axel riding in a wagon when he had a choice.

Axel said as he stepped up into the saddle, "I

wanted to know what it was like having a million dollars in gold tagging along behind me."

The men nodded, smiling.

"Floose," said Axel, "is this canyon ready to come down?" He looked all around as he asked.

"You bet it is, Axel," said Floose. He pulled a cigar from inside his riding duster and stuck it into his mouth. "Just tell me when. I'll light 'er up."

"I'm staying here to help you," said Axel. He nodded ahead along the trail where the canyon opened down onto a long stretch of flatlands. "All of yas stay in front of Denton and the wagon. Floose and I will wait until we see this wagon top down out of sight out there. As soon as you get there, stop and wait for us." He eyed Denton Spears, who sat with a double-barreled ten-gauge shotgun propped up beside him. Next to the shotgun stood a Winchester repeating rifle.

"Boys, right there is enough gold to make us all rich for the rest of our lives," said Axel. "Don't none of you start thinking about doing something stupid." He looked from one face to the next. Each man nodded, getting the message. Then he made a gesture with his hand, and Spears slapped the reins across the team horses' backs and sent them forward.

Almost a half hour later, on the other side of the downturn onto the flatlands, as Denton sat with the ten-gauge in his hands and the men sat their horses in front of him, Dallas Ryan stood in his stirrups craning his neck and looking back. "Here they come!"

The others craned up in their saddles for a look, except for Denton Spears. He sat watching the men. A moment later Axel and Floose had joined them, both smoking cigars. "Let's go," said Axel, giving his horse a nudge with his boot heels, waving the men ahead of him.

"Ain't we going to wait, make sure it blows?" said Spears.

"If it doesn't blow, there ain't nothing we can do about it now," said Axel. "We spotted a high rise of dust while we were lighting the fuses. Looked like no less than fifty *federales* coming." He looked back, judging the time. "I'd say they're getting there, right about now."

The men started heeling their horses forward. Spears raised his reins and started to give the horses a slap of leather. But at that moment a tremendous explosion rocked the earth beneath them, causing the horses to almost stagger in place for a second. *"Whooo-eee!"* said Floose, looking back over his shoulder at the high-rising cloud filled with fire, dust and rock. "Did we lift that sucker or what?"

"Check it out, Charlie," said Axel, relaxing some now that he knew the fuses had done their job. He puffed on the cigar.

Floose turned his horse, batted his boots to its sides and raced back to the rise in the trail. He circled his horse a couple of times, staring back into the billowing aftermath of the explosion. Then he stretched upward in his stirrups and waved his hat back and forth at Axel Capp. "Nobody made it through that storm!" he shouted, laughing aloud, booting his horse back toward the others.

"Well, then," said Axel, relaxing even more, "looks like we've bucked the tiger and won, boys." He looked around at the faces of the men who also seemed to relax as dust and bits of small rock showered down around them. "But let's not get sloppy. Everybody ride a tight saddle tonight. Things keep going this way, tomorrow we'll be crossing the border onto free ground! They ain't about to come over there looking for us."

"Then, by God! We've just about done it," Spears laughed. He put the team horses forward at an easy pace. The rest of the men divided up, half staying behind the wagon, half in front. Axel Capp allowed both riders and wagon to get a few feet ahead of him. With one more quick look back toward the rising dust from the explosion, he put his boot heels to his horse and rode on.

A full three hours later, the dust still hung in the air above the closed-off canyon when Combs, Hector and Doc Cain arrived at the same rise in the trail where the wagon had sat. Looking back upon the canyon, Doc said, "I expect Axel thinks it's all going his way about now."

"He has every right to," said Hector, examining the tall plume of smoke. "The question is, did all of the soldiers perish in the canyon, or had the explosion already happened when they got there?"

"It would make it lots easier on us if they went up with the powder kegs," said Doc Cain. "But I doubt if we're that lucky."

"It's a good possibility they're riding back right now," said Combs, "getting ready to go the same way we went."

"Yep, let's play it like they're right behind us," said Doc.

He turned his horse in the direction of the wagon tracks and heeled it forward. Hector and Combs followed. They rode at a quick steady pace for the next hour, only stopping once for a few minutes to rest the animals, knowing that they were gradually gaining ground on the slower-moving wagon.

Thirty yards to their left the land sloped upward to

a plane running parallel to the trail, which they climbed about a hundred feet, giving them a good view in all directions. Ten minutes later after pushing the horses a little harder along the higher trail, Doc Cain spotted rising dust and stopped long enough to raise the binoculars to his eyes. Scanning down onto the flatlands he saw the rear of the wagon, the men riding behind it and Axel Capp a few cautious yards farther back.

"There they are right now," said Doc. "They've slowed down some. I reckon they don't want to blow the team horses out." He chuckled and added, "Looks like Axel doesn't trust anybody around all that gold."

"That's good," said Combs. Then he said aloud as if Axel Capp could actually hear him, "You take real good care of our gold for us, Axel, you back-stabbing sonsabitch, you!"

Doc Cain lowered the binoculars. "There's a water hole four or five miles ahead. If we get there fast and get watered, we can get ahead of them and be above the wagon when the trail swings over here closer to us."

"You mean it will swing over within shooting distance," said Combs.

"Yeah, something like that." Doc gave Combs and Hector a stiff grin. "I wouldn't mind sticking a couple of shots down their shirts from up here. What about you, after all they put us through, trying to jackpot us?"

"It sounds good to me," said Combs. "The more you knock down now, the less we'll have to deal with later." They both looked at Hector.

"I do not care how many of them you kill, so long as you leave one alive to drive our gold across the border." He jerked his horse around and booted it forward, taking the lead, the other two following close behind.

They rode on, pushing hard for the next five miles toward the water hole, staying far enough back from the edge of the land fault to keep from being sky-lighted as they passed the wagon and the riders below. Their horses were strong and resilient. The water and a few moments rest grazing on sparse clumps of wild grass brought them back to service. As evening shadows grew long across the land, the three had tied their horses in a stand of cottonwood and taken a position, lying prone along the edge of a stone cliff. Below them they watched the trail lead man, horse and wagon ever closer.

"The way I figure," said Doc, "is that I can take two before they get down and cover up behind that wagon. We don't want to hold them up too long, take a chance of any *federales* catching up to them." He grinned. "We've got to keep them protecting our gold."

"Why not take out Axel Capp right off?" said Combs. "He's the one who set this up and was ready to get us killed."

"He's the leader," said Doc. "Do you suppose the others will have enough sense to make it to the border without him in charge?"

"I don't know why not," said Combs, "it's a straight ride from here."

"All right, I'll take him out then," said Doc, "if you're sure that's what you both want." He took his time adjusting the long scope on the big 50-caliber buffalo rifle, casting them a sidelong glance. "But then he's out of it for good, there's no more we can do to him. No matter what we do, we can't make him itch or sweat, or cuss the bastards that just gut shot him and left him lying dead while they ride off with that gold he went to all the trouble to haul back for them." He let out a short dark laugh under his breath. "Sometimes killing a dirty bastard like Axel Capp is the very *last* thing you want to do."

Combs and Hector looked at one another. Turning to Doc Cain, Bobby Combs spoke for both of them, saying, "You're the one shooting, Doc, it's your call."

Doc smiled to himself without answering and laid the long gun barrel out over three flat rocks he'd stacked for a shooting stand. He rested his face back a safe distance from the scope, looked down through it and watched the band of riders grow larger within the narrow circle of his vision. "What about you first, Murphy?" he whispered to himself, steadying the crosshairs onto the chest of Joe Murphy, who rode along in front of the wagon.

On the flatlands Denton Spears had just raised a canteen to his parched lips and took a sip when he heard Joe Murphy let out a loud grunt and stiffen in his saddle. As the shot resounded, Spears caught a glimpse of Murphy's blood spilling out of his back in a long red mist. "He's shot!" Spears shouted, grabbing the Winchester as he jerked the team of horses to a halt and yanked back hard on the brake lever and set it. He jumped over the wagon seat, bounded over the tarpaulin-covered stack of gold and swung the Gatling gun toward the ridgeline above them, three hundred yards away.

Hearing the shot and seeing that Joe Murphy had fallen from his saddle, the rest of the men reined their horses back and forth wildly, their pistols drawn, their eyes scanning the ridgeline.

"All of yas get down!" Axel Capp bellowed, already jumping down from his horse and leading it quickly up close behind the wagon. "Get down here, Denton," he said, "before you get your head shot off. That Gatling gun won't do anything for you from that distance!"

"From what distance?" shouted Spears, ducking down behind the stack of gold.

"I saw the smoke," said Axel. "It came all the way from up there! Too far out of range for anything we've got! Have you still got a field lens?"

"Yeah," said Spears. He hurried to the driver seat and came back carrying a dusty telescope. He pitched it to Axel.

The rest of the men had dropped from their saddles and crowded around behind the wagon. "What the hell are *federales* doing carrying long-range shooters?" Ace Tinsdale asked, frantically scanning the ridgeline, as did the others.

"It's not *federales*," said Axel, raising the telescope to his eye.

"Then who is it?" said Spears from inside the wagon.

"I don't know," said Axel, "it might just be one man. But if it's *federales*, why haven't they shot the team horses? Once they did that, the gold ain't going nowhere, that's for sure!"

The men looked at one another, knowing he was right. "Then, by God," said Millard Trent, standing up out of a crouch and taking a step back toward his horse, "I ain't letting one sonsabitch pin us—"

"Get down, you stupid bastard!" shouted Axel, grabbing him, pulling him down as a puff of dust rose up from the trail five feet behind them, followed by the loud distant explosion.

"Lord have mercy!" said Trent in a shaky voice. "He 'bout put that one right in my gullet!" He stood up into a crouch and hurried in closer to the back of the wagon.

Axel dusted himself off and stayed back a few feet, crouched and gazing through the telescope farther along the trail to where the land above them sloped back down to the flatlands. The evening sun cast a dark shade along the bottom edge of the land fault, too black for whoever was up there to see into it. "We've got to make a run for it, to the shade over there."

"He'll pick us off one at a time!" said Ace Tinsdale.

"I don't think so, Ace," said Axel. "I believe whoever it is, he doesn't want to kill all of us. He knows this gold ain't worth spit without people to move it."

"Yeah, but while we're riding there," said Tinsdale, "what's to keep him from—"

"It's Doc Cain. Son of a bitch!" said Axel, cutting him off, looking upward through the telescope.

"Cain?" said Spears in surprise. "How the hell would he have gotten out of that bank alive!"

"Simple," said Axel Capp, "he never went in there in the first place. He's not as big a fool as I played him for." He scanned back and forth, having only caught a quick look at Doc, and wanting to see if anyone was with him. Then he moved in closer to the wagon and shouted loudly toward the ridge, "Doc! I seen it's you. What is it you want?"

No reply came from the ridgeline. Axel waited a moment longer then called out again, "Doc Cain! Whatever you want . . . you've got it! Gold? You've got a share coming! You and whoever is with you! Is that a deal? Truce?"

A silence passed, then Doc's voice echoed down to the flatlands, saying, "I can't hear you! You son of a bitch!"

"Well, there we have it," said Axel. "It's Doc Cain all right. There's no telling who's with him . . . Bobby Combs, no doubt. We've got to get to that shade and stay in it till dark sets in."

"Then what?" said Spears.

"I'll show you then what," said Axel. "When he comes down off there, we'll be waiting for him."

Atop the ridgeline, Doc Cain watched the riders mount quickly and follow the wagon across the flatlands into the shadows. Turning to Combs and Hector as he scooted back and stood up, he said, "They're headed for cover. I missed the second one, but that's all right. We'll thin them down some more before we take the gold from them."

The three mounted and followed the high trail as it sloped down gradually. They rode long after dark until the moonlight on their right showed that they had made it to the flatlands.

Speaking quietly, Doc Cain said, "We'll have to be careful. If they pulled up out of their cover at dark, they could be anywhere along here."

No sooner than the words came out of his mouth, shots rang out in the darkness, one of them lifting Hector from his saddle and tossing him to the ground. Gunfire exploded to their right behind the black outline of rock. Bullets whistled past Doc's and Combs' heads. Hector's horse bolted away; Doc and Combs followed it. Neither man slowed his horse down until they rounded a thick stand of rock, hearing the bullets pound it from the other side.

"Damn!" said Doc, "they must have heard us coming down off the trail! I reckon they've moved out quicker than I thought they would! I got Hector killed," he added with remorse.

"Ain't nobody blaming you, Doc," said Combs.

"Hector knew this business as well as we do." He had his pistol out and cocked, searching for a target in the moonlight.

"Don't shoot back," said Doc. "They can't hit us if they can't find us. We're still in the game. Let's not tip our hand."

In a moment the firing ceased. A moment later Axel Capp's voice called out in the night, "Doc? Damn ole hoss! You sure took it personal, me jackpotting all of you that way. Come on out now. We'll let you back in with us. No harm done, eh? What do you say?"

Doc and Combs had to force themselves not to empty their guns in the direction of Axel's voice.

"Looks like you left somebody laying in the dirt out there. Better go back and get him. Can't leave a pal to die that way, can you?"

Doc bit his lip.

"Doc!" Hector Ruiz shouted loudly in a strained voice, "don't come back for me. Keep going! Don't let him get—"

Hector's voice was silenced abruptly by a volley of gunfire. "I'll be dogged," said Axel, "that was my ole *amigo*, Hector, wasn't it?"

When they heard Axel's words followed by a dark laugh, Doc Cain bit his lip and whispered to himself, his hand tight around his pistol, "Laugh you son of a bitch. We'll get you." He and Combs pulled their horses back silently and moved away deeper into the darkness.

After a moment Spears said to Axel, "I think he's moved out on us."

"Yeah, me too. There's another rider with him," said Axel, "I caught a glimpse of two horses high-tailing it for cover."

"We need to stay right on them," said Spears. "Dog

them until they can't stand it, get rid of them for once and for all!" In his excitement he stepped back away from the their rock cover and snatched up his horse's reins.

"Whoa, now! Not in the dark, we're not," said Axel. "I just wanted to let them know they're not messing with choirboys here. Tonight we're going to rest these horses, keep that team from blowing out on us. Come morning we're heading on for the border. We can't waste no more time here, let the *federales* catch up to us. We'll just have to put up with Doc Cain and his friend for a while longer."

"But with that long-range shooter, he can pick us all off one at a time!" said Ace Tinsdale, standing beside Spears.

"But he won't," said Axel. "He shot Joe Murphy just to show us he could. He must've taken it hard, me jackpotting him. But right now he wants us alive, able to take care of this gold until we get it across the border."

"Damn it," said Spears, "things was going so good."

"Things still are," said Axel. "Once we get across that border, I know ambush spots like Doc Cain ain't never dreamed of. If he makes it past them, I'll kill the old sonsabitch on the street in Redemption. Him and whoever's with him. To hell with them."

"That's something else we've got to deal with," said Spears, "that damned ranger."

"To hell with him too. He won't believe what's heading his way." Axel grinned to himself. "Anybody gets between me and this gold, I'll kill them all, deader than hell."

Chapter 20

The ranger stood on the boardwalk in front of the express office and watched the stagecoach roll into Redemption from the southeast, leaving a large rise of dust behind it. When the horses came to a halt and the passenger compartment door swung open, Horace Meaker came running up out of nowhere and stood like an eager pup, his bowler hat in hand, waiting to assist Territorial Judge Cornell Shelby down from the coach. Sam shook his head, stepped off the boardwalk and over to the stage.

"Judge Shelby," said Meaker, reaching out a hand to the big white-haired man holding a walking cane with a silver lion's head for a handle. "I'm Councilman Horace Meaker, Your Honor. I'm the one who telegraphed you."

"Indeed," said the big burly judge. He examined Meaker's thin extended hand skeptically. He shook it briefly, then let it go. His attention went directly to the ranger. "Now, then, Ranger Burrack, tell me what kind of mess you have gotten yourself embroiled in here, young man."

"No mess at all, Your Honor," Sam said, respectfully. He took off his hat out of courtesy.

"Oh?" said Judge Shelby, peering around at Horace Meaker above the wire-rimmed spectacles perched on his thick nose, then back to the ranger. "I have it from Councilman Meaker here that you have shot and incarcerated a town councilman, turned loose a suspected murderer and killed an innocent man in the middle of the street! Perhaps I'm being a bit overly sensitive, Ranger. But, yes, I certainly do call that a mess!"

"Begging your pardon, Your Honor," said Sam, "I didn't mean to treat the matter lightly." The ranger saw that the judge had taken Councilman Meaker's allegations with a grain of salt. Giving Horace Meaker a harsh stare before replying to the judge's question, he said, "I shot a corrupt town councilman who tried to shoot me in the back because I had exposed him for what he is. I could have killed him, but I didn't. He's in a cell charged with assault and attempted murder of a lawman—namely *me*. I turned a man loose who was being falsely accused of killing Sheriff Dolan. That man was Henry Dove, Your Honor. The only reason I didn't turn him loose the day I got here was because I feared for his life. I had no legal right to hold him here."

"Henry Dove?" said the judge with a disbelieving look. "It so happens that I've known Henry Dove for years. That man is by no means a murderer." Again he looked at Meaker above his spectacles.

"Right, Your Honor," said Sam, continuing. "And the man I killed in the street was one of the Rio Sagrado Gang, a fellow named Bo Altero, who really was involved in Sheriff Dolan's death. I tried to take him in, he decided he'd rather die instead. I agreed with him."

"See, Judge Shelby?" said Meaker, pointing a slim

delicate finger for emphasis, "This ranger seems to think it's up to him who lives and dies!"

Sam cut a glance to Horace Meaker. "I deliberately kept myself from killing Councilman Avondale because I wanted to hear who else he might implicate after he spent a few days in a jail cell next to Giles Capp. I'm looking forward to seeing if your name is mentioned, Councilman."

Horace Meaker looked nervous all of a sudden.

"You did say Giles Capp, Ranger Burrack?" the judge said. "Not his older brother, Axel?" The judge looked surprised and troubled. The stage driver had stepped down, bringing the judge's worn leather valise with him and dropping it beside the judge. Horace Meaker leaned to pick it up, but Judge Shelby brushed him aside with his silver-tipped cane.

"No," said Sam, "but I expect to be hearing from Axel and the rest of the gang most anytime."

"I see," said the judge, his troubled look growing even more so, "and I expect your intentions are to arrest him for the outstanding murder charges against him?"

"That's right, Your Honor," said Sam.

"Then I have some bad but important news for you, Ranger," the judge said. "I'm afraid the murder charge against Axel Capp has been dropped."

"What?" The ranger looked shocked. "Axel is a stone-cold killer, Your Honor! Who did something like that?"

"I'm afraid I'm the one who dropped those old murder charges, Ranger," said Judge Shelby.

"But why?" Sam asked.

"I had no choice," said the judge. "Axel Capp hired the famous Chicago attorney, Burtrim Forbes. It appears Axel has learned to buy his way through the courts the same way he has been buying his way into local politics." He gave Meaker a look of disgust. But Meaker didn't seem to notice. The look on the councilman's face told Sam that his mind was working quickly.

"Maybe we'd better talk about this in private," said Sam.

The judge looked away from Meaker and back to the ranger. "Why? It is a matter of public record after all. Axel Capp is free of any and all charges against him in this territory. It's that simple."

"Any and *all* charges?" Sam asked.

"Well, of all charges in this territory, any that my court is aware of," said the judge.

"I see," said the ranger with resolve. "Then he can ride in here any time he feels like it, and there's nothing I can do about it?"

"There you have it, Ranger," said the judge. He looked off toward the hotel a block away. "Come, walk with me. We can discuss the charge you have against Giles Capp, and this Councilman Avondale as well." He turned to Councilman Meaker and said grudgingly, "If you wish to say anything on Councilman Avondale's behalf, you can join us."

"Uh . . . no thank you, Your Honor," said Meaker, suddenly seeming to have more pressing business to attend. "I'm sure we'll get an opportunity to talk more about it later." He backed away a step, nodded as a way of excusing himself, then turned and hurried away.

"What put him in such a hurry to get away from here?" asked the judge, stooping to pick up his valise.

Reaching down ahead of him and picking up the valise, Sam said, "I expect he can't wait to get the word to Axel Capp that he's free to come here and do as he pleases, Your Honor."

"Oh, I see . . ." said the judge. He gave the ranger a knowing look.

The ranger nodded with a trace of a smile. "I get the idea you knew that all along, Your Honor."

"Don't ever think I enjoy turning these killers loose, Ranger," said the judge, ambling along using his lion-head cane. "But like you, I must abide by the law, chapter and verse."

"I understand, Your Honor," said Sam. "The only difference those murder charges being dropped will make is the way Axel Capp comes to town. He's not going to stand for his brother hanging for the murder of Sheriff Dolan, no matter what."

Judge Shelby shook his head slowly, the troubled look coming back to his brow. "I trust you will have sufficient proof of this murder charge, Ranger?" he said.

"I have an eyewitness," said Sam, "a saloon owner who saw the whole thing."

"Then you better see to it he stays alive for the trial," said the judge, shaking his head again in dark contemplation.

"Don't worry, Your Honor. I'm not going to let anything happen to him," said the ranger.

"That might be easier said than done, even for you, Ranger," the judge said as they walked along the street. He looked around in both directions, noting that the boardwalk along the Even Odds Saloon was not crowded with drinkers and that the big wooden star out front of the sheriff's office had been repaired. He smiled in satisfaction at how peaceful Redemption had become. "Although, I have to admit you've done a remarkable job here."

"I had help, Your Honor," said the ranger, nodding toward Sheriff Watts and Julie Ann Dolan, who walked toward them from the sheriff's office. "The new sheriff here was appointed by Avondale. But instead of turning out to be a puppet for the outlaws, he's put himself into the job, learning to be a good lawman."

"Oh?" Judge Shelby looked Sam up and down. "Then I'm sure you played a hand it that too."

Sam said, "There had to be some good in him for it to ever come out." He didn't mention the incident involving the money he'd taken off of Henry Dove. Watts had made it right as far as he was concerned.

When Watts and Julie Ann came up to them, the ranger introduced them both to the judge. Judge Shelby tipped his hat to Julie Ann. Turning to shake Watts' hand, he said in his gruff voice, "Ranger Burrack has said some good things about you, Sheriff. I hope you'll stand good for it."

Watts nodded modestly. "I'll sure try my best, Judge." He gave Sam a look of gratitude as the four began walking toward the hotel.

"And you, young lady," the judge said to Julie Ann, "I'm terribly sorry about what happened to your father. But now I think it's time you get out of here and go on with your life, don't you?"

"I'll be staying until I see my father's murderers hang," Julie Ann said firmly.

"That's understandable," said the judge. "I must warn you, though, watching a man hang is not a pleasant thing."

"I'm aware of that, Judge Shelby," Julie Ann said firmly, "but nevertheless, I'm going to do it."

Shooting Watts a glance, the judge asked, "Sheriff,

you are a bachelor, I trust, the same as Ranger Burrack?"

The three paused silently for a moment, surprised at Judge Shelby asking such a question. Finally Watts stammered, "Well, I—that is, yes, I am a bachelor. Why do you ask, Judge?"

"Just curious." Judge Shelby smiled, staring toward the hotel as they walked on. Dismissing the subject, the judge reached into his loose-fitting coat with his free hand, pulled out a folded piece of paper and handed it to Watts. "I've already given Ranger Burrack the bad news. Here, you can read it for yourself."

Watts read silently for a moment, then stopped cold when he got to the part that said all charges against Axel Capp had been dropped by a higher court. "How can this be, Ranger?" Watts asked, waving the paper slightly. "He never even went to court, stood trial or nothing else?"

Answering for the ranger, Judge Shelby said, "He didn't have to, Sheriff. He had an attorney appear for him. He'd never been arrested on the charge. He lives outside the United States." The judge tossed his free hand in disgust. "It's all perfectly legal, I assure you." The judge and Julie Ann continued on toward the hotel. But Sam and Watts stood for a moment longer.

Scratching his head, Watts said, "I swear, Ranger, there's times I look at how the law works and wonder what it is I've gotten myself into, trying to uphold it." He gave Sam a strange puzzled look. "Don't you ever wonder the same thing?"

Sam offered a tired half smile. "Only when I let myself think too much about it." He nodded at the piece of paper in Watts' hand. "That court order only means something to folks like us and the judge. All it means to Axel Capp is that he got a chance to thumb his nose at the law one more time. It's not as if he'll see he's free of these charges then quit breaking the law, and never have to pay for the things he's done. He'll go right on until either the noose goes around his neck or somebody puts a bullet in him. Don't let the paperwork bother you."

"He'll still come here looking for his brother?" said Watts.

"Yep," said Sam. "And my hunch is, he's not going to wait around to see his brother go to trial."

"He'll try to break him out?" Watts asked.

"He'll try," said Sam, walking on toward the hotel behind Julie Ann and the judge.

In the shadows at the edge of an alley across the street, Meaker stood back behind Danny Boy Wright and Snake Bentell, who stared secretively at the ranger and Sheriff Watts. "Whatever the sheriff was reading sure wasn't making him very happy," said Snake.

"See?" said Meaker, eagerly, "that's probably the court decree! I'm telling you I heard it straight from the judge's mouth! He said the murder charges against Axel Capp are dropped! Gone! Finished!" Meaker waved his hands back and forth in his excitement. "I just came from the saloon. You should have seen Swain's face when I gave him the news!"

"Try to hold your water, Councilman," said Danny Boy, watching Meaker's wild antics. "What's got you so froggy anyway? You used to creep around like a damn mouse."

"My friend and political associate, Willis Avondale, is in a legal bind. I'm doing what any man would do for a friend! I'm looking for help! If it comes from Axel Capp riding in and shooting that pesky lawman, so be it."

"Hear that?"—Snake grinned at Danny Boy. "He called the ranger *pesky.*"

"Yeah, I heard it," said Danny Boy. Dismissing Snake's idea of humor, he said to Meaker, "We're both ready to ride out of here and let Axel know what's going on." He pointed a finger into the councilman's chest. "But you're going to have to get us some guns and ammunition. We can't ride through the badlands to the border unarmed."

"All right, I'll get you both some firearms," said Meaker, trying to get the two gunmen to hurry. "Meanwhile, go get your horses and meet me back here in half an hour!"

From the boardwalk in front of the hotel, the ranger caught a glimpse of Danny Boy and Snake Bentell as they stepped out of the alley and headed for the livery barn. He also saw Horace Meaker head quickly toward the mercantile store. Putting two and two together, he said idly to Sheriff Watts, "It looks like the news of Axel Capp's good fortune is about to come bounding to him."

Sheriff Watts looked at the two outlaws hurrying to the livery barn. "Want me to stop them, find a reason to hold them here?"

"No, let them go," said the ranger, giving Judge Shelby a knowing glance. "It's time those two got out of town anyway. They've stayed out of trouble about as long as they can stand." He looked at Julie Ann and Watts and added, "I better go talk to Swain, make sure he don't cave over Axel Capp being free to come and go as he pleases."

Chapter 21

For two days Axel Capp and his gang had been plagued by Doc Cain and the long-range rifle. In the night hours as Axel had led his men and wagon across a stretch of badlands and across the border, Millard Trent had made the mistake of rolling a smoke and striking a match in the darkness. No sooner than Axel heard the flare of the match, he'd said over his shoulder, "Put that fire out!" But his warning came too late. A shot ripped through Trent's back and sent him tumbling forward out of his saddle.

"Damn it, Trent!" said Axel as he and Denton Spears both dropped to the ground and crawled quickly over to the fallen outlaw. "He almost gut-shot you day before yesterday! Didn't you learn anything?"

Trent groaned and said in a broken voice, "I reckon not."

"I can patch him up some and put him up on the wagon till we can get him some help," said Spears.

"What help?" said Axel. "He's done for, and we know it." He looked down at Trent, saying, "You know that too, don't you, Millard?"

"I figured . . . as much," Trent gasped.

"Patch him up then," Axel said to Spears, knowing

it would look bad to the rest of the men if he left one of them lying wounded and dying, "but don't put him in the wagon. We've got to keep the weight low on them team horses."

"He can't sit in a saddle," said Spears.

"Yes he can, can't you, Trent?" Axel asked the wounded man.

"Hell, yes, I can ride," Trent said in a failing voice.

Axel patted Trent's shoulder, then said to Spears, "Get him moved a few yards before you do anything. We've got to get out of Doc's gun sight. We're across the border now. They'll be wanting to make their move on us at any time."

The gang hurriedly moved farther along the thin trail. Fifty yards away, they found a place for Spears and Ace Tinsdale to attend to Trent's gaping wound. Then they helped the dying man atop his saddle and moved out, Axel Capp wanting to put as much distance as he could between them and the deadly buffalo rifle. As daylight streaked on the horizon, Axel brought the men to a halt once again and looked back at the long stretch of flatlands behind them.

"All right, men," said Axel. "Here's where we're going to lose them. Now that we're heading into some rock country, that buffalo rifle's worth a lot less to him than it was on the flats." He nodded at two towering stands of rock at the base of the rocky hills in front of them to the right of the trail. He said to Ace Tinsdale and Dallas Ryan, "Ace, you and Dallas get up there with your repeaters. Stay up there till you force them to go around. It'll take them all day, and it'll give us time to cut off the main trail into another direction. They'll never pick our trail back up agin."

"Where are we going to meet back up with yas?" Ryan asked. He and Tinsdale were already prepared to spring forward and climb the rough terrain to find themselves a shooting position.

"We'll be at the old Cub Sanders Mine site. We're going to rest there before we push on into to Redemption."

Before the two men turned to ride off to the right and disappear onto a thinner path leading to the stand of rock, Axel stopped them with a raised hand, saying, "Hold it!"

All the men turned their attention to the sound of horses coming toward them down the hill trail at a steady pace. Guns came up quickly, cocked and ready. But Axel's raised hand halted any action as he recognized Snake Bentell and Danny Boy Wright hurrying along, waving their hats in the morning light.

"Axel! It's us! Don't shoot!" shouted Snake.

"Hold your fire, men," Axel said quietly.

Moments later, Snake and Danny Boy brought their tired horses to a halt in front of Axel, Snake wiping his shirtsleeve across his forehead. "Damn, we sure are glad to see you, Axel," Snake said. "We rode most of yesterday and all last night!"

"All right, Snake," said Axel, impatiently, "you found us. Now, out with it!"

Danny Boy's eyes searched back and forth along the wagon, the mounted Gatling gun and the tarpaulin-covered load until they stopped on Spears' threatening expression looking back at him.

Snake said, "Your brother, Giles, is in jail, charged with murdering Sheriff Dolan! Andrew Swain jackpotted him for it!"

"Damn it!" said Axel. "What about Avondale? That sonsabitch is supposed to be keeping things like this from happening! What about that sheriff he hired? Floose said he'd turned hardheaded. Did he ever come around to our thinking?"

"Hell, no," said Snake, "the new sheriff never did come around. He's even gotten worse, hanging around with that ranger! And Avondale's got himself thrown in jail too!" said Snake, "for trying to kill the ranger!"

Axel gave Charlie Floose a look. Floose shrugged. "See? It's gotten worse since I left."

Axel looked back across the flatlands toward Mexico. "Well, I've worn out my welcome in Old Mex. Looks like the territory is going to have to get used to us being around here for a while. "Looks like I'm going to have to kill Swain, bust my brother out of jail and take care of this ranger in the meantime."

"But that ain't all," said Snake. "Here's some good news for you. The territorial judge arrived in Redemption and said you've been cleared of them old murder charges."

It took a second for Axel to realize what Snake had said. Finally he chuckled and said in a bemused tone, "Ain't that something? I'd been thinking about riding to Yuma, get my money back from that attorney and shooting some holes in him. Now he's come through and got my charges dismissed." He laughed out loud; the others joined in, laughing with him.

"We knew you'd want to hear that straightaway," said Snake. "So Danny and me hightailed it toward Mexico, not knowing where we'd meet up with you along here!" He grinned widely.

But as Snake had spoken, Axel had taken the time to note the guns in the two men's holsters. Snake carried a short, rusty, single-shot small caliber rodent pistol. Danny Boy carried a fancy, pearl-handled gentleman's pocket revolver. Both were guns that Councilman Meaker had picked up for them.

"Don't try getting too friendly with me," Axel said flatly to them. "Floose told me how you let that ranger take your shooting irons."

"Axel, we never *let* him have our guns," said Snake. "The fact is, this ranger ain't like nothing we've ever seen. Danny Boy thinks he's a spook of some sort, and damned if I ain't started to believe it myself!"

Axel rested his hand on his pistol butt and said, "Snake, I ever hear you say something like that again, I'll have to kill you. Do you understand me?"

Snake's face reddened. "I understand," he said quietly.

Axel nodded at the guns on their hips. "I won't ask where you got these guns, because I don't want to hear what you're liable to tell me." He nodded forward. "Get up there in front of me with Floose, see if he's got any shooting gear he can lend you."

"I'm all lent out," said Floose, looking back at them from where he rode in front of the wagon.

"Well," said Axel, "it looks like the first thing when we get to town, you two are going to get your guns back from that ranger." He looked at Ace Tinsdale and Dallas Ryan and said firmly, "Well, what are you waiting for?"

"Nothing, Axel, we're gone," said Tinsdale. The two turned their horses again and rode away at a gallop.

Danny Boy and Snake looked at one another, not liking the idea of having to face the ranger again. But they kept silent, nodded and moved to the front of the wagon. Sidling up to Floose, Snake asked in a whisper as he gestured toward the wagon, "What's under the tarp, Charlie?"

"Gold," Floose said matter-of-factly, giving the two another shrug.

"Gold?" Danny Boy whispered in awe.

As Axel rode forward, Spears asked from his driving seat alongside him, "You ain't going to go riding right into town, bold as brass, are you?"

"You better believe I am," said Axel. "I was going to ride in before, when I was wanted for murder . . . so you can bet there ain't a damn thing going to keep me out now."

"What about Giles?" asked Spears. "Are we going to bust him out of jail?"

"Bust him out? Hell, no." Axel grinned. "I'm going to walk in, take the cell key and open the door for him." He gave Spears a flat stare and added, "That is, after I step over that ranger's dead carcass in the middle of the street."

Beside Floose, Danny Boy looked over at Millard Trent, who rode leaning dangerously forward in his saddle, bowed at the waist, his back and chest covered with bloody makeshift bandages. "What happened to Trent?" Danny Boy asked in a whisper.

"Doc Cain shot him," Floose said bluntly, staring straight ahead.

"Doc Cain?" said Danny Boy, looking surprised.

"Yeah," said Floose, "he's an old gunman Axel dragged in to help us out on a robbery."

"I *know* who he is," said Danny Boy.

"Danny Boy knows everything about every gunman who ever lived," said Snake Bentell in a sarcastic tone. "Don't get him started on it."

Danny Boy ignored his remark. "I never thought I'd hear that Doc Cain was riding with us! The fact is, I thought he died years ago."

"I bet Trent wishes to hell he was," said Floose. "He's also killed Joe Murphy."

"Jesus," whispered Danny Boy. "What's been going

on in old Mex?" As he spoke his eyes went back to the tarpaulin-covered stack of gold in the wagon and to the Gatling gun standing loaded and ready behind it.

"It's a long story," Floose grinned, still staring ahead.

"I've got all day," said Danny Boy, still eyeing the stack of gold in the wagon bed.

On their high perches atop the tall stone buttes overlooking the trail, Dallas Ryan and Ace Tinsdale watched the rise of dust grow closer across the flat-lands in from the direction of the border. "Not to complain," said Ryan, "but if I'd been Axel, I think I might have done things a little different. I don't be-lieve I would have jackpotted a man like Doc Cain. It ain't right treating a man that way, no matter how you look at it."

"It ain't right, but it's done," said Ace Tinsdale. "And it's too damn late for how you or I might have done things. Axel is the boss." He adjusted the sight on his repeater rifle as he stared out at the two oncom-ing riders.

On the flat sandy trail over a mile away, Doc Cain's eyes went to the stand of rock in the distance where the trail turned up into the rugged hills. "We'll have company waiting for us up there," he said.

"Want to circle wide of the trail?" asked Bobby Combs. "We can pick it up later."

"No we can't," said Doc, "not for another forty miles or more. This is the place where you can give a man the slip even if you're leaving wagon tracks two yards wide. There's dozens of smaller trails leading off between here and where we'd get back on. We don't have time to check every one of them after we waste a day circling." As he spoke he drew his horse down to a slower pace, glancing at the rising sun in the east as if judging its upward climb in the early morning sky.

"Then what do you want to do?" Combs asked. "Just charge in and hope for the best?"

"Yep." Doc offered a thin smile. "But we're going to do it with the sun on our side." He nodded up toward the east. "If we slow down now and time it just right, that sun will walk us right up that trail past them, while it blinds anybody trying to draw a bead on us."

Combs looked at him and said, "It sounds like you've been here before, Doc."

"I've been everywhere before," Doc replied.

Stopping for a while as if to rest their horses, the two stalled and waited until a brilliant beam of light broke over the eastern horizon. They stepped back into their saddles and moved forward with deliberation, watching the sunlight grow more and more intense on their right. Finally when they'd reached a distance of less than two hundred yards from where the trail swung upward between the two towering rock buttes, Doc jerked his hat from his head and shouted, "All right, give it hell!" Slapping the horse's rump as he hammered his boot heels to its sides.

Atop the butte on the left of the trail, Ace Tinsdale rubbed his eyes and said, "Damn, here they come running, and I can't see squat!"

Dallas Ryan craned his neck and visored his hand to the left side of his face, squinting against the sun glare. "This Doc Cain is a lot smarter than Axel Capp figured him to be." Lifting his rifle, then coming up off of his belly into a crouch, he added, "While I still got time, I'm getting over on that other butte!"

"You're just cutting out on me?" Ace Tinsdale asked.

"What did I just say, Ace?" said Ryan. "I never cut out on nobody in my life. The way the sun's coming, if I stay here we'll be lucky we don't shoot ourselves!"

"I've got a feeling Doc Cain knew it," said Ace, trying to focus on the two fast approaching figures in the glittering sunlight."

"Well, no shit!" Ryan said sarcastically. "You just now figuring that out?" Dusting his knees, he moved away across the narrow butte to the thin footpath that meandered down to where they'd tied their horses. When he'd reached the horses, he heard the first shots resound in from less than a hundred yards away. He shook his head when he heard Ace Tinsdale's rifle return fire wildly, knowing Ace couldn't see a thing.

"Stupid sumbitch," Ryan said to himself. He untied the horses, stepped into his saddle and rode away, leading Tinsdale's horse by its reins. "Ain't no need in you waiting for him," he said to the horse over his shoulder.

On top of the butte, Ace Tinsdale had ducked down close to the ground as bullets sliced the air over his head. His eyes watered from the intense sunlight. "Jesus!" he said, "how the hell did I let myself get talked into this?"

He managed to squint and take a quick peep down as Doc Cain and Bobby Combs streaked inside the shelter of the butte, giving up the sunlight, but no longer needing it now that Tinsdale couldn't get a shot straight down at them. The firing stopped, and Tinsdale looked across at the empty butte across the trail where Dallas Ryan was supposed to be. "Aw hell . . ." he sighed, realizing he'd been abandoned. "Ryan, you low-down, dirty bastard."

In the deafening silence beneath a whir of desert wind, Tinsdale scooted around on his belly until his position faced toward the spot where the footpath came up onto the flat top of the butte. Moments passed as he lay still and visualized the two men creeping up on foot. Finally a voice called out from just beneath the rocky edge, "Your pal is gone, horses and all!"

"Doc Cain, is that you?" said Tinsdale.

"Yep, it's me and Combs," said the old gunman.

"I've sure gotten myself in a spot, ain't I?" Tinsdale tried to chuckle.

"That you have," said Doc.

A silence passed, then Tinsdale said, "Is killing me the only way you'll have this thing turn out, Doc?"

"How else can you see it?" Doc asked.

"Well . . . I'm afoot, lightly armed," said Tinsdale. "I can't see myself being much of a threat to you."

"Yeah, so?" said Doc.

"Come on, Doc, don't make me beg you," said Tinsdale. "Let me walk out of here . . . what do you say?"

Without asking Combs anything, Doc waited for a moment then said, "I said yes, but Bobby here says no way in hell. Not after the way you boys lied to us, mislead us, tried to get us killed. Bobby thinks you're going to have to die for it."

"Hell's fire, Bobby," said Tinsdale. "You ought to know that was all Axel's doings. I didn't even know he was going to use you new men as decoys until it was too late to stop it! Now, that's the damned truth! Far as I was concerned, there was enough gold to go around!"

"Where's Axel headed with that gold?" Combs called out.

"If I tell you, are you still dead-set on killing me?" Tinsdale asked, his voice taking on a bartering tone.

"The way it stands right now, you've got nothing to lose, everything to gain," Combs said firmly.

"All right," said Tinsdale, "let me come down off this butte before it turns into a furnace. I'll tell you everything I heard them say before they left here."

"Lay your guns down there, Tinsdale," said Doc Cain. "They'll be waiting for you if you climb back up."

Ace Tinsdale let out a relieved breath and let his rifle lay on the ground. He lifted his pistol from his holster and laid it beside the rifle. "I'm coming over," he said, rising to his feet with his hands in the air. "To hell with Axel Capp and his crazy brother."

Chapter 22

Doc Cain and Bobby Combs sat atop their horses with their wrists crossed and watched Ace Tinsdale begin his climb back up the side of the butte to where he'd left his guns. "I don't know if I can recall a time when any one man told me that much without stopping to rest awhile," said Doc.

Combs smiled slightly and said, "He told everything but his ma's birth date. I was about ready to tell him to shut up."

Doc nodded. "Bobby, I've got a good feeling about this gold. I've got a hunch we're going to get every last bar of it, just you and me."

"Have you ever had a hunch like that before?" Bobby asked.

Doc Cain's brow clouded. "Sure I have. But this time I believe it's going to work out. I can damned near feel myself running my hands across that German gold."

"Good," said Bobby. "Here's hoping your hunch is right." He watched Tinsdale disappear from sight. "What about this Ranger Burrack? I've heard of him . . . he's not known as a light piece of work. Look what he done to Junior Lake and his gang."

"I know all about it," said Doc. "Seems like I've been hearing about a lot of ole boys like us running *into* this ranger, but I never hear of any of us getting *past* him."

"Same here," said Combs. "Maybe we'd do better going right to the hills around the Cub Sanders Mine and take our chances finding where the gold is hidden."

"Hu-uh," said Doc. "There's too many blind spots and twists and turns in that area. It could be a setup at best. Besides, I've lived too long to start chasing hidden gold. Now that we know what's of interest to Axel Capp, let's make this game a little easier on ourselves." He grinned. "While they're busy hiding that gold, I say we go to Redemption, get our hands on Axel's brother and stand him before Axel with a gun to his head. That ought to get Axel's undivided attention."

"Make him bring the gold to us," Bobby said, pondering it for a moment."

"Something like that," said Doc, straightening in his saddle and turning his horse to the trail.

Turning his horse right beside him, Bobby said, "We're still going to be stepping up against that ranger."

"I know," said Doc, "that's the part that bothers me. I ain't ashamed to admit when facing a man troubles me, and facing that ranger troubles me something awful."

Bobby Combs nodded in agreement. "All right, then, what do you say?"

Doc took a breath and said with resolve, "I say if we ride hard, we'll be in Redemption by nightfall." He batted his heels to his horse and sent it upward along the rocky trail.

Twelve miles ahead of Doc and Combs, Axel stood high in his stirrups and looked back down the winding trail while the wagon and the men turned onto a steeper trail, the surface of which consisted of flat, smooth solid rock. "I didn't hear enough shooting back there to suit me," he said to Charlie Floose, who sat his horse only a few feet away, already wetting his bandanna from a canteen. He wrapped the cool wet bandanna around his neck against the rising morning heat.

"Maybe Ace and Dallas blasted them as soon as they got into range," said Floose.

"Yeah, maybe," said Axel, "but I don't think so." He sat quietly for a moment, contemplating. Floose wasn't at all surprised when Axel said, "Ride back down there and see if you spot anybody coming up on this side of the buttes."

Floose just looked at him for a second, then said with a puff of a breath, "Whatever you say, Axel." He reined his horse roughly around and started down the steep trail they'd just climbed. But before he'd gone ten feet, he spotted the rise of dust climbing into the air off of the trail below. "Axel! Here comes horses now!"

"Tinsdale and Ryan?" asked Axel Capp.

Standing high in his stirrups, Floose searched the trail until he caught a glimpse of Ryan leading Tinsdale's horse through a clear·spot in the rocks along the trail. "Naw, bad news," said Floose. "Looks like Ace won't be joining us. Ryan's bringing his horse in."

"Damn it," said Axel, but then he settled and almost smiled to himself, realizing there would be one less person to share the German gold with. "Well, I suppose that was why the firing didn't last long." He rode over beside Floose and said, "Wait here for him.

Then both of yas check the trail behind you before you come up and join us."

"What if we can't find you, Axel?" said Floose. "Those hills around the mining country can get a man lost really quick."

"Hell's fire, Floose!" said Axel, getting impatient with him. "It won't be but just a few minutes! Don't you trust all of us that far?" His hand rested on his holstered Colt.

"Sure I trust you, Axel," said Floose. "I just meant that that country is easy to get lost in!"

"Well, you and Ryan try real hard, Floose," said Axel with a critical scowl. "If you get lost, raise your noses in the air and sniff for gold." He jerked his reins and rode away.

Floose became skittish as soon as the silence set in around him. So when Ryan topped a rise in the trail and saw him, Floose raised his hat and waved it vigorously. The suddenness of coming upon Floose almost caused Ryan to rear his horse up in surprise. "Jesus, Floose! Let somebody know you're around!" he snapped.

"I did," Floose snapped right back, "that's why I waved my hat."

"Well, I don't like to be sprung upon that way," Ryan said, not letting it go.

"What happened to Ace?" Floose asked, looking the spare horse up and down.

"Them sonsabitches killed him," said Ryan, putting on a face of remorse. "We fought them to a standstill, me and ole Ace. But they got lucky . . . shot him dead."

"You brought his horse along?" Floose asked, for no particular reason.

"Yes, I did," Ryan replied indignantly. "What of it?"

"Nothing, Dallas, damn!" said Floose. "I was just commenting about it."

"Are the others far ahead?" Ryan asked, looking off along the upward trail.

"Not far," said Floose, the two of them turning their horses and moving along, looking back over their shoulders. "Axel and I saw you leading Tinsdale's horse up the trail. He left me to wait for you."

"Is he riled about me coming on alone?" asked Ryan.

"That's a peculiar thing to ask," said Floose. "Why would he be?"

"I don't know." Ryan shrugged. "I thought I'd ask."

"Then you better ask him for yourself soon as we catch up to him," said Floose. "I don't like getting too far away from that gold."

"Neither do I," said Ryan, giving his horse a nudge.

Within moments they had caught up with Axel and the others, the team horses laboring slowly with their heavy load. As soon as Dallas Ryan reined in beside Axel Capp, he started telling him about the gunfight and how Tinsdale had fallen beneath a hail of bullets. But to Ryan's relief, Axel didn't seem too interested in hearing it right then.

Instead he said, "Save it for later, Ryan. We've got a stiff ride ahead of us." He did look back along the trail and say, "Did you two at least slow them down any?"

"Sure we did," said Ryan. "I can't swear to it, but I believe I got one of their horses."

"One of their horses, eh?" said Axel. "Good work."

He nudged his horse away from him, leaving Ryan to wonder if he meant it or if he was being sarcastic. They pushed on.

It was mid-afternoon when they saw the black-streaked hills surrounding the long abandoned Cub Sanders mining project. Before riding down the switchback trail to what looked like an endless row of boarded-up mine shaft entrances, Axel called the men in around him.

"Men," he ordered, "just so nobody tries to pull any double-crosses or goes around thinking anybody else is about to, here's the way we're going to do things." He looked around to make sure everybody saw his serious expression. "Before we split up that gold, we're going into Redemption and take care of business. I'm taking that ranger down, and I want everybody here helping me doing it. We're sticking this wagon down into a mine shaft and hiding it good and proper. Then we're boarding the shaft back up, sweeping away our tracks and taking the team horses with us when we go to town. Even if somebody found that gold, they can't take it without a team of horses to pull the wagon."

"I'm staying here with the gold, and the Gatling gun to protect it," said Denton Spears, looking all around.

"Just so you don't go wondering if Denton might get tempted here by himself with all the gold," said Axel. "We're leaving him provisions for a couple of days, but we're taking *his* horse with us too. Anybody got any questions?"

The men looked at one another, satisfied with the plan. Even if they weren't, there was nothing that could be said about it. Axel wasn't about to split up the gold before he got Giles out of jail, for fear that once the men had their share they might ride off without joining him against the ranger.

But Dallas Ryan did venture forward and ask, "What if Doc and Combs shows up here?"

"I thought you said you shot one of their horses?" Axel snapped at him.

"Well, I'm pretty sure I did," said Ryan, "but suppose I'm wrong?"

Axel gave him a dark gaze. "If Doc and Combs could happen to know where we were headed and happened to show up, I think that Gatling gun would trim their toenails real good. What do you think, Denton?"

Spears said, "I think they had us pressed out there with that long range rifle, but we're on my terms here . . . with that big gun ready to start bucking."

"Besides," said Axel, "if Doc is still on our trail, we ought to know it by nightfall. We're going on into the mining project, get a good night of food and rest. Come morning, we're heading into Redemption, see about bagging ourselves a ranger."

It was after dark when Doc Cain and Bobby Combs rode into town from a narrow side street, their wet horses frothed and streaked with sweat and sand. Even though the main street was empty, they deliberately avoided it and rode along the alleyway behind the jail, looking the back door over closely. "It's been a long time since I pulled a jailbreak," Doc said in a lowered tone. "What about you?"

"I've never pulled one, Doc," Combs whispered in reply. "But it's never looked all that difficult to me."

"You're right, it's not." Doc nodded and smiled slightly, liking Combs' game attitude. "Bobby, I wish you'd been around twenty years ago. We'd both been out of robbing and owning railroads by now."

"It's not too late yet, Doc," Bobby said. "Once we get our gold we might buy us a railroad, have us a railcar custom built."

They rode on in silence to the livery barn, where Doc stayed back in the shadows while Combs slipped inside through a back door and came out moments later leading three fresh horses, each of them saddled and ready for the road.

"How hard did you hit him?" Doc asked, stepping down from his tired horse.

"Not too hard," said Combs. "I figure ten, fifteen minutes he'll be come staggering out to the sheriff's office."

"We best hurry," said Doc. He untied his saddle boot and dropped his saddle in the dirt. He slipped the bit from his horse's mouth and dropped the bridle to the ground as well. He gave a halfhearted slap across the horse's rump. The tired animal bolted away, but only a few feet before stopping and turning toward a water trough beside the livery corral.

Combs had already dropped the saddle and bridle from his tired horse and sat atop a big bay waiting for him, holding the reins to a big dun and a powerful-looking silver-gray standing beside him. Doc tied his saddle boot into place, shoved the buffalo gun into it and took the reins to the dun.

"I never like doing anything on an untried horse," Doc said quietly, stepping up into the saddle.

"Neither do I," said Combs, "but I don't see that we've got much choice. These three were the only horses in the barn. It's either these or hitch rail horses. The hitch rails looked a little slim coming in."

They turned the three horses and trotted them as

quietly as possible along the same direction they'd taken into town. When they got to the main trail where their hoofprints disappeared into a thousand others, they turned back to Redemption, cut wide of the main trail and came in from the other end of town. They put their horses at a walk along the dark shadows behind the main street then stopped in an alley where they could see the soft glow of a lamp in the window of the sheriff's office.

"Now all we can do is wait," said Doc, almost to himself. Five minutes later he broke the tense silence, asking, "How hard did you say you hit him?"

"Not that hard, Doc," said Combs, looking a little curious himself about what was taking so long.

But even as they stared at one another, wondering in the darkness, they heard a groaning voice across the street and looked over at the wobbly figure walking unevenly toward the sheriff's office. "Help!" the voice of the old livery hostler bleated. "I've been robbed! Help! Sheriff!"

"It's about time," Doc whispered, pulling his fresh horse back a step, seeing the lamp in the office window glow brighter.

At the door of the sheriff's office, the hostler knocked loudly. Having already heard the old man calling out to him, Watts opened the door and the old hostler almost fell into his arms. "Earl, what's happened?" Watts asked, helping the old man to a chair.

A block away, in the parlor of the hotel where Sam had sat talking quietly with Julie Ann Dolan, he'd heard the sound of Earl Piercy's voice and stood up from the small two-party sofa. "I've got to go," he said, snatching his gun belt from a chair back next to the sofa and buckling it around his waist quickly.

Julie Ann stood up beside him. "I understand," she

said. "It seems we're never going to get a chance to be together."

"We will, I promise," Sam said, tying his holster down deftly, turning, grabbing his sombrero from the chair seat. "You stay here, there might be trouble."

"Trouble or not, I'm coming," said Julie Ann, hurrying along behind him, out the door and to the sheriff's office.

Across the street in the alley, Combs murmured in the darkness, "There he goes."

Doc whispered, "You figure that's the ranger?"

"One of them is. Either this one is or the one who opened the door," Combs replied. Making a pistol with his hand, he pointed his finger at the running figures along the boardwalk and said, softly, "Bang."

Chapter 23

"We can't both go after them," said Sam, looking up from the saddles and bridles lying on the ground. He looked both directions in the darkness. He rolled one of the wet saddles over with the toe of his boot, studying it. Then he looked Watts up and down, saw his mussed hair and his shirttail hanging out of his trousers, and said, "I was still up anyway."

"I feel like I ought to be the one to have to go, Sam," said Watts. "It's my job to go more so than yours. This is a town sheriff's work, not a ranger's."

"Guarding prisoners is a town sheriff's work too," said Sam, turning back toward the hotel, where he'd left his horse tied to a hitch ring in the rear stable area.

As the ranger walked out of sight, Watts turned to Julie Ann and, seeing her fold her arms across herself and sigh quietly, he said, "I'm awfully sorry, Miss Julie. I know the two of you wanted to be alone."

Julie Ann looked a little embarrassed and said, "No, please don't apologize. It isn't your fault, Sheriff Watts." She looked down at the ground, the discarded saddles, the hoofprints leading off into the darkness. "My father being a sheriff, I grew up expecting this sort of thing. I'm accustomed to accepting disrupted plans." She smiled. "Now, if you'll excuse me." She turned quietly and walked back toward the hotel. On the main street she caught a glimpse of the ranger riding out of sight in the direction of the prints. She sighed and said to herself, "Julie Ann Dolan, are you sure you want another lawman in your life?" She smiled to herself and shook her head slowly.

Watching her idly from the alley across the street, Doc whispered to Combs as the ranger rode away, "And that's how easy it is, Bobby. We must be living right."

"I'm sure of it," Combs said, smiling. They sat quietly for a moment watching Julie Ann walk up onto the porch in front of the hotel and through the door.

"Let's get it done," said Doc, backing his horse deeper into the darkness and turning it around in the alley. The two rode quietly but quickly along the back of businesses, leading the third horse behind them. Reaching a darker spot where they crossed the street unseen, they followed another alley to the rear door of the sheriff's office.

"Do you think that was the ranger who rode out of here?" Combs asked.

"Odds are, yes, it was him," Doc Cain whispered in reply. "But I suppose it doesn't make a lot of difference right now. We're bringing Giles Capp out of there no matter who's guarding him."

They stepped down, tied the horses to a telegraph pole and walked to the rear door of the sheriff's office. Lifting his Colt from his holster, Doc Cain whispered to Combs, "Go around front, get ready." He watched Combs disappear around the corner of the building, then he knocked quietly on the wooden door.

From within the jail, Watts asked, "Who's there?"

Doc mumbled something under his breath, just loud enough to be heard but not understood.

"What?" Watts asked, his voice sounding closer to the door, Doc even hearing his boots walking across the floor toward him.

Doc mumbled something again.

"I can't understand a word you're saying," came Watt's reply through the door. "Speak up!"

Doc Cain emptied his Colt into the middle of the door and stepped back, checking in both directions while he hurriedly reloaded and waited for Bobby Combs. He heard Combs' boots running across the floor. Within another second, Combs lifted the latch and swung the door open. Doc looked down as he stepped over Watts, who lay gasping for breath on the floor, his chest covered with blood.

"Hurry it up, Bobby," he said. "Everybody for five miles around heard all that shooting."

Giles Capp saw the two men and began immediately pulling his boots on. "Axel sent yas, right?" he said from his cell.

"That's right," said Doc. "we're here to get you out."

As he spoke to Giles, Combs ran to the wall where the key to the cells hung by a brass ring. He grabbed the ring and hurried over to Giles' cell.

In the next cell, Willis Avondale only sat on the side of his cot looking stunned. But Crazy Man Lewis hurriedly pulled on his boots and stepped over to his cell door. He watched with a slight smile of anticipation. But when Giles came out of his cell and no one turned to open Lewis' cell door, Lewis rattled it and said, "Hey, what about me?"

Doc gave him a look, saying, "Sorry, nobody mentioned you in this deal."

"Hey, Giles, what the hell?" said Lewis, rattling the cell door again.

"He's with me, let him out," said Giles, starting to take a step toward the gun cabinet.

Bobby Combs blocked his way and gave him a nudge toward the rear door. "Get going, Giles, the whole town is up and coming by now!"

Giles gave Crazy Man a sheepish look on his way to the bullet-riddled rear door.

"Giles, Gawdamn it!" shouted Lewis. He shook the iron door violently.

"Let him out," said Giles, taking a stand. "I don't want him doffing me for leaving him here!"

Doc and Combs looked at one another. "All right, I'll let him out. Keep moving."

Doc snatched the brass ring from Bobby's hand and pitched it to Lewis' outstretched hand as Bobby gave Giles a shove out the back door. Doc hurried out behind them, seeing the brass ring fly through the air.

"Damn it to hell!" shouted Lewis, missing the brass ring, grasping wildly for it as it hit the iron bars and bounced away from the cell onto the wooden floor. He dropped down flat onto his stomach and stretched his arm out through the bars toward the key ring. It was less than an inch past the tips of his struggling fingers. "Giles, you son of a bitch! I'll kill you!" Lewis shouted.

Climbing atop the waiting horse, Giles asked, "What did he say?"

"Never mind!" said Doc Cain, nodding toward the sound of townsfolk shouting back and forth along the main street. "He's got the key, don't worry about him!"

Giles started to say something else, but his words were cut off by Combs reaching out with his hat in hand and slapping the big silver-gray on its rump. The horse bolted forward between Doc and Combs onto the back trail out of town. Behind them came a long string of cursing from the open rear door as Crazy Man Lewis scratched and clawed the floor, unable to reach the keys. Finally, for all his effort, he managed to hook the tip of a finger over the brass ring and pull it to him.

"There, by God!" Lewis shouted to himself, his breath heaving in his chest. He quickly unlocked the cell and raced over to the gun cabinet. Finding the cabinet locked, he cursed loudly again, turned to the back door and bounded over Sheriff Watts, who lay groaning in a pool of blood.

"There's one!" a voice called out. Two townsmen in nightshirts pointed at Lewis running along the alley toward the livery barn. "Jailbreak!" the two men shouted.

"Ha!" said Crazy Man Lewis, running wildly into the barn, to the stall where his big stallion had been kept. Seeing the stall door standing open caused his jaw to drop open. "Where the hell is my horse? My horse has been stolen!" He looked back and forth frantically, seeing no other horses in the barn. From the rear door came the old livery hostler, carrying a lantern, holding a wet rag to his swollen head with his free hand.

"They're all stolen!" said old Earl. "There were three good horses here. They knocked me in the head and took them!"

Crazy Man Lewis let out a sad hysterical laugh. "Giles Capp did this to me? He brought me here, got me arrested . . . now he's stolen my horse?"

Outside the barn townsmen lurked with pistols and rifles, listening to Lewis rave. When he came out the

door wiping his eyes on his shirtsleeve, he only gave
a passing glance at the guns pointed at him and kept
walking.

"All right, mister! Stop right there!" said a voice.

"Aw, shut up!" Lewis replied. He kept walking, ignoring the guns.

"Hey, where do you think you're going!" asked another townsman in a nervous voice.

"Back to jail," Lewis said over his shoulder.
"Where the hell else do you think I'd go? I'm not
leaving town on foot!" He walked stiffly back to the
jail and through the bullet-riddled door. "Pardon me,"
he said as he stepped around Julie Ann, who sat cra-
dling the wounded sheriff in her arms, awaiting the
doctor.

"Whoever did this is nothing but low despicable
cowards!" Julie Ann shrieked as Lewis walked into
his cell and swung the door shut behind himself.

"Ma'am, I couldn't agree more," said Lewis, dropping down onto his cot.

Having heard the shots before he reached the main
trail, the ranger realized he'd been tricked. He'd spun
the big Appaloosa around and raced back to town,
arriving at the sheriff's office as the doctor stood up
from Sheriff Watts and began rolling his shirtsleeves
down. Watts was barely conscious, but he looked up at
the ranger and said, "I failed . . . I let them get away."

The ranger stooped down beside Julie Ann, who
held Watts' bloody hand. "No, Sheriff, this mistake
was mine. They set me up and caught me cold."

"I still . . . failed," Watts whispered. "Failed at
being a lawman."

"No, you haven't failed, Watts," said Sam. "You
started off wrong, but you redeemed yourself. You

cleared an innocent man and set him free when there was no gain in it for you. That's what a *true* lawman does . . . that's the most important thing for a true lawman *ever* to do."

Watts looked up at him with a realization coming into his tired eyes. "Thanks, Ranger."

"Don't thank me, Sheriff, not yet," said Sam. Glancing at the bullet-riddled door, then at the empty cell where Giles Capp had been, he said, "Wait until I get them. And I will get them, you've got my word on that."

Watts nodded weakly and drifted off.

Julie Ann's tear-streaked face turned to the ranger. "Sam, is he . . . is he going to die," she whispered.

The ranger looked up at the doctor with a questioning expression. "No, he's going to live, ma'am," said the doctor. "Only two of the bullets did any real damage . . . one in the chest and one in the shoulder. The one in his chest went through. I'll have to remove the one in his shoulder when we get him over to my office." He looked around at the townsmen gathered on the boardwalk and motioned them inside. "Get over here and carry him," he said. Looking at the ranger, the doctor said, "We've sent for the judge to come look after things here for the time being."

"Good." Sam stood up, helping Julie Ann to her feet. "Are you all right?" he asked.

She nodded. "Yes, I'll be all right. I know you have to go after them. I'll stay and see if I can help the doctor in any way."

Sam patted her arm, then walked over to the cell and looked in at Crazy Man Lewis and Avondale. The councilman shrank beneath the ranger's cold stare, but not Lewis. He stood up and stared back at the ranger, saying, "Don't give me that look. I came back and turned myself in. You can ask this idiot!" He jerked his head toward Avondale.

Avondale said, "It's true, Ranger, he did. I saw it all!"

"Was it Axel Capp himself, or just his men?" Sam asked them both.

"I never saw any of these men before, Ranger," said Councilman Avondale.

"There was only two of them, Ranger," said Lewis in a calm voice. "One was a young fellow about your age. Believe it or not the other one was Doc Cain."

"Doc Cain?" said Sam. "I thought he was dead."

"So did I," said Lewis, "but it was him all right. He wore that same tall top hat I saw him wearing years ago."

"He's not even wanted for anything anymore that I know of," said the ranger." He eyed Lewis closely. "Why'd you come back here, Crazy Man? Why are you telling me all this?"

Lewis had been talking calmly, but now his voice took on a wild bitter tone. "Why? I'll tell you why! Because they stole my gawdamned horse! That's why!" As he spoke he stepped forward and gripped the bars tightly. "Run them down and kill them, Ranger! Shoot them to pieces, a little at a time! Make them beg you to kill them—"

"That's enough of that kind of talk, Crazy Man," said the ranger. "You're starting to scare the other prisoner." He nodded at Avondale.

Lewis tossed a glance at Avondale, then looked back at the ranger grumbling under his breath.

Looking over at the locked gun cabinet, Sam said thinking aloud, "That's odd. Giles didn't try to get his gun out of there." He looked back at Lewis. "Did one of them give him a gun?"

"Nope," said Lewis. "The more I think on it, the more I realize, they didn't seem to want him to get into the gun cabinet." Lewis cocked his head slightly. "Now, I call that peculiar, don't you, Ranger?"

Sam didn't answer. Instead he turned in time to see the townsmen carrying Watts out the front door, Julie Ann right behind them. Earl, the stable hostler, had walked over, closed the rear door and dropped the latch on it. "Can you stay here and keep an eye on these prisoners until the judge gets here?"

"I'm here already, Ranger," said the judge from the front door, stepping in no sooner than the others were out and on their way to the doctor's office.

"Once I get on their trail, Judge Shelby, I don't know how long I'll be gone," Sam said. "You might have to deputize somebody to look after things here for a while."

"I'm certain I can manage to look after these two," said the judge, looking down his nose at Lewis and Avondale. "I am more than qualified." He looked the ranger up and down. "You get those rapscallions, Ranger Burrack. Bring them back here and watch me nail their proverbial hides to the wall!"

"Yes, Your Honor," said Sam. "I'm on my way."

Chapter 24

In the middle of the night, the ranger left Redemption on his Appaloosa at a fast clip, carrying no more provisions for himself than a canteen of water and a small canvas bag packed with coffee beans and jerked beef. Another small bag carried grain for his stallion. Standing beside Judge Shelby on the boardwalk in front of the doctor's office, Julie Ann Dolan sighed and watched man and horse disappear into the night.

Judge Shelby said quietly, "If romance with a lawman is *difficult*, young lady, one must conclude that romance with a territory ranger is *impossible.*"

Julie Ann was a bit taken aback by the judge's remark. But she was too tired to protest. Instead she said with a weary smile, "I have lived with the difficulties of being a lawman's *daughter* for most of my life. I'm not sure I owe the *law* any more than that."

"Then steer your life away from that one, young lady," said the judge, nodding at the darkness in the direction the ranger had taken.

Julie Ann looked at him expectantly, as if asking him to justify such a remark. But the judge only said gently, "Child, don't you already know all the reasons why?"

As the two turned and walked inside the doctor's office, the ranger rode deeper into the darkness, stopping every few hundred yards to jump down from his saddle and examine the ground, making sure the three sets of fresh hoofprints had not eluded him. Behind him the lights in Redemption had grown small by the time he reached the main trail. He followed the fresh tracks, distinguishing them among the hundreds of other hoofprints by the dirt they had kicked in their urgency.

When the tracks veered off of the main trail, Sam stopped only long enough to look back toward Redemption for a second to get his bearings. From there he needed no hoofprints to tell him where the three men were headed. They had to be hurrying for the cover of the hills. Any other direction would have left them exposed on miles of barren desert flatland come daylight. He heeled the Appaloosa into a steady pace, conserving the animal, knowing that come daylight that pace would have to change, least he himself be caught in the open crossing the desert floor.

As soon as the first grainy light of dawn allowed him and his mount to see the trail more clearly, he called upon the strength of the big stallion to close the gap between him and the men he followed. Putting the stallion into a race against the rising sun, he reached the cover of the hills and started upward along the winding rock-walled trail, letting the stallion cool itself out and set its own pace.

At mid-morning he studied the three sets of prints closely at a watering hole while the stallion drank its fill. But when he led the animal away from the water and followed the prints on foot for a few yards, he noted that one horse had drifted off away from the other two. His senses piqued, wondering if one rider had stayed behind and lay above him at that very minute ready to spring an ambush.

"I know it too," he whispered as the stallion snorted and grumbled under its breath, as if warning of some impending danger. Lifting his Colt from his holster, Sam walked quietly in the same direction as the single set of prints.

Stepping around the edge of a tall jagged rock with his Colt cocked and pointed, he saw the dun standing crooked, favoring a limp front hoof, a saddle still on its back. Upon seeing the ranger, the horse shied and tried to bolt away, but its injured leg wouldn't allow it. "Easy, boy," Sam said gently, wrapping Black Pot's reins around a spur of rock and stepping over closer to the lamed animal. Holstering his pistol, he rubbed a reassuring hand down the horse's shoulder, picked up its dangling reins, then lifted the injured leg carefully and examined it.

"You've picked up a bad stone bruise," he said as if the horse could understand him. Lowering the hoof gently to the ground, he looked all around, weighing the horse's chances of surviving until its bruise healed. Then he dropped the saddle from its back, slipped the bit from its mouth and dropped its bridle. "You've got water," he said, backing away toward his waiting stallion. "You'll find yourself some graze when you get hungry enough."

He stepped atop his stallion, knowing that it wouldn't be long until he came upon the three men, two of them now sharing a horse. "Take up, Black Pot," he said to the stallion, "looks like the desert just dealt us a stronger hand than we had starting out." He rode on.

In the heat of mid-afternoon, he stepped down from the stallion and eased over to the edge of the trail.

He gazed down at the three men and the two horses on the switchback trail a hundred feet beneath them. "Got you, Doc Cain," he whispered, stooping down and raising his rifle to his shoulder. He started to draw a bead on Doc, but before he settled in for the shot, he watched Doc raise the buffalo rifle waist-high and give Giles Capp a shove toward the horses. Only then did he notice that Giles' hands were bound together by a strip of rawhide.

"What have we here," Sam whispered to himself, lowering his rifle an inch, deciding to wait and watch for a moment.

On the switchback trial, Giles stumbled on his way to the horses and looked back at Doc and Combs. "I don't know what makes you think my brother won't kill you both once this is over! He'll hunt you down like dogs!"

Doc said sarcastically, "That's real smart thinking, Giles, telling us something like that. Makes us want to go ahead and kill you and your brother, you idiot." He gave Giles another push. "Now, get on that horse, so I can smell your stink the rest of the way."

"Hey, I didn't mean it," said Giles. "I just lost my head when you shoved me. I don't know how much you're going to ask him, but he'll give it . . . to get me back alive, he'll pay whatever you ask."

"That's more like it," said Doc, giving Bobby a look and a slight grin. "Now you're starting to use your brain. As bad as your brother double-crossed us, it's hard to not want to put a bullet in your head and leave you nailed to cottonwood for him to find his way here."

From above them, the ranger only made out a little of what was said. But that didn't matter, he'd seen enough to know what was going on. Doc Cain and his

partner hadn't broken Giles out for Axel Capp. They
had broken him out to hold him captive. This could
change things, he thought, lowering his rifle. He
watched the three men mount up and move away
along the trail. Then he backed away, took up his
reins, mounted up and followed. There might be a
way to get both of the Capp brothers after all.

Axel Capp led the group of riders along the winding
hill trail through a maze of tall rock. He was no longer
worried about who rode behind him now that the
wagon load of gold sat safely tucked away inside a
mine shaft under Denton Spears' watchful eyes. A few
steps behind Axel rode Dallas Ryan, Rod Sealey and
Curly Barnes. Behind them came the others, Danny
Boy Wright, Snake Bentell. Charlie Floose rode at the
rear, leading Spears' horse and the team of wagon
horses on a lead rope. Beside him Millard Trent rode
low in his saddle, looking more dead than alive.

Approaching a turn in the trail, Axel stopped
abruptly and threw his hand to his gun butt at the
sudden sight of Bobby Combs stepping his horse out
into full view. Bobby carried a stick with a dirty rag
tied to the end of it. Seeing Axel on the verge of
snatching up his gun, Combs called out, "Keep it holstered, Axel, if you don't want to see your brother try
to fly." His words carried an echo among the rocks as
he pointed the stick upward to the edge of a barren
stone cliff eighty feet above them.

"Jesus! It's Giles!" Dallas Ryan whispered, having
stepped his horse up beside Axel Capp.

As the riders looked up, Giles Capp stepped dangerously close to the edge of the cliff, being prodded
there by the long barrel of Doc Cain's buffalo rifle.

"That's Doc Cain behind him," said Combs. "If you

have doubts about that being your brother, Giles, Doc wouldn't mind at all slicing something off of him, pitching it down to you."

"I recognize my brother," said Axel, getting right down to business, knowing that what Combs said was true. "What is it you want?"

"We want the same thing we started out wanting before you jackpotted us," said Combs. "We want our share of the take." He pointed the dirty rag at Axel as he spoke, adding, "Only you have to know, our share has gone up a few notches."

In spite of his brother standing at the edge of a cliff with a gun to his head, Axel Capp had to test the situation a little. He nodded over his shoulder at the two wagon horses standing beside Charlie Floose and said, "As you can see the wagon's gone. All we've got left are the horses that pulled it."

"I see," Combs said flatly, glancing at the team of horses and taking note of the third horse as well. Nodding in resolve, he called out to Doc Cain, saying, "Drop the hammer, Doc! Let him fly!"

"Whoa! No! Hold it!" Axel Capp shouted loudly, his echo booming along the rock walls, overlapping itself like waves on a beach. He threw both hands in the air as if to hold his brother up on the cliff. "Damn, Combs! Let me finish! I meant we don't have it with us! The wagon is hidden!"

"That's what I thought you might have meant," Combs said in a critical tone, their echoing words intertwining and drifting away together. He gave a slight wave of the dirty rag for Doc Cain. Axel and his men watched wide-eyed and tense as Doc pulled Giles back a step from the edge of the cliff. Axel appeared relieved.

"Now, let me make sure you understand something,

Axel," said Combs. "Doc and I will stand for no
bluffs, no tricks, no shots called that we won't fire."
He lowered the dirty rag across his lap. "We both
want that gold, but we can both live without it. Doc
wants to kill your brother as bad as I do, just to make
sure you have to watch him die." He paused, but only
for a second. Then he said, "Now, you tell me what's
going to happen next."

"All right," Axel Capp said quickly, "we're going
right now to the gold. Does that suit you?"

"Yep, that's a damn good start," said Combs.
"Where is the wagon?"

Already thinking about Denton Spears and the big
Gatling gun awaiting whoever came snooping around
the mine shaft, Axel called out, "It's underground, in
a mine shaft at the old Cub Sanders mining project.
Do you know the place?"

"I've heard of it," said Combs. "I'm certain Doc
will know where it's at."

"Well, bring him and Giles down here," said Axel.
"We can all ride there together."

"Say something else that stupid, Axel," said Combs,
"see if we don't splatter your brother's brains all over
the badlands."

"I meant nothing by it," said Axel. "I'm going along
with whatever you tell me to do. You tell me how you
want us to play this out."

"Then start riding," said Bobby Combs. "We'll be
right behind you."

"But what if we get separated?" said Axel. "I don't
want you killing Giles, thinking we cut out on you."

"You try *real* hard not to lose us," said Combs.
"You can bet we'll be doing the same." He nudged
his horse slowly back behind the steep rock cover.

"Jesus!" Dallas Ryan whispered again as Combs disappeared from sight.

"Is that all you know how to say?" Axel snapped at him. Above them Doc and Giles had also vanished. He looked back over his shoulder and shouted loudly, "Floose, get the hell up here!" Again, his echo blared. "I want them horses right here beside me."

From the rear, Charlie Floose hurried forward leading the two horses. "What are we going to do, Axel?" he asked with a worried look as he slid his horse down and jerked the lead rope to settle the team horses beside him.

Axel gave a nervous look back and forth and above them, and replied as if he might be overheard, "What the hell do you think we're going to do? They've got Giles! We're going to give them what they want!"

"Jesus!" said Ryan, "he never made it clear how much they want. It could be any amount!"

"Yeah? And what if it is?" said Axel, his hand on his gun butt again. "That's Giles we're talking about! My kid brother! I ain't letting him die if I can keep from it!"

"Jesus!" said Ryan, "take it easy. I didn't mean nothing by it!"

"Let me hear you say *Jesus* one more time, Ryan!" Axel threatened. "So help me God, I'll kill you!"

Ryan shied back, keeping his mouth shut.

Axel looked around at the rest of the men. "Turn around, Gawdamn it! We're heading back to the mines."

"What about Redemption, that damned ranger?" Snake Bentell asked as the horses began turning on the narrow trail.

"Snake, shut the hell up!" said Axel. Then he

shouted at all of the men. "Can any of you just do what I tell you without giving me a bunch of lip over it?" He pushed his horse through them until once again he was in the lead, headed back in the opposite direction. "Floose! Get up here with me! I told you I want them damn horses beside me!"

Charlie Floose shook his head in exasperation, but hurried along through the other riders until he once again had the horses standing alongside Axel Capp.

As they headed back along the path, forty yards above them where he'd taken up a position in the cover of rock, the ranger ducked down and listened as the horses hooves clicked and echoed along the rock trail. He'd gotten a good look at Charlie Floose, one of Sheriff Dolan's killers. He'd heard Axel call him by name. He'd heard enough to know there was gold involved in whatever bad blood lay between Axel Capp and the two outlaws holding his brother prisoner. That was good enough for him. He knew they were headed for the old Cub Sanders Mine project. He knew a shortcut. With a hard ride and a little luck, he would be there, waiting for them.

Chapter 25

At the Cub Sanders mining project, Denton Spears had done exactly as Axel had told him to do. He'd waited until everybody rode out of sight, then carried the big Gatling gun out of the mine shaft, found himself a nice rock perch overlooking the entrance to the shaft and set himself up a firing position. He hadn't liked the idea of being left without a horse; but for the kind of money he was going to make off of this job, he supposed he could put up with it. It would only be for a day or two—long enough for Axel and the men to kill that ranger and get back here with his brother Giles.

Spears sipped tepid water from his canteen and watched the winding trail stretch in and out of sight down through the walls of tall barren rock. On the ground near the Gatling gun stand, he'd built a small fire to boil a pot of coffee. As soon as the coffee began to smell strong enough, he set the pot aside to simmer and quickly put out the fire. No harm done he thought, looking up at the last wisp of gray smoke drifting away on the warm air.

But coming up a thin steep path across the rock land above the mine project, the ranger saw the slight-

est waft of smoke rise twenty yards to his left as if
coming up out of the earth. He reined over closer,
and he drew his stallion to a halt. Stepping down from
his saddle, he led the tired animal forward silently.
From the edge of his higher precipice, he looked down
at the top of Spears' hat as the man racked his boot
sole back and forth on the ground, putting out the last
glowing embers of the fire. Breathing a sigh of relief,
the ranger looked down past the Gatling gun at the
entrance of the mine on the lower ground beneath it.
"We made the *hard ride*, Black Pot," he whispered to
the big stallion. "Now here's that *little luck* we were
hoping for."

He stepped back, looking all around at the vast rock
hillsides that made up the mining project. He knew
that had it not been for that single rise of smoke, he
could have either spent days wandering the project
looking for the right mine shaft, or else he might have
ridden right into the sights of the big gun waiting
above him. Thanking his luck, Sam walked the tired
stallion back ten feet from the edge and took down
the coiled lariat from his saddle horn.

On the rock perch below, Denton Spears had
capped his canteen of tepid water and laid it aside,
favoring a cup of hot coffee even in the afternoon
heat. Taking his gloves off and rounding his finger in
a tin cup to wipe dust from it, he poured the cup full
and set the pot out of the way, planning on it lasting
him the rest of the day and into the night. He sipped
the coffee and stared once again out along the winding
trail. When he felt something hit his hat brim from
above, he swiped a startled hand at it, spilling some
of his coffee.

"What the hell!" he shouted. Then he felt something drop across his chest. "What the—!" He started

to speak again but his words got cut off as the ranger gave a hard yank of the rope, drawing it tight around Spears' throat, lifting him halfway to his feet.

Spears raised his left hand, grasping the taut rope above him. Realizing what was going on, he snatched his pistol from his holster with his right hand while his feet began thrashing back and forth beneath him, seeking purchase on the rocky ground, but losing touch with it more and more. Just as he tried to raise the gun and shoot, his body took a quick jerk upward, so hard that it caused him to let go of his gun and grab the rope on his throat with both hands. His boot heels scraped wildly on the sheer rock wall behind him. But finding no hold there, soon they stopped scraping and only bucked and kicked until one boot flew from his foot and bounced down the rocks, landing near the front entrance of the mine shaft.

On the cliff above, the ranger watched the taut rope gradually stop twanging and turn still. He stood beside the stallion a moment longer, then reached up, unwrapped the lariat from the saddle horn enough to let out some slack, then unwrapped it the rest of the way when he felt the weight of Denton Spears' dead body rest on the rock perch below.

Sam walked the stallion to a safe spot in the shade of a tall standing rock and left him there while he walked the rounded surface of the cliff and found a steep footpath leading down to where Denton Spears lay with a stunned expression on his dead blue face. The ranger's intention had been to move the Gatling gun to a better location overlooking the entrance; but upon closer consideration he realized Spears had found the best spot. From where the gun sat, once the riders arrived at the entrance to the mine, the gun had them cut off from riding back out to the trail.

"Good choice," the ranger said to himself. He picked up the dropped coffee cup, wiped dirt from the rim of it, filled it and sat looking down the winding trail as he sipped from it.

Axel and his men rode up the last few yards of the switchback, stopped out front of the mine shaft and stepped down from their saddles. They gave their horses a shove out of the way. Axel looked up and all around for any sign of Denton Spears, knowing he was up there somewhere. In order to tip off Spears, he called out to the trail behind him, saying loudly, "Doc Cain, Bobby Combs . . . here it is! Bring my brother in here! I'll take him . . . you take your share of the gold, the way we agreed, all right?"

A few yards back along the trail, still covered by tall rock walls on either side of them, Doc Cain called out, "Who does the third horse belong to, Axel?"

"It's just a spare horse," Axel called back to him.

"I think you're lying, Axel," said Doc. "If you are, you can kiss your brother good-bye. Tell him for me, Giles."

Giles called out in a frightened voice, "Axel, listen to him, don't try any crazy bullshit! This man is ready to kill me here!"

"What? Are you kidding?" Axel tried to sound stunned by the idea that he might try some sort of trick. "I'm doing whatever I have to, to keep you *from* getting killed!"

Above them the ranger sat hunkered down behind the Gatling gun, his hand lying on the crank, ready to raise up and fire as soon as the time was right.

A silence passed. Axel Capp grew anxious. "Come on in, Doc. I'm on the square with you, so help me!"

"All right, Axel, we're coming in," said Doc. Another moment passed, then Doc and Combs came in
on foot, Giles standing pressed between them. The
buffalo rifle was gone, replaced by a sawed-off shotgun. A short strip of rawhide ran from Giles' neck to
the shotgun barrel, keeping the tip of the barrel a few
inches from the back of his head.

"Aw, come on, now, Doc," said Axel, "that ain't
necessary! We're all serious men here . . . we can trust
each other more than this, can't we?"

"The longer you talk, the madder I'll get. I bet I
have to say to hell with the gold and just blow this
idiot's head off," said Doc. The three of them finally
stepped inside the Gatling gun's firing range. Sam
raised up slightly, enough to get his hand into position
on the gun handles.

"Easy, Doc," said Axel. "There's no need in that.
It's all going your way. We're about to get this settled.
Stay calm."

"I'm calm," said Doc. "Bring up the gold, let's get
this over with, right now!"

"That's what I say," said Axel, raising a hand in
the air, trying to give Spears a signal to hold his fire
until the shotgun came away from Giles' head. Once
they gave Doc and Combs their share of the gold,
there would be an opportunity to open fire on them.
"What's it going to take, Doc," he asked, "say ten
bars to each of yas?"

Doc gave him a flat stare. "We would have gotten
more than that to begin with, Axel. Now that you
double-crossed us, it's going to take more . . . lots
more."

Beside Axel, Dallas Ryan's temper flared. But
seeing him taking a step forward, Axel grabbed his

arm, saying, "Take it easy, Dallas, everything is going to be all right." As he spoke, Doc and Combs came closer, with Giles between them.

Above them, the ranger saw that he had everybody in the right position. "Here we go," he said to himself. Without hesitation he opened fire, fanning the big gun back and forth, the shots kicking up dirt and rock, tearing through flesh and bone.

Thinking it was Denton Spears manning the Gatling gun, Axel cried out, "No! Stop! Not now, you stupid bastard!" As he ducked back behind a thick support timber at the entrance to the mine, he saw Curly Barnes fall dead, three gaping bullet holes in his chest. Beside him, Rod Sealey lay dying, moaning softly, both hands gripping his bloody groin. Millard Trent, already wounded, fell backward and onto his knees when a bullet opened a fresh wound in his upper chest. He looked almost relieved as he fell forward onto his face.

Axel looked quickly at Doc Cain, who stood with his back against a steel ore buggy sitting abandoned on a set of rails that ran up from an adjoining shaft. He noted that Doc was holding the shotgun but Giles was no longer tied to the barrel. Instead, Giles was screaming, lying against the front of the mine entrance, slapping smoke and flames from the back of his head where the shotgun had gone off just as he'd ducked away from it.

As suddenly as the Gatling gun fire had started, it stopped. Axel Capp took that second of silence to shout up at the rock perch, "Denton, Damn it! Hold your fire! Can't you see he's got Giles?" Giving a look toward Doc and Combs, Axel saw the shotgun was again pointed at Giles, from less than ten feet away.

Above them, the ranger called down, "This is Arizona Ranger Sam Burrack. Giles Capp, Charlie Floose, you are both under arrest for the murder of Sheriff Mack Dolan.

"Oh, God!" Danny Boy Wright shouted hysterically at the sight of the ranger standing up above them behind the Gatling gun. "It's him! He's not human!" In a panic he started running to his horse, but a shot from the ranger's big Colt nailed him high in the back of his shoulder and drove him to the ground. Danny Boy lay sobbing and writhing, dying in the dirt.

"Everybody stay put," the ranger called down. "I'm not finished. I'm also arresting Doc Cain and the man riding with him, for jailbreak and aiding an escaped prisoner." He looked all around at the men taking cover in and around the entrance to the mine shaft. "Once these four men come forward and give themselves up, the rest of you are free to leave."

A stunned silence set in as the men tried to digest the ranger's words and intentions. From their hiding positions, even Doc Cain and Axel Capp gave one another a disbelieving look. Finally Axel broke the silence, saying, "Ranger, you are one crazy sonsabitch, if you think you're taking *any of us* to jail, especially my kid brother!" He jumped out of hiding long enough to fire two quick pistol shots up at the rock perch where the ranger stood. "You ain't nothing, Ranger!" He laughed long and loud and shouted to his men, "Get to the horses and rush him, boys!" But when he ducked back into cover, his hand clasped his belly, where warm blood gushed from a bullet hole.

"Damn, he shot me!" Axel said in surprise, staring down at his bloody belly as the men tried to rush from behind their cover and fire upward at the ranger, making their way to their loose horses. "I ain't even wanted anymore, the sonsabitch shot me!"

Sam dropped down amid the heavy gunfire and once again put the Gatling gun into play. This time he kept the bullets pouring out of it relentlessly, causing the big support timber to splinter and tremble until it slipped sideways. Dirt and rock broke loose and fell into a heavy shower.

As Dallas Ryan and Charlie Floose ducked inside the mine shaft, the heavy gunfire followed them, ricocheting, knocking out chunks of rock all around them. Seeing dirt begin to spill down from the ceiling, Floose shouted, "We can't stay in here! He'll shoot it down around us!"

The Gatling gun fell silent for a moment. "I sure as hell ain't going out there!" Ryan shouted. But then he looked back along the mine shaft and saw more dirt, this time filled with larger rocks, falling from the ceiling. "Damn! It's coming down! What about our gold?"

Floose didn't answer. Instead he took advantage of the lull in the firing to run back out of the shaft and ducked down beside Axel Capp, who lay leaning back against the steel-ore buggy. Beside him sat Doc Cain, holding both Axel's pistol and his own, looking up toward the Gatling gun.

"Axel!" shouted Charlie Floose, "what are we going to do? We're all trapped here!"

"All?" Doc Cain said, with a dark bitter laugh. "You better look around you, fool! He's about wiped you Rio Sagrado boys out for good!"

"We ain't whipped yet," said Axel, trying to struggle to his feet, blood pouring from his belly.

"Yeah, you look it," said Doc Cain, reloading his pistol, taking a bandanna from around his neck and stuffing it down onto Axel's belly. "Hold this on it." He looked at Bobby Combs' body lying at his feet, then said to Axel, "I ought to kill you myself, you dirty rotten bastard, setting us up, doing us that way!" He cocked his pistol and jammed it against Axel's temple.

But Axel just cut a glance at him, gave a stiff pained grin and said, "You have to admit I got you good, Doc!"

Doc Cain stared at him and shook his head. "Yeah, damned if you didn't." He uncocked the pistol and looked up among the rocks. "And this sumbitching ranger got us all." He laughed a little.

Axel managed to laugh with him, a broken weak wheeze of a laugh. He said, "Where's Giles? He better not be hurt!"

"I'm still up," said Giles, a few feet away, taking cover beside Snake Bentell behind the bodies of Rod Sealey and Curley Barnes, Sealey's dead hands still clamped onto his wounded groin. In the melee Giles had managed to work his hands free of the rawhide strips binding them and had picked up Bobby Combs' pistol. His hair still smoked from the close shotgun blast earlier. He gave Doc Cain a hard look and said, "You came damned near blowing my head off!"

"That was exactly my intention," Doc replied, wiping the blood from Axel's pistol and sticking it into his bloody hand. "We get out of this, there's still a lot of making up we've got to do. I ain't coming this far and not getting my share of that gold." He glanced again at the rock perch above them and said, "What's he waiting for up there?"

From across the clearing eight yards away, the ranger called out, "Giles Capp, Charlie Floose, Doc Cain and the man riding with him. Any of you that's still alive come on out. You're under arrest."

"I'll be damned," said Doc Cain to the others. "He

had us cold from up there. But he's brought it down
here to us." He gave Axel a curious look. Then he
called out to the ranger. "Why'd you do that, Ranger?
Huh? Why'd you come down here?"

"I didn't want to shoot you down like tin ducks,"
said the ranger. "Everybody comes out now and be-
haves themselves, I take them in, they get a fair trial."

"A fair trail for killing a lawman?" Floose said.
"Who the hell wants that? No thanks, Ranger, I'll take
me chances face to face." He looked at the others and
said, "Let's all make a move at once. He can't take
us all down."

Doc Cain looked around slowly from body to body
on the ground, then said, "Damned if he ain't done
pretty good at it so far."

"You know what I mean," said Floose, "he can't
do it without that Gatling gun." He looked at Axel
and asked, "What do you say, Axel? To keep me and
Giles from hanging? Are you with me?"

"Hell, yes," said Axel, his voice failing him fast.
Floose looked back at Doc Cain. "Are you with us
or not?"

"Yeah, why not?" said Doc. "I'll count three. Everybody go out shooting at once." He searched the
bloody faces. "Ready. One, two, three! Let's go!"

Floose, Giles and Snake bolted forward from their
cover, shouting and firing as one. But not only did
Doc Cain stay behind cover, he grabbed Axel Capp
and held him down as well.

"You sonsabitch!" said Axel, too weak to struggle.
Doc Cain grabbed his pistol barrel and pointed it
down away from him.

Giles Capp managed to get one shot off at the
ranger before the ranger's big Colt exploded and blew
him backward past his brother and against the already

loosened support timber, knocking it farther out of place. Charlie Floose dropped to his knee, taking a close steady aim at the ranger; but it did him no good. The ranger's next shot rolled him backward and dropped him dead on his face. Snake had fired twice, missing both times. On his third shot he let out a scream as the Ranger turned and dropped him with a shot through his heart. A ringing silence followed. Sam stared at the ore buggy and said, "Doc, why did you do something like that?"

"I wanted to be the last one standing, Ranger," said Doc, standing slowly, wiping the blade of his boot knife back and forth slowly onto his trouser leg. Stepping out from behind the ore buggy, he grinned, stooped down warily and slid the knife back into his boot well. He stood up slowly and straightened his battered top hat on his head. Nodding over his shoulder at the mine entrance, he said, "There's nearly a million dollars worth of German gold in there." He gave the ranger a questioning stare.

"Imagine that," Sam said flatly, his Colt hanging at his side, smoke still curling slowly up the barrel, caressing the back of his hand.

"Hey, I'm not joking," said Doc Cain. "Come on, I'll go show you."

"Stay where you are, Doc Cain," said the ranger. "You're under arrest."

"Ranger," said Doc, lowering his voice secretively even though there was no one to hear, "don't you get it? There's just us two left. We can drop the pretense." The ranger watched his hand tighten on the pistol. "All that gold? Huh?" Doc's grin broadened. "Doesn't this raise any possibilities for you?"

"You're under arrest, Doc. Drop the gun," said Sam. "I'm not saying it again."

"I can't do it, Ranger," said Doc. "This was going to be my last job. I need that money! I'm getting old! I can't go to prison again."

"You'll be out in a year or so, Doc," said the ranger. "Better think about it."

"Out in a year, facing what?" said Doc, his hand still gripping the pistol. "A job swamping saloons, tending livery? Huh-uh, this is it for me. You ain't stopping me, 'less you kill me."

"I understand," said the ranger, "make your play."

But Doc hesitated and said, "Damn, what's wrong with you, that you won't take the gold? Why not?"

"It ain't mine, Doc," Sam said flatly. "Now, make your play."

"Aw-hell," said Doc, turning loose of the pistol, letting it fall to the ground, "what's the use? All right, I'm going to jail, Gawdamn it to hell!" He spit at the ground and kicked the pistol away from his feet. "There, I'm done! Are you satisfied?" He jerked the top hat from his head and snatched out a wadded-up bandanna and blotted it to his forehead. "You are too hardheaded to listen to reason."

"Don't do it, Doc," Sam warned him, raising the big Colt, cocking it, watching his hand disappear behind the top hat.

Doc Cain let out a breath of exasperation and said, "Son of a bitch! You beat all I ever saw." He flipped a two-shot derringer to the ground and said, "There, let's get going. The quicker I get to prison, the sooner I get out."

"That's the spirit," said Sam, taking a step forward, lowering his pistol again, reaching for a set of handcuffs behind his back. But before he even got within reach of Doc Cain, a rumbling rose up from the mine shaft as timber after timber snapped like match sticks in the belly of the mine. Dallas Ryan let out one short scream from inside the mine.

"Look out," Sam shouted at Doc Cain, dropping flat to the ground as a blast of dust blew out of the shaft, carrying bits of wood and rock.

Sam lay with his arms over his head until he felt the dust settling atop him. Standing, coughing and fanning his hat, he called out, "Doc? Are you all right?" He walked out of the heaviest concentration of looming dust and looked all around. Raising his pistol he called out again as he searched back and forth. "Doc? Can you hear me? Where are you?" But then he stopped himself and said no more, realizing he wasn't about to get an answer. His eyes searched the numerous footpaths snaking up into the maze of barren rock. After a moment he shook his head slightly and walked toward the spooked horses that stood huddled on the other side of the small clearing. "I'll be seeing you, Doc," he said aloud to himself.

Epilogue

All eyes along the street turned to the ranger as he rode into Redemption leading a long string of horses, all but three of them with a body draped over their saddle. At the end of the string, one of the team horses carried the Gatling gun, the other the stand and ammunition. Judge Shelby had spotted Sam through his hotel window and hurried down to the boardwalk to meet him at the hitch rail out front of the sheriff's office. On his way past the Even Odds Saloon, the ranger noted that the main doors were closed and padlocked. No sooner than he stopped, still looking in that direction, Judge Shelby said to him bluntly, "If you're wondering why its closed, its because Andrew Swain hanged himself last night."

Sam just looked at him.

"Yeah, he sure did." Judge Shelby nodded in affirmation. "He came to me scared to death that the Capps would kill you, and come here after him." He looked at the long string of bullet-riddled bodies and said, "Poor devil couldn't handle the kind of life he fancied for himself, not even for one more day."

"That's a shame. How's Sheriff Watts?" Sam asked.

Shelby gave him a narrowed gaze and said, "The sheriff's doing good. He's being well attended, if you know what I mean." He cocked a brow implying something.

"No, I guess I don't," said Sam.

"I mean Miss Dolan is taking good care of him . . . hasn't left his side for a moment."

"I understand," said Sam, stepping down from his saddle. Dismissing the subject, he pointed back along the string of bodies. "There's the Rio Sagrado Gang, the Capp brothers and all."

"I'm sure in the end Axel put up a fight for his brother, and you had to kill him?"

"The fact is, I didn't kill Axel," said Sam. "I shot him, but Doc Cain killed him."

"Doc Cain, eh?" said Shelby. "I bet he turned out to be the hardest one to kill?"

"You could say that," said Sam. "He's not dead. He got away. There's a wagon load of German gold out there buried under a hillside. We'll have to contact the Mexican government, let them make arrangements to come get it."

The judge smiled. "Think they might find Doc out there digging for it?"

"I doubt it," said Sam. "Doc didn't strike me as a digger." As he spoke his eyes drifted to the sheriff's office. "Who's watching the prisoners?"

"Nobody right now," said the judge. "The only one left is Manifred Lewis. I let Avondale go, on the condition that he resign his position and leave the territory. He left here with Horace Meaker—they both seemed eager to leave." He gave Sam a level stare, letting him know there would be no discussing the matter.

"Then I may just as well let Crazy Man go too," said Sam. "With Giles dead, I doubt he'll be trying to kill anybody . . . not around here anyway."

The judge looked him up and down. "She's at the doctor's office right now, if you want to see her."

Sam didn't answer.

"When you see things working out the way they should, it's best to step out of the way and let them, don't you think so, Ranger?"

"Her father was a lawman," said Sam. "She told me she's use to this kind of life."

"Her father was a town *sheriff,* Ranger," the judge pointed out with a raised finger for emphasis. "We both know there's a world of difference."

"I know," said Sam. Nodding at the bodies, he said, "Will you handle the paperwork on this bunch?"

"I'd be happy to oblige," said the judge. "So, this was the first town you ever tamed?"

Sam didn't reply.

"Well, you did a striking job if it is," said Shelby.

Sam tied the lead rope to the string of horses and bodies to the hitch rail. Taking Black Pot's reins, he walked away from Judge Shelby to the sheriff's office without another word. The judge watched him walk away; he looked the bodies over again and shook his head slowly. "Yep, a striking job," he chuckled under his breath.

Inside the sheriff's office, the ranger walked back to the cell where Crazy Man Lewis stood up from the edge of his cot and stared at him through the bars. Sam took the key from its peg and unlocked the cell door. Swinging the door open, he said, "You're free to go, Crazy Man."

Manifred Lewis didn't leave right away. He walked forward, taking his time, and stopped in the open cell doorway. "I ain't going to be that easy to get rid of, Ranger," he said in a spiteful tone. He placed his right hand on the iron door frame and leaned there belligerently. "You see, nobody calls me Crazy Man."

"All right, then, Manifred," said Sam, "Now, come on out." He held the cell door open wide.

But Manifred didn't move. "Another thing . . . I ain't forgot about you banging my head into that barn timber. See, I ain't leaving this town until you and me face off in the street. I'm going to see blood, Ranger." He gave a wide cruel grin. "I'm going to see some pain. I'm going to—" His words turned into a scream as the ranger swung the iron door hard, slamming his gun hand against the iron door frame.

"Oh, God! It's broke!" Lewis shrieked in pain "You broke my hand! My gun hand!" Tears streamed down his cheeks. He bowed at the waist, holding his crushed gun hand and walking in a short circle trying to still the throbbing pain.

"Is it?" the ranger asked idly. He walked over to the gun cabinet, took out Lewis' wrapped-up gun belt and checked the gun, making sure it wasn't loaded on his way back. "Maybe you better stop by the doctor's, have him take a look at it."

He shoved the gun belt up under Lewis' arm while Lewis still walked around bowed in pain. Guiding Lewis across the office, he opened the front door and gave him a shove. Then he closed the door without another word, walked to the window and watched Crazy Man stagger along toward the livery barn in pain, still bowed at the waist. Sam knew the gunman's hand wasn't broken, just close to it. And he knew Crazy Man wasn't going to the doctor's. He'd go to some cool stream somewhere, soak his hand, wrap it in a wet rag and wait it out. That was how a gunman did things, he told himself. That was probably what he would do himself . . . wait out the pain.

He stood at the window for a moment and looked down across the street, watching the reflections in the store window. He looked down at the circles on the window ledge and smiled slightly to himself. "You helped me find your killers, didn't you, Sheriff? You showed me the way you watched this town . . . the way you kept things in order." He looked back into the window across the street and saw Julie Ann's reflection as she stepped out of the doctor's office and started along the boardwalk. As if answering a question, he said, "I reckon I owe you this much, Sheriff Dolan."

Sam walked out of the empty sheriff's office, stepped down, mounted the big Appaloosa stallion and turned it to the street, into the passing traffic of horses, buggies and freight wagons. Behind him he thought he heard her call out his name. But he didn't look around. Instead he turned the stallion into the alley that ran to the rear of town. And he rode the length of it until it came to a side trail out of town. He left quietly, as if slipping away from a gathering through the back door, unnoticed . . . not wanting himself to be missed there.